Arabian Nights and Days

NAGUIB
MAHFOUZ

Translated by
Denys Johnson-Davies

Doubleday
New York London Toronto
Sydney Auckland

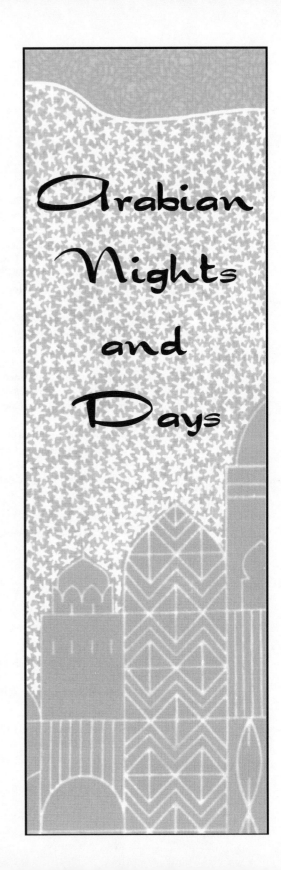

Arabian
Nights
and
Days

PUBLISHED BY DOUBLEDAY
a division of Bantam Doubleday Dell Publishing Group, Inc.
1540 Broadway, New York, New York 10036

DOUBLEDAY and the portrayal of an anchor with
a dolphin are trademarks of Doubleday,
a division of Bantam Doubleday Dell
Publishing Group, Inc.

Arabian Nights and Days was first published in Arabic in 1979,
under the title *Layali alf lela.*
Protected under the Berne Convention.

This translation is published by arrangement with
The American University in Cairo Press.

Library of Congress Cataloging-in-Publication Data

Maḥfūẓ, Najīb, 1912–
  [Layālī alf laylah. English]
  Arabian nights and days / Naguib Mahfouz ; translated by Denys
Johnson-Davies. — 1st ed.
    p. cm.
    I. Title.
PJ7846.A46L3913   1995
892'.736—dc20   94-6457
                                                              CIP

ISBN 0-385-46888-1
Copyright © 1979 by Naguib Mahfouz
English translation copyright © 1995 by
The American University in Cairo Press

1   3   5   7   9   10   8   6   4   2

CONTENTS

SHAHRIYAR   1

SHAHRZAD   3

THE SHEIKH   5

THE CAFÉ OF THE EMIRS   8

SANAAN AL-GAMALI   11

GAMASA AL-BULTI   29

THE PORTER   51

NUR AL-DIN AND DUNYAZAD   77

THE ADVENTURES OF UGR THE BARBER   106

ANEES AL-GALEES   130

QUT AL-QULOUB   145

ALADDIN WITH THE MOLES ON HIS CHEEKS   157

THE SULTAN   172

THE CAP OF INVISIBILITY   179

MA'ROUF THE COBBLER   194

SINDBAD   207

THE GRIEVERS   222

Arabian
Nights
and
Days

Shahriyar

Following the dawn prayer, with clouds of darkness defying the vigorous thrust of light, the vizier Dandan was called to a meeting with the sultan Shahriyar. Dandan's composure vanished. The heart of a father quaked within him as, putting on his clothes, he mumbled, "Now the outcome will be resolved—your fate, Shahrzad."

He went by the road that led up to the mountain on an old jade, followed by a troop of guards; preceding them was a man bearing a torch, in weather that radiated dew and a gentle chilliness. Three years he had spent between fear and hope, between death and expectation; three years spent in the telling of stories; and, thanks to those stories, Shahrzad's life span had been extended. Yet, like everything, the stories had come to an end, had ended yesterday. So what fate was lying in wait for you, O beloved daughter of mine?

He entered the palace that perched on top of the mountain. The chamberlain led him to a rear balcony that overlooked a vast garden. Shahriyar was sitting in the light shed by a single lamp, bare-headed, his hair luxuriantly black, his eyes gleaming in his long face, his large beard spreading across the top of his chest. Dandan kissed the ground before him, feeling, despite their long association, an inner fear for a man whose history had been filled with harshness, cruelty, and the spilling of innocent blood.

The sultan signaled for the sole lamp to be extinguished. Darkness took over and the specters of the trees giving out a fragrant aroma were cast into semi-obscurity.

"Let there be darkness so that I may observe the effusion of the light," Shahriyar muttered.

Dandan felt a certain optimism.

"May God grant Your Majesty enjoyment of everything that is best in the night and the day."

Silence. Dandan could discern behind his expression neither contentment nor displeasure, until the sultan quietly said, "It is our wish that Shahrzad remain our wife."

Dandan jumped to his feet and bent over the sultan's head, kissing it with a sense of gratitude that brought tears from deep inside him.

"May God support you in your rule forever and ever."

"Justice," said the sultan, as though remembering his victims, "possesses disparate methods, among them the sword and among them forgiveness. God has His own wisdom."

"May God direct your steps to His wisdom, Your Majesty."

"Her stories are white magic," he said delightedly. "They open up worlds that invite reflection."

The vizier was suddenly intoxicated with joy.

"She bore me a son and my troubled spirits were put at peace."

"May Your Majesty enjoy happiness both here and in the hereafter."

"Happiness!" muttered the sultan sharply.

Dandan felt anxious for some reason. The crowing of the roosters rang out. As though talking to himself, the sultan said, "Existence itself is the most inscrutable thing in existence."

But his tone of perplexity vanished when he exclaimed, "Look. Over there!"

Dandan looked toward the horizon and saw it aglow with hallowed joy.

Shahrzad

Dandan asked permission to see his daughter Shahrzad. A hand-maid led him to the rose room with its rose-colored carpet and curtains, and the divans and cushions in shades of red. There he was met by Shahrzad and her sister Dunyazad.

"I am overwhelmed with happiness, thanks be to God, Lord of the Worlds."

Shahrzad sat him down beside her while Dunyazad withdrew to her closet.

"I was saved from a bloody fate by our Lord's mercy," said Shahrzad.

But the man was barely mumbling his thanks as she added bitterly, "May God have mercy on those innocent virgins."

"How wise you are and how courageous!"

"But you know, father," she said in a whisper, "that I am un-happy."

"Be careful, daughter, for thoughts assume concrete forms in palaces and give voice."

"I sacrificed myself," she said sorrowfully, "in order to stem the torrent of blood."

"God has His wisdom," he muttered.

"And the Devil his supporters," she said in a fury.

"He loves you, Shahrzad," he pleaded.

"Arrogance and love do not come together in one heart. He loves himself first and last."

"Love also has its miracles."

"Whenever he approaches me I breathe the smell of blood."

"The sultan is not like the rest of humankind."

"But a crime is a crime. How many virgins has he killed! How many pious and God-fearing people has he wiped out! Only hypocrites are left in the kingdom."

"My trust in God has never been shaken," he said sadly.

"As for me, I know that my spiritual station lies in patience, as the great sheikh taught me."

To this Dandan said with a smile, "What an excellent teacher and what an excellent pupil!"

The Sheikh

Sheikh Abdullah al-Balkhi lived in a simple dwelling in the old quarter. His dreamy gaze was reflected in the hearts of many of his old and more recent students and was deeply engraved in the hearts of his disciples. With him, complete devotion was no more than a prologue, for he was a Sheikh of the Way, having attained a high plane in the spiritual station of love and contentment.

When he had left his place of seclusion for the reception room, Zubeida, his young and only daughter, came to him and said happily, "The city is rejoicing, father."

"Hasn't the doctor Abdul Qadir al-Maheeni arrived yet?" he inquired, not heeding her words.

"Maybe he's on his way, father, but the city is rejoicing because the sultan has consented that Shahrzad should be his wife and he has renounced the shedding of blood."

Nothing dislodges him from his calm, however: the contentment in his heart neither diminishes nor increases. Zubeida is a daughter and a disciple, but she is still at the beginning of the Way. Hearing a knock at the door, she left, saying, "Your friend has come on his usual visit."

The doctor Abdul Qadir al-Maheeni entered. The two of them embraced, then he seated himself on a mattress alongside his friend. As

5

usual the conversation was conducted in the light from a lamp in a small recess.

"You have no doubt heard the good news?" said Abdul Qadir.

"I know what it is my business to know," he said with a smile.

"Voices are lifted in prayer for Shahrzad, showing that it is you who primarily deserve the credit," said the doctor.

"Credit is for the Beloved alone," he said in reproof.

"I too am a believer, yet I follow promises and deductions. Had she not been a pupil of yours as a young girl, Shahrzad would not, despite what you may say, have found stories to divert the sultan from shedding blood."

"My friend, the only trouble with you is that you overdo your submission to the intellect."

"It is the ornament of man."

"It is through intellect that we come to know the limits of the intellect."

"There are believers," said Abdul Qadir, "who are of the opinion that it has no limits."

"I have failed in drawing many to the Way—you at the head of them."

"People are poor creatures, master, and are in need of someone to enlighten them about their lives."

"Many a righteous soul will save a whole people," said the sheikh with confidence.

"Ali al-Salouli is the governor of our quarter—how can the quarter be saved from his corruption?" inquired the doctor, suddenly showing resentment.

"But those who strive are of different ranks," the sheikh said sadly.

"I am a doctor and what is right for the world is what concerns me."

The sheikh patted his hand gently and the doctor smiled and said, "But you are goodness itself and good luck."

"I give thanks to God, for no joy carries me away, no sadness touches me."

"As for me, dear friend, I am sad. Whenever I remember the God-fearing who have been martyred for saying the truth in protest against the shedding of blood and the plundering of property, my sadness increases."

"How strongly are we bound to material things!"

"Noble and God-fearing people have been martyred," bewailed Abdul Qadir. "How sorry I am for you, O my city, which today is controlled solely by hypocrites! Why, master, are only the worst cattle left in the stalls?"

"How numerous are the lovers of vile things!"

Sounds of piping and drumming reached them from the fringes of the quarter and they realized that the people were celebrating the happy news. At this the doctor decided to make his way to the Café of the Emirs.

The Café of the Emirs

The café was centered on the right-hand side of the large commercial street. Square in shape, it had a spacious courtyard, with its entrance opening onto the public way and its windows overlooking neighboring sections of the city. Along its sides were couches for the higher-class customers, while in a circle in the middle were ranged mattresses for the common folk to sit on. A variety of things to drink were served, both hot and cold according to the season; also available were the finest sorts of hashish and electuaries. At night many were the high-class customers to be found there, the likes of Sanaan al-Gamali and his son Fadil, Hamdan Tuneisha and Karam al-Aseel, Sahloul and Ibrahim al-Attar the druggist and his son Hasan, Galil al-Bazzaz the draper, Nur al-Din, and. Shamloul the hunchback.

There were also ordinary folk like Ragab the porter and his crony Sindbad, Ugr the barber and his son Aladdin, Ibrahim the water-carrier and Ma'rouf the cobbler. There was general merriment on this happy night, and soon the doctor Abdul Qadir al-Maheeni had joined the group that included Ibrahim al-Attar, Karam al-Aseel the millionaire, and Sahloul the bric-a-brac merchant and furnisher. That night they had recovered from a fear that had held sway over them; every father of a beautiful virgin daughter felt reassured and was promised a sleep free from frightening specters.

"Let us recite the Fatiha over the souls of the victims," several voices rang out.

"Of virgins and God-fearing men."

"Farewell to tears."

"Praise and thanks be to God, Lord of the Worlds."

"And long life to Shahrzad, the pearl of women."

"Thanks to those beautiful stories."

"It is nothing but God's mercy that has descended."

The merriment and conversation continued until the voice of Ragab the porter was heard saying with astonishment, "Are you mad, Sindbad?"

And Ugr, who was keen to put his nose into everything, asked, "What's got into him on this happy night?"

"It seems he's come to hate his work and is tired of the city. He no longer wants to be a porter."

"Does he have ambitions to be in charge of the quarter?"

"He went to a ship's captain and kept insisting till he agreed to take him on as a servant."

Ibrahim the water-carrier said, "Whoever gives up an assured livelihood on dry land to run away after some vague one on water must be really crazy."

"Water that from earliest times has derived its sustenance from corpses," said Ma'rouf the cobbler.

To which Sindbad said defiantly, "I am fed up with lanes and alleys. I am also fed up with carrying furniture around, with no hope of seeing anything new. Over there is another life: the river joins up with the sea and the sea penetrates deeply into the unknown, and the unknown brings forth islands and mountains, living creatures and angels and devils. It is a magical call that cannot be resisted. I said to myself, 'Try your luck, Sindbad, and throw yourself into the arms of the invisible.' "

Nur al-Din the perfume-seller said, "In movement is a blessing."

"A beautiful salutation from a childhood comrade," said Sindbad.

Ugr the barber demanded sarcastically, "Are you making out that you're upper-class, porter?"

"We sat side by side in the prayer room receiving lessons from our master, Abdullah al-Balkhi," said Nur al-Din.

"And, like many others, I contented myself with learning the rudiments of reading and religion," said Sindbad.

"The dry land will not be lessened by your leaving, nor the sea increased," said Ugr.

At this the doctor Abdul Qadir al-Maheeni said to him, "Go in God's protection, but keep your wits about you—it would be good if you were able to record the wonderful sights you come across, for God has ordered us to do so. When are you departing?"

"Tomorrow morning," he muttered. "I leave you in the care of God the Living, the Eternal."

"How sad it is to part from you, Sindbad," said his comrade Ragab the porter.

Sanaan
al-Gamali

I

Time gives a special knock inside and wakes him. He directs his gaze toward a window close to the bed and through it sees the city wrapped around in darkness. Sleep has stripped it of all movement and sound as it nestles in a silence replete with cosmic calm.

Separating himself from Umm Saad's warm body, he stepped onto the floor, where his feet sank into the downy texture of the Persian carpet. He stretched out his arm as he groped for where the candlestick stood and bumped into something solid and hard. Startled, he muttered, "What's this?"

A strange voice issued forth, a voice the like of which he had never heard: the voice of neither a human nor an animal. It robbed him of all sensation—it was as though it were sweeping throughout the whole city. The voice spoke angrily, "You trod on my head, you blind creature!"

He fell to the ground in fear. He was a man without the tiniest atom of valor: he excelled at nothing but buying and selling and bargaining.

"You trod on my head, you ignorant fellow," said the voice.

"Who are you?" he said in a quaking voice.

"I am Qumqam."

"Qumqam?"

"A genie from among the city's dwellers."

Almost vanishing in terror, he was struck speechless.

"You hurt me and you must be punished."

His tongue was incapable of putting up any defense.

"I heard you yesterday, you hypocrite," Qumqam continued, "and you were saying that death is a debt we have to pay, so what are you doing pissing yourself with fear?"

"Have mercy on me!" he finally pleaded. "I am a family man."

"My punishment will descend only on you."

"Not for a single moment did I think of disturbing you."

"What troublesome creatures you are! You don't stop yearning to enslave us in order to achieve your vile objectives. Have you not satisfied your greed by enslaving the weak among you?"

"I swear to you . . ."

"I have no faith in a merchant's oath," he interrupted him.

"I ask mercy and plead pardon from you," he said.

"You would make me do that?"

"Your big heart . . ." he said anxiously.

"Don't try to cheat me as you do your customers."

"Do it for nothing, for the love of God."

"There is no mercy without a price and no pardon without a price."

He glimpsed a sudden ray of hope.

"I'll do as you want," he said fervently.

"Really?"

"With all the strength I possess," he said eagerly.

"Kill Ali al-Salouli," he said with frightening calm.

The joy drowned in an unexpected defeat, like something brought at great risk from across the seas whose worthlessness has become apparent on inspection.

"Ali al-Salouli, the governor of our quarter?" he asked in horror.

"None other."

"But he is a governor and lives in the guarded House of Happiness, while I am nothing but a merchant."

"Then there is no mercy, no pardon," he exclaimed.

"Sir, why don't you kill him yourself?"

"He has brought me under his power with black magic," he said with exasperation, "and he makes use of me in accomplishing purposes that my conscience does not approve of."

"But you are a force surpassing black magic."

"We are nevertheless subject to specific laws. Stop arguing—you must either accept or refuse."

"Have you no other wishes?" said Sanaan urgently. "I have plenty of money, also goods from India and China."

"Don't waste time uselessly, you fool."

In utter despair, he said, "I'm at your disposal."

"Take care not to attempt to trick me."

"I have resigned myself to my fate."

"You will be in my grasp even if you were to take refuge in the mountains of Qaf at the ends of the world."

At that, Sanaan felt a sharp pain in his arm. He let out a scream that tore at his depths.

II

Sanaan opened his eyes to the voice of Umm Saad saying, "What's made you sleep so late?" She lit the candle and he began to look about him in a daze. If it were a dream, why did it fill him more than wakefulness itself? He was so alive that he was terrified. Nevertheless he entertained thoughts of escape, and feelings of grateful calm took control of him. The world was brought back to its proper perspective after total ruin. How wonderful was the sweetness of life after the torture of hellfire!

"I take refuge in God from the accursed Devil," he sighed.

Umm Saad looked at him as she tucked scattered locks of hair inside the kerchief round her head, sleep having affected the beauty of her face with a sallow hue. Intoxicated with the sensation of having made his escape, he said, "Praise be to God, Who has rescued me from grievous trouble."

"May God protect us, O father of Fadil."

"A terrible dream, Umm Saad."

"God willing, all will be well."

She led the way to the bathroom and lit a small lamp in the recess. Following her, he said, "I spent part of my night with a genie."

"How is that, you being the God-fearing man you are?"

"I shall recount it to Sheikh Abdullah al-Balkhi. Go now in peace that I may make my ablutions."

As he was doing so and washing his left forearm, he stopped, trembling all over.

"O my Lord!"

He began looking aghast at the wound, which was like a bite. It was no illusion that he was seeing, for blood had broken through where the fangs had penetrated the flesh.

"It is not possible."

In terror he hurried off toward the kitchen. As she was lighting the oven, Umm Saad asked, "Have you made your ablutions?"

"Look," he said, stretching out his arm.

"What has bitten you?" the woman gasped.

"I don't know."

Overcome by anxiety, she said, "But you slept so well."

"I don't know what happened."

"Had it happened during the day . . ."

"It didn't happen during the day," he interrupted her.

They exchanged an uneasy look fraught with suppressed thoughts.

"Tell me about the dream," she said with dread.

"I told you it was a genie," he said dejectedly. "It was a dream, though."

Once again they exchanged glances and the pain of anxiety.

"Let it be a secret," said Umm Saad warily.

He understood the secret of her fears that corresponded to his own, for if mention were made of the genie, he did not know what would happen to his reputation as a merchant on the morrow, nor to what the reputation of his daughter Husniya and his son Fadil would be exposed. The dream could bring about total ruin. Also, he was sure of nothing.

"A dream's a dream," said Umm Saad, "and the secret of the wound is known to God alone."

"This is what one must remind oneself," he said in despair.

"The important thing now is for you to have it treated without delay, so go now to your friend Ibrahim the druggist."

How could he arrive at the truth? He was so burdened with anxiety that he was enraged and boiled with anger. He felt his position going from bad to worse. All his feelings were charged with anger and resentment, while his nature deteriorated as though he were being created anew in a form that was at variance with his old deep-rooted gentleness. No longer could he put up with the woman's glances; he began to hate them, to loathe her very thoughts. He felt a desire to destroy everything that existed. Unable to control himself, he pierced her with a glance filled with hatred and resentment, as though it were she who was responsible for his plight. Turning his back on her, he went off.

"This is not the Sanaan of old," she muttered.

He found Fadil and Husniya in the living room in a dim light that spilled out through the holes of the wooden latticework. Their faces were distraught at the way his excited voice had been raised. His anger increased and, very unlike himself, he shouted, "Get out of my sight!"

He closed the door of his room behind him and began examining his arm. Fadil boldly joined him.

"I trust you are all right, father," he said anxiously.

"Leave me alone," he said gruffly.

"Did a dog bite you?"

"Who said so?"

"My mother."

He appreciated her wisdom in saying this and he agreed, but his mood did not improve.

"It's nothing. I'm fine, but leave me on my own."

"You should go to the druggist."

"I don't need anybody to tell me that," he said with annoyance.

Outside, Fadil said to Husniya, "How changed father is!"

III

For the first time in his life, Sanaan al-Gamali left his house without performing his prayers. He went at once to the shop of Ibrahim the druggist, an old friend and neighbor in the commercial street. When the druggist saw his arm, he said in astonishment, "What sort of dog was this! But then there are so many stray dogs . . ."

He set about making a selection of herbs, saying, "I have a prescription that never fails."

He boiled up the herbs until they deposited a sticky sediment. Having washed the wound with rose water, he covered it with the mixture, spreading it over with a wooden spatula, then bound up the arm with Damascene muslin, muttering, "May it be healed, God willing."

At which, despite himself, Sanaan said, "Or let the Devil do what he may."

Ibrahim the druggist looked quizzically into his friend's flushed face, amazed at how much he had changed.

"Don't allow a trifling wound to affect your gentle nature."

With a melancholy face, Sanaan made off, saying, "Ibrahim, don't trust this world."

How apprehensive he was! It was as though he had been washed in a potion of fiery peppers. The sun was harsh and hot, people's faces were glum.

Fadil had arrived at the shop before him and met him with a beaming smile which only increased his ill humor. He cursed the heat, despite his well-known acceptance of all kinds of weather. He greeted no one and scarcely returned a greeting. He was cheered by neither face nor word. He laughed at no joke and took no warning note at a funeral passing. No comely face brought him pleasure. What had happened? Fadil worked harder in order to intervene as far as possible between his father and the customers. More than one inquired of Fadil in a whisper, "What's up with your father today?"

The young man could only reply, "He's indisposed—may God show you no ill."

IV

It was not long before his condition was made known to the habitués of the Café of the Emirs. He made his way to them with a gloomy countenance and either sat in silence or engaged only in distracted conversation. He no longer made his amusing comments; quickly dispirited, he soon left the café.

"A wild dog bit him," Ibrahim the druggist said.

And Galil the draper commented, "He's utterly lost to us."

While Karam al-Aseel, the man with millions and the face of a monkey, said, "But his business is flourishing."

And the doctor Abdul Qadir al-Maheeni said, "The value of money evaporates when you're ill."

And Ugr the barber, the only one among those sitting on the floor who would sometimes thrust himself into the conversation of the upper-class customers, said philosophically, "What is a man? A bite from a dog or a fly's sting . . ."

But Fadil shouted at him, "My father's fine. It's only that he's indisposed—he'll be all right by daybreak."

But he went deeper and deeper into a state that became difficult to control. Finally, one night he swallowed a crazy amount of dope and left the café full of energy and ready to brave the unknown. Disliking the idea of going home, he went stumbling around in the dark, driven on by crazed fantasies. He hoped for some action that might dispel his rebellious state of tension and relieve it of its torment. He brought to mind women from his family who were long dead and they appeared before him naked and in poses that were sexually suggestive and seductive, and he regretted not having had his way with a single one of them. He passed by the cul-de-sac of Sheikh Abdullah al-Balkhi and for an instant thought of visiting him and confiding to him what had occurred, but he hurried on. In the light of a lamp hanging down from the top of the door of one of the houses he saw a young girl of ten going on her way, carrying a large metal bowl. He rushed toward her, blocking her way and inquiring, "Where are you going, little girl?"

"I'm going back to my mother," she replied innocently.

He plunged into the darkness till he could see her no more.

"Come here," he said, "and I'll show you something nice."

He picked her up in his arms and the water from the pickles spilt over his silken garment. He took her under the stairway of the elementary school. The girl was puzzled by his strange tenderness and didn't feel at ease with him.

"My mother's waiting," she said nervously.

But he had stirred her curiosity as much as her fears. His age, which reminded her of her father, induced in her a sort of trust, a trust in which an unknown disquiet was mixed with the anticipation of some extraordinary dream. She let out a wailing scream which tore apart his compassionate excitement and sent terrifying phantoms into his murky imagination. He quickly stifled her mouth with the trembling palm of his hand. A sudden return to his senses was like a slap in the face, as he came back to earth.

"Don't cry. Don't be frightened," he whispered entreatingly.

Despair washed over him until it demolished the pillars on which the earth was supported. Out of total devastation he heard the tread of approaching footsteps. Quickly he grasped the thin neck in hands that were alien to him. Like a rapacious beast whose foot has slipped, he tumbled down into an abyss. He realized that he was finished and noticed that a voice was calling, "Baseema . . . Baseema, my girl."

In utter despair he said to himself, "It is inevitable."

It became clear that the footsteps were approaching his hiding-place. The light from a lamp showed up dimly. He was driven by a desire to go out carrying the body with him. Then the presence of something heavy overtook his own collapsing presence, the memory of the dream took him by storm. He heard the voice of two days ago inquiring, "Is this what we pledged ourselves to?"

"You are a fact, then, and not a dire dream," he said in surrender.

"You are without doubt mad."

"I agree, but you are the cause."

"I never asked you to do something evil," the voice said angrily.

"There's no time for arguing. Save me, so that I can carry out for you what was agreed."

"This is what I came for, but you don't understand."

He felt himself moving in a vacuum in an intensely silent world. Then he again heard the voice, "No one will find a trace of you. Open your eyes and you will find that you are standing in front of the door of your house. Enter in peace, I shall be waiting."

V

With a superhuman effort Sanaan took control of himself. Umm Saad did not feel that his condition had deteriorated. Taking refuge behind his eyelids in the darkness, he set about calling to mind what he had done. He was another person; the killer-violator was another person. His soul had begotten wild beings of which he had no experience. Now, divested of his past and having buried all his hopes, he was presenting himself to the unknown. Though he hadn't slept, no movement escaped him to indicate that he had been without sleep. Early in the morning there came the sound of wailing. Umm Saad disappeared for a while, then returned and said, "O mother of Baseema, may God be with you."

"What's happened?" he asked, lowering his gaze.

"What's got into people, father of Fadil? The girl's been raped and murdered under the elementary school stairway. A mere child, O Lord. Under the skin of certain humans lie savage beasts."

He bowed his head until his beard lay disheveled against his chest.

"I take my refuge in God from the accursed Devil," he muttered.

"These beasts know neither God nor Prophet."

The woman burst into tears.

He began to ask himself: Was it the genie? Was it the dope he had swallowed? Or was it Sanaan al-Gamali?

VI

The thoughts of everyone in the quarter were in turmoil. The crime was the sole subject of conversation. Ibrahim the druggist, as he prepared him more medicine, said, "The wound has not healed, but there is no longer any danger from it." Then, as he bound his arm with muslin, "Have you heard of the crime?"

"I take refuge in God," he said in disgust.

"The criminal's not human. Our sons marry directly they reach puberty."

"He's a madman, there's no doubt of that."

"Or he's one of those vagabonds who haven't got the means to marry. They are milling around the streets like stray dogs."

"Many are saying that."

"What is Ali al-Salouli doing in the seat of government?"

At mention of the name he quaked, remembering the pact he had made, a pact that hung over his head like a sword. "Busy with his own interests," he concurred, "and counting the presents and the bribes."

"The favors he rendered us merchants cannot be denied," said the druggist, "but he should remember that his primary duty is to maintain things as they are for us."

Sanaan went off with the words, "Don't put your trust in the world, Ibrahim."

VII

The governor of the quarter, Ali al-Salouli, knew from his private secretary Buteisha Murgan what was being said about security. He was frightened that the reports would reach the vizier Dandan and that he would pass them on to the sultan, so he called the chief of police, Gamasa al-Bulti, and said to him, "Have you heard what is being said about security during my time in office?"

The chief of police's inner calm had not changed when he had learned about his superior's secrets and acts of corruption.

"Excuse me, governor," he said, "but I have not been negligent or remiss in sending out spies. However, the villain has left no trace and we haven't found a single witness. I myself have interrogated dozens of vagabonds and beggars, but it's an unfathomable crime, unlike anything that has previously happened."

"What a fool you are! Arrest all the vagabonds and beggars—you're an expert on the effective means of interrogation."

"We haven't the prisons to take them," said Gamasa warily.

"What prisons, fellow? Do you want to impose upon the public treasury the expense of providing them with food?" said the governor in a rage. "Drive them into the open and seek the help of the troops—and bring me the criminal before nightfall."

VIII

The police swooped down on the plots of wasteland and arrested the beggars and vagabonds, then drove them in groups into the open. No complaint and no oath availed, no exception was made of old men. Force was used against them until they prayed fervently for help to God and to His Prophet and the members of his family.

Sanaan al-Gamali followed the news with anxious alarm: he was the guilty one, of this there was no doubt, and yet he was going about free and at large, being treated with esteem. How was it that he had become the very pivot of all this suffering? And someone unknown was lying in wait for him, someone indifferent to all that had occurred, while he was utterly lost, succumbing without condition. As for the old Sanaan, he had died and been obliterated, nothing being left of him but a confused mind that chewed over memories as though they were delusions.

He became conscious of a clamor sweeping down the commercial street. It was Ali al-Salouli, governor of the quarter, making his way at the head of a squadron of cavalry, reminding people of the governor's power and vigilance, a challenge to any disorder. As he proceeded he replied to the greetings of the merchants to right and left. This was the man he had undertaken to kill. His heart overflowed with fear and loathing. This was the secret of his torment. It was he who had chosen to liberate the genie from his black magic. It was the genie alone who had done this. His escape was conditional on his doing away with al-Salouli. His eyes became fixed on the dark, well-filled face, pointed beard and stocky body. When he passed in front of the shop of Ibrahim the druggist, the owner hurried up to him and they shook hands warmly. Then, passing before Sanaan's shop, he happened to glance toward it and smiled so that Sanaan had no choice but to cross over and shake him by the hand, at which al-Salouli said to him, "We'll be seeing you soon, God willing."

Sanaan al-Gamali returned to the shop, asking himself what he had meant. Why was he inviting him to a meeting? Why? Was he finding the path made easy for him in a way he had not expected? A shudder passed through him from top to toe. In a daze he repeated his words, "I'll be seeing you soon, God willing."

IX

When he lay down to sleep that night the other presence took control and the voice said mockingly, "You eat, drink, and sleep, and it is for me to exercise patience!"

"It's an onerous assignment. Those with such power as yourself do not realize how onerous," he said miserably.

"But it's easier than killing the little girl."

"What a waste! I had long been thought of as among the best of the good."

"External appearances do not deceive me."

"They were not simply external appearances."

"You have forgotten things that would bring sweat to one's brow with shame."

"Perfection is God's alone," he said in confusion.

"I also don't deny your good points, and it was for this that I nominated you to be saved."

"If you hadn't forced your way into my life, I wouldn't have got myself involved in this crime."

"Don't lie," he said sharply. "You alone are responsible for your crime."

"I don't understand you."

"I really judged you too favorably."

"If only you'd just left me alone!"

"I'm a believing genie and I told myself, 'This man's goodness exceeds his wickedness. Certainly he has suspicious relations with the chief of police and doesn't hesitate to exploit times of inflation, but he is the most honest of merchants, also he is charitable and undertakes his religious devotions and is merciful to the poor.' Thus I chose you to be saved, to be the saving of the quarter from the head of corruption, and the saving of your sinful self. Yet instead of attaining the visible target, your whole structure collapsed and you committed this repugnant crime."

Sanaan moaned and kept silent, while the voice continued, "The chance is still there."

"And the crime?" he asked helplessly.

"Life gives opportunities for both reflection and repentance."

"But the man is an impregnable fortress," he said in a voice clinging to a vestige of hope.

"He will invite you to meet him."

"That seems unlikely."

"He will invite you—be sure and be prepared."

Sanaan thought for a while, then inquired, "Will you promise me deliverance?"

"I chose you only for deliverance."

So exhausted was Sanaan that he fell into a deep sleep.

X

He was getting ready to go to the café when Umm Saad said, "There's a messenger from the governor waiting for you in the reception room."

He found the private secretary, Buteisha Murgan, waiting for him with his sparkling eyes and short beard.

"The governor wants to see you."

His heart beat fast. He realized that he was going off to commit the gravest crime in the history of the quarter. Perhaps it worried him that Buteisha Murgan should be acquainted with the circumstances surrounding his visit, but he took reassurance in Qumqam's promise.

"Wait for me," he said, "till I put on my clothes."

"I shall go ahead of you so as not to attract attention."

So the man was bent on keeping the secret nature of the meeting, thus facilitating his task. He began anointing himself with musk, while Umm Saad watched, nursing a sense of unease that had not left her since the night of the dream. She was held by a feeling that she was living with another man and that the old Sanaan had vanished into darkness. Without her noticing, he slipped into his pocket a dagger with a handle of pure silver that he had received as a gift from India.

XI

Ali al-Salouli received him in his summer mansion at the governorate's garden, appearing in a flowing white robe and with his head bare, which lessened the awe his position bestowed. A table stood in front of him on which were assembled long-necked bottles, glasses, and various nuts, dried fruits, and sweets, which gave evidence of conviviality. He seated him on a cushion alongside him and asked Buteisha Murgan to stay on.

"Welcome to you, Master Sanaan, true merchant and noble man."

Sanaan mumbled something, hiding his confusion with a smile.

"It is thanks to you, O deputy of the sultan."

Murgan filled three glasses. Sanaan wondered whether Murgan would stay until the end of the meeting. Maybe it was an opportunity that would not be repeated, so what should he do?

"It's a pleasant summer night," said al-Salouli. "Do you like the summer?"

"I love all seasons."

"You are one of those with whom God is content, and it is by His complete contentment that we start a new and productive life."

Impelled by curiosity, Sanaan said, "I ask God to complete His favor to us."

They drank, and became elated and invigorated from the wine.

"We have cleansed our quarter of riffraff for you," al-Salouli continued.

"What firmness and determination!" he said with secret sadness.

"We scarcely hear now of a theft or other crime," said Buteisha Murgan.

"Have you discovered who the culprit is?" asked Sanaan cautiously.

"Those confessing to the crime number over fifty," said al-Salouli, laughing.

Murgan laughed too, but said, "The true culprit is doubtless among them."

"It's Gamasa al-Bulti's problem," said al-Salouli.

"We must also increase the exhortations at the mosques and at religious festivals," said Murgan.

Sanaan was beginning to despair, but then al-Salouli gave a special sign to Murgan, who left the place. Even so, the guards were dispersed throughout the garden and there was no way of escape. But not for an instant was he unmindful of Qumqam's promise.

"Let's close the discussion of crimes and criminals," said al-Salouli, changing his tone of voice.

"May your night be a pleasant one, sir," said Sanaan, smiling.

"The fact is that I invited you for more than one reason."

"I'm at your disposal."

"I would like to marry your daughter," he said confidently.

Sanaan was amazed. He was saddened too about an opportunity that was fated to miscarry before it was born. He nevertheless said, "This is a big honor, the greatest of happiness."

"And I also have a daughter as a gift for your son Fadil."

Chasing away his bewilderment, Sanaan said, "He's a lucky young man."

For a while the other was silent and then continued, "As for the final request, it relates to the public welfare."

There gleamed in Sanaan's eyes an inquiring look, at which the governor said, "The contractor Hamdan Tuneisha is your relative, is he not?"

"Yes, sir."

"The point is that I have made up my mind to construct a road alongside the desert the whole length of the quarter."

"A truly excellent project."

"When will you bring him to me here?" he asked in a meaningful tone.

Feeling how ironic the situation was, he said, "Our appointment will be for tomorrow evening, sir."

Al-Salouli gave him a piercing glance and inquired with a smile, "I wonder whether he will come duly prepared?"

"Just as you envisage," said Sanaan with shrewd subtlety.

Al-Salouli laughed and said jovially, "You're intelligent, Sanaan— and don't forget that we are related!"

Sanaan suddenly feared he would summon Buteisha Murgan, and he said to himself, "It's now or the chance will vanish forever."

The man had facilitated things for him without knowing it by relaxing and stretching out his legs and turning over on his back, his eyes closed. Sanaan was immersed in thoughts about the crime and hurling himself into what destiny still remained to him. Unsheathing the dagger, and aiming it at the heart, he stabbed with a strength drawn from determination, despair, and a final desire to escape. The governor gave a violent shuddering, as though wrestling with some unknown force. His face was convulsed and became crazily glazed. He started to bring his arms together as though to clutch at the dagger, but he was unable to. His terrified eyes uttered unheard words, then he was forever motionless.

XII

Trembling, Sanaan stared at the dagger, whose blade had disappeared from sight, and at the gushing blood. With difficulty he wrested his eyes away and looked fearfully toward the closed door. The silence was rent by the throbbing in his temples, and for the first time he caught sight of the lamps hanging in the corners. He also noted a wooden lectern decorated with mother-of-pearl on which rested a large copy of the Quran. In all his agonies he pleaded to Qumqam, his genie and his fate. The invisible presence enveloped him and he heard the voice saying with satisfaction, "Well done!" Then, joyfully, "Now Qumqam is freed from the black magic."

"Save me," said Sanaan. "I abhor this place and this scene."

The voice said with sympathetic calm, "My faith prevents me from interfering now that I have taken possession of my free will."

"I don't understand what you're saying," he said in terror.

"Your fault, Sanaan, is that you don't think like a human being."

"O Lord, there is no time for discussion. Do you intend to abandon me to my fate?"

"That is exactly what my duty requires of me."

"How despicable! You have deceived me."

"No, rather I have granted you an opportunity of salvation seldom given to a living soul."

"Did you not interfere in my life and cause me to kill this man?"

"I was eager to free myself from the evil of black magic, so I chose you because of your faith, despite the way you fluctuated between good and evil. I reckoned you were more worthy than anyone else to save your quarter and yourself."

"But you did not make clear your thoughts to me," he said desperately.

"I made them sufficiently clear for one who thinks."

"Underhand double-dealing. Who said I was responsible for the quarter?"

"It is a general trust from which no person is free, but it is especially incumbent upon the likes of you, who are not devoid of good intentions."

"Did you not save me from my plight under the stairway of the elementary school?"

"Indeed it was difficult for me to accept that you should, by reason of my intervention, suffer the worst of endings without hope of atonement or repentance, so I decided to give you a new chance."

"And now I have undertaken what I pledged myself to you to do, so it is your duty to save me."

"Then it is a plot and your role in it is that of the instrument, and worthiness, atonement, repentance, and salvation are put an end to."

He went down on his knees and pleaded, "Have mercy on me. Save me."

"Don't waste your sacrifice on the air."

"It's a black outcome."

"He who does good is not troubled by the consequences."

"I don't want to be a hero!" he cried out in terror.

"Be a hero, Sanaan. That is your destiny," said Qumqam sorrowfully.

The voice began to fade as it said, "May God be with you and I ask Him to forgive both you and me."

Sanaan let out a scream that reached the ears of Buteisha Murgan and the men of the guard outside.

Gamasa al-Bulti

I

The soul of Sanaan al-Gamali floated in the air of the Café of the Emirs, and its habitués were overcome with distress.

They had witnessed his trial and heard his full confession, and they had seen the sword of Shabeeb Rama the executioner as he chopped off his head. He had a good status among the merchants and the notables, and belonged to that minority that was held in affection by the poor. In front of all these his head had been cut off and his family made destitute. His story was circulated on every tongue, and the hearts of the quarter and the whole city were stirred. The sultan Shahriyar recalled it many a time, and in the café, whose atmosphere had been softened by the harbingers of autumn, Hamdan Tuneisha the contractor said, "God the Creator and Owner of Dominion, Who disposes as He will in His affairs, says to something 'Be' and it is. Who among you would have imagined such a fate for Sanaan al-Gamali? Sanaan rape and strangle a young girl of ten? Sanaan kill the governor of the quarter at his first meeting with him?"

"If one regards the genie as far-fetched, the story becomes a riddle," said Ibrahim the druggist.

"Perhaps it was being bitten by the dog," said the doctor Abdul Qadir al-Maheeni. "If that were the root cause, then the fantasies of some malignant disease that was not treated as it should have been become possible."

"There is no one," said Ibrahim the druggist heatedly, "more experienced than me in the treatment of dog bites, the last being Ma'rouf the cobbler. Isn't that so, Ma'rouf?"

To which Ma'rouf, from his place among the common people, answered, "Thanks be to God Who accomplished the blessing of the cure."

"And why shouldn't we believe the story of the genie?" asked Ugr the barber.

"They exceed human beings in number," said Ibrahim the water-carrier.

"Death has no need of causes," said Sahloul the bric-a-brac merchant.

"I have had so many experiences with genies," said Ma'rouf the cobbler, at which Shamloul the hunchback, the sultan's buffoon, said, "We know that genies avoid your house in fear of your wife."

Ma'rouf gave a smile of submission to his destiny, although the jest met with no success in the lugubrious atmosphere.

Galil the draper said, "Sanaan has been ruined, as has his family."

Karam al-Aseel, the millionaire with the face of a monkey, said, "To extend a helping hand to his family would be regarded as challenging authority. There is no strength or power other than God."

"The thing I fear the most," said Ibrahim the druggist, "is that people will shun his family for fear of the evil power of genies."

Hasan the son of Ibrahim the druggist said, "It is out of the question that anything will change my relationship with Fadil Sanaan."

"He says to something 'Be' and it is," repeated Hamdan Tuneisha the contractor.

II

Gamasa al-Bulti the chief of police set off toward the river to indulge in his favorite pastime of fishing. He had given it up for forty days as an act of mourning for his superior, Ali al-Salouli. He was also sorry for the murderer, by virtue of their being neighbors and the long-standing friendship that had made the two families one. It had been he who had arrested him, he who had thrown him into prison, and he who had sent him to court and had finally handed him over to the executioner, Shabeeb Rama; he, too, who had hung his head above his house, had confiscated his possessions and had driven his family from their home to ruin. Though known for his severity and sternness, his serenity had been disturbed and he had been sad at heart—for he had a heart despite the fact that many did not think so. In fact, this heart loved Husniya, Sanaan's daughter, and he had been on the point of asking for her hand had events not intervened.

Today the weather was beautiful and limpid autumn clouds wandered in the sky. His love, though, had been trampled underfoot by the wheel of circumstance.

He left his mule with a slave, then pushed the boat out to the middle of the river and cast his net: drops of relaxation in the maelstrom of brutish and arduous work. He smiled. In no time a mutual understanding had grown between him and the new governor, Khalil al-Hamadhani. From where did Shahriyar get these governors? The man had given himself away at the very first test—the confiscated properties of Sanaan. He had taken possession of a not inconsiderable portion of them and had fed Buteisha Murgan on them; he had also given Gamasa his share. What remained was assigned to the exchequer. Gamasa had taken his share despite his sadness at his friend's fate, giving himself the excuse that to refuse would mean a challenge to the new governor: in his heart there was a place for emotions and another place for avidity and hardness. He said to himself, "He who's too decent goes hungry in this city." And he asked himself in fun, "What would become of us if a just governor were to take over our affairs?" Had not the sultan himself killed hundreds of virgins and many pious men? How light were his scales when measured against other great rulers!

He breathed deeply: it was truly a beautiful day, the sky dappled with clouds, the air mild and perfumed with the aroma of grass and water, the net filling up with fish. But where was Husniya? Sanaan's family was now living in a room in a residential building, after all that luxury, the jewels and the stables. Now Umm Saad makes sweetmeats that gladden the hearts of guests, while Fadil hawks them around. As for Husniya, she awaits a bridegroom who won't come. Did a genie really bring you down, or was it a dog's bite that destroyed you? I shall not forget your glazed looks and your appeal to me for help, "My family, Gamasa!" It is out of the question that anyone should stretch out a helping hand to your family. Your son Fadil, too, was born a man with his pride. You have perished, Sanaan, and what is past is past. If your genie is truly a believer, let him do something. What an extraordinary sultanate this is, with its people and its genies! It raises aloft the badge of God and yet plunges itself in dirt.

Suddenly his attention was drawn to his hand. The heaviness of the net boded well. Joyfully he brought it in till it was alongside the boat. But he saw not a single fish!

III

Gamasa al-Bulti was amazed. It contained nothing but a metal ball. He took it up dejectedly, turning it over in his hands. Then he threw it into the bottom of the boat. It made a deep resounding sound. Something strange happened: it was as though it were about to explode. What looked like dust emanated from it, swirling right up into the air until it embraced the autumn clouds. Once the dust had vanished it left a presence that crouched over him, and he was filled with a sensation of how overpowering it was. Despite his familiarity with dangerous situations, Gamasa trembled with terror. He realized that he was in the presence of a genie that had been freed from a bottle. He couldn't stop himself from calling out, "Protection from harm, by our Lord Solomon!"

"How sweet is freedom after the hell of imprisonment!" said a voice whose like he had not heard before.

With a dry throat al-Bulti said ingratiatingly, "Your liberation has been achieved at my hands."

"Tell me, first of all, what God has done with Solomon."

"Our Lord Solomon has been dead for more than a thousand years."

His head swaying with elation, the other said, "Blessed is the wish of God, which imposed upon us the decree of a human being, whose dust does not ascend to our fire, and that human is the one who has punished me for a lapse of the heart, may God in His mercy forgive worse."

"Congratulations on your freedom. Go off and enjoy it."

"I see that you're keen to make your escape," he said mockingly.

"Seeing that I was the means to your being liberated."

"I was freed by nothing but destiny."

"And I was destiny's instrument," said Gamasa eagerly.

"During my long imprisonment," said the other, "I became filled with anger and the desire for revenge."

"Pardoning when one can is one of the natural characteristics of noble people," implored Gamasa.

"You people are skilled at memorizing, quoting, and hypocrisy, and in proportion to your knowledge must be your reckoning, so woe to you!"

"We wage a continuous struggle with ourselves, with people, and with life," said Gamasa al-Bulti entreatingly, "and the struggle has victims that cannot be numbered, and hope is never lost in the mercy of the Merciful."

"Mercy is for him who deserves mercy," said the genie sternly. "God's vastnesses are spread with the opportunities granted to those who have adhered to wisdom. Thus mercy is due only to those who strive, otherwise offensive smells would spoil the purity of the air illuminated by divine light, so don't make corruption an excuse for corruption."

"We believe in mercy even when we are chopping necks and cropping heads."

"What a hypocrite you are! What's your job?"

"Chief of police."

"What titles! Do you perform your duty in a manner that pleases God?"

"My duty is to carry out orders," said Gamasa apprehensively.

"A slogan suitable for covering up all sorts of evils."

"I am in no position to do anything about that."

"If you are called upon to do good, you claim you are incapable; and if you are called upon to do evil, you set about it in the name of duty."

Gamasa was in a tight corner. The warnings fell upon him and he backed away to the edge of the boat, trembling. At the same time he felt the penetration of a new presence taking control of the place. He knew that another genie had arrived and he was convinced that he was lost. The newcomer addressed the first genie, "Congratulations on your freedom, Singam."

"Thanks be to God, Qumqam."

"I haven't seen you for more than a thousand years."

"How short they are when measured against life, and how long they are if spent in a bottle!"

"I too landed in the snares of magic, which is like prison in its torture."

"No harm afflicts us that does not come from human beings."

"During the period of your absence many were the events that occurred, so maybe you'd like to catch up on what you missed."

"Indeed, but I would like to take a decision about this human."

"Let him be for now. In no way is he going to slip from your grasp if you need him, but don't take a decision while you're in a rage. No genie among us ever perished except as a prey to his anger. Let's go to the mountains of Qaf and celebrate your liberation."

"Till we meet, O chief of police," said Singam, addressing al-Bulti.

The controlling presence began to dwindle until it disappeared altogether. Gamasa regained the freedom of his limbs, but collapsed on the deck of the boat, his strength drained away. At the same time he was intoxicated with the hope of escape.

IV

Gamasa al–Bulti jumped ashore and was met by a slave, who bowed down to him, then set about folding up the net.

"There's not a single fish in the net," he remarked.

"Were you looking in my direction when I was in the boat?" asked Gamasa, his throat dry.

"All the time, master."

"And what did you see?"

"I saw you casting the net, and then I saw you waiting and drawing it in. That's why I was astonished to find it empty."

"You didn't see any smoke?"

"No, sir."

"And you didn't hear a strange sound?"

"None."

"Perhaps you nodded off."

"Not at all, master."

It was impossible for him to have doubts about what had happened. It was more real than reality itself. In his memory was engraved the name Qumqam, as was that of Singam. He recalled in a new form the confessions of Sanaan and it seemed to him now that his old friend had been an unfortunate victim. He wondered anxiously what the unseen could be holding for him.

V

He buried his secret in his bosom. Even his wife Rasmiya did not know of it. It was a secret that weighed heavily upon him, but what could be done? If one day he divulged it, he would harm his position and lose his post. He stayed awake nights thinking about the consequences and resolved to be cautious. Singam, it would appear, was a believing genie and would be mindful of the good turn he had done by freeing him, even though by accident. He slept following the dawn prayers for a while, then awoke in a better mood. He was by nature strong and would defy difficulties and misgivings. He had got onto friendly terms with al-Salouli and al-Hamadhani, and Singam was no more intractable than they.

As they were drinking their morning milk, Rasmiya said to him, "Yesterday our old neighbor Umm Saad paid me a visit."

Suddenly his nerves tautened. He appreciated the danger of the visit in the way a policeman would who knew the secrets behind particular circumstances.

"A poor widow, and yet . . ." he said with distaste.

He hesitated for an instant, then continued, "But her visiting us is harmful to my position."

"Her situation is heartrending."

"It's the situation of the world, Rasmiya, but let's leave to God what is His."

"She came with the hope that you could help her in making a petition to the governor to return the family properties."

"What a foolish woman!" he exclaimed.

"She said that God did not hold the sins of the fathers against the sons."

"It is Shahriyar himself who pronounced the judgment."

Then he said frankly, "Sanaan was my friend but what had been decreed came to pass. Perhaps the killing of the girl after raping her does not count as anything when measured against the killing of the governor of the quarter, for the sultan regards the blow directed against his representative as being aimed against his person, and the sultan is still a bloodthirsty ruler despite his unexpected change of heart. Do not, therefore, encourage her to pay you frequent visits, or a curse will descend upon us, a curse under which we shall be powerless." Downcast, the woman kept silent.

"I am as sad as you are," he said, "but there is nothing we can do about it."

VI

He was truthful in what he said: his sorrow for Sanaan's family did not dissipate, and the origin of that did not lie solely in passionate love. He had liked the man before he had liked his daughter. He was not always devoid of good sentiments and religious remembrances, but he found no objection to practicing corruption in a corrupt world. The truth was that in the quarter there was no heart like his for mingling black with white. So it was that he invited Fadil Sanaan to his house on a visit shrouded with secrecy.

The young man came in his new attire, consisting of a gallabiya and sandals, the garb of a peddler. Gamasa seated himself beside him in the reception room and said, "I am pleased, Fadil, that you are facing up with such courage to the way things have turned out for you."

"I thank God who has preserved my faith after the loss of position and wealth."

Truly impressed, Gamasa said, "I summoned you in deference to our long acquaintance."

"May God bless you, sir."

He looked at him for a while, then said, "If it weren't for that I would have allowed myself to arrest you."

In amazement Fadil inquired, "Arrest me? Why, sir?"

"Don't pretend not to know. Has not the evil that engulfed you been enough for you? Seek your livelihood far from associating with destructive elements who are the enemies of the sultan."

"I am nothing but a peddler," said Fadil with a pallid face.

"Stop dissimulating, Fadil. Nothing is hidden from Gamasa al-Bulti, and my first task, as you know, is to pursue the Shiites and the Kharijites."★

"I am not one of them," said Fadil in a low voice. "Early in my life I was a student of Sheikh Abdullah al-Balkhi."

"I too was a student of his. Many graduate from the school of al-

★ A sect of dissenters in early Islam.

Balkhi—people of the Way and people of the Prophet's Sunna, Sufis and Sunnis. Some devils who deviate from the Path also graduate."

"Be sure, sir, that I am as far as can be from those devils."

"You have very many companions from among them."

"I have nothing to do with their doctrines."

"It starts as innocent friendship, then comes degeneration—they are madmen, they accuse the rulers of unbelief and they delude the poor and the slaves. Nothing pleases them, not even fasting in the month of Ragab. It is as though God has chosen them to the exclusion of His other worshipers. Be on your guard against falling into the same fate as your father, for the Devil has all kinds of ways and means. As for me, I know nothing but my duty. I have pledged my loyalty to the sultan, as I have to the governor of the quarter, in exterminating the apostates."

"Be assured, sir," said Fadil in a listless tone, "that I am very far distant from the apostates."

"I have given you fatherly advice, so keep it in mind," said Gamasa.

"Thank you for your kindness, sir."

Gamasa began scrutinizing his face in search of points of similarity between him and his sister Husniya. For some moments he was lost in the ecstasy of love. Then he said, "There's one more matter: I would ask you to inform your mother that to present a petition for the return of the family property would be regarded as a challenge to the sultan. There is no power or strength other than through God."

"That is also my opinion, sir," said Fadil meekly.

The meeting ended secretly, as it had begun. Gamasa wondered whether one day he would be given the chance of summoning him that he might ask for Husniya's hand.

VII

Perhaps Sanaan al-Gamali's crime was the sole momentous event that occurred during the time Gamasa al-Bulti was in office. No one charged him with being responsible for it, especially after it was known about the genie's intervention in the matter. This, however, did not apply to what was happening in the quarter at present, for several incidents of highway robbery within the city's walls had followed in succession with disquieting frequency: money and goods were seized and men were assaulted. Gamasa al-Bulti was assailed by the anger of a capable policeman possessed of self-confidence. He dispatched plain-clothed men to outlying places and had patrols out day and night. He himself searched suspect places, but the incidents continued to occur, making a mockery of his activity, and not a single criminal was arrested.

Karam al-Aseel the millionaire said in the Café of the Emirs, "Security was better in the time of the late al-Salouli."

"There wasn't a single highway robber at that time apart from himself," said the doctor Abdul Qadir al-Maheeni, laughing.

"Gamasa al-Bulti," said Ugr the barber, "is the worst possible."

He, after all, saw for himself how such gentlemen behaved when he brought them his services as a barber to their homes.

"Security," said Ibrahim the druggist, "is the very lifeblood of trade, while trade is the livelihood of the people. I propose that some of us go as a deputation to al-Hamadhani, the governor of our quarter."

VIII

Khalil al-Hamadhani summoned Gamasa al-Bulti to the house of government.

"The city is going to rack and ruin and you're snoring away fast asleep," he said severely.

"I haven't been sleeping and I haven't been lax," said the chief of police in a frustrated tone.

"One judges by how things turn out."

"My hands are tied."

"What do you want?"

"The vagabonds who had previously been arrested are now beginning to take revenge."

"It has been established from Sanaan's confession that they were innocent."

"Which is why they are taking revenge. They must be re-ar-rested."

The governor said heatedly, "The vizier Dandan was annoyed at their being arrested the first time and won't allow it again."

Gamasa al-Bulti said sadly, "In any case I'm waging a battle against a force that doesn't let up."

"You've got to have security under control or I'll dismiss you."

Gamasa al-Bulti left the house of government feeling demeaned for the first time in his life.

IX

He was angry about being insulted and his strong and defiant nature took control of him. His tendencies toward good became submerged and disappeared to faraway depths. He reacted to the defeat with the savagery of a man who regards anything as permissible in defense of his authority. Authority had completely absorbed him and had created of him something new so that he had become oblivious to the goodly words he had learned at the hands of the sheikh in the prayer room in the time of innocence. Quickly he gathered his aides and poured upon them the stream of invective he had endured in the hall of the headquar-ters, opening wide the windows of hellfire. Whenever a new incident took place he arrested tens of people and tortured them unmercifully. As a result of this, his pursuit of the Shiites and the Kharijites decreased so that they were able to redouble their activity. They composed secret newssheets that were full of indictments of the sultan and the men in charge of affairs and which demanded that the Quran and the Prophet's Traditional Sayings should become the basis for legal rulings. Becoming frantic, he also arrested many of them, so that an air of dread hung over the whole quarter and all went in fear and trembling. Al-Hamadhani found the violence of the steps being taken shocking. Yet he closed his eyes in his desire to find an end to the incidents. Despite all that, they increased in number and violence.

X

Though defeated, Gamasa al-Bulti refused to admit it. He began spend-
ing many nights at the police headquarters until the pressure of work
affected his unusual strength. Once, overcome by sleep in the room
where he worked, he yielded to it like a wounded lion. He did not
achieve the hoped-for rest, however, but was cast under the weight of a
being who took over his entire body.

"Singam!" he whispered in bewilderment.

The voice came to him, invading his very being, "Yes, chief of
police."

"What has prompted you to come?" he asked him, in loathing.

"The stupidity of those who claim they are intelligent."

Suddenly Gamasa's mind saw the light.

"Now we know," he said, "the secret of the brigands of whom no
one can find any trace."

"Now only?"

"How could I guess that you are their master?"

"Admit, despite your conceit, that you are stupid."

He asked Singam defiantly, "How is it that you are so little worried about stealing people's property when mention of God is constantly
on your lips?"

"My anger has fallen only upon that group of people who take
advantage of other human beings!"

Gamasa sighed and said, as though talking to himself, "I shall lose
my job because of this."

"You too are of the corrupt group of people."

"I am incomparable in the way I perform my duty."

"And money come by dishonestly?"

"Merely the crumbs that fall from the tables of the great."

"A shameful excuse."

"I'm living in the world of humans."

"And do you know about the great?"

"Every tiny detail. They are nothing but thieves and scoundrels."

"Yet you protect them with your sharp-cutting sword," the voice said, scornfully, "and you attack their enemies, who are honorable people of sound opinion and judgment."

"I am executing orders and the path I tread is clear."

"Rather are you pursued by the curse of protecting criminals and persecuting respectable people."

"Any man who thinks when doing such a task as mine perishes."

"Then you're a mindless instrument."

"My mind is solely in the service of my duty."

"An excuse that tends to nullify the humanity of a human."

An idea flashed within him and doors and windows opened before him.

"The fact is that I am not satisfied with myself," he said ruefully.

"Sheer lies!"

"I have never succeeded in uprooting noble inner voices. They always converse with me in the silence of the night."

"I don't find any trace of them in your life."

"I require," he said slyly, "some force to support me when I need it."

"But you are chasing away the noble voices just as you do honest men."

"I put myself on trial," he said challengingly.

"Make plain what you mean."

"Put your power to supporting me rather than thwarting me."

"What do you want?"

"To do away with the criminals and to rule the people justly and honestly."

A peal of laughter rang out, filling the universe.

"You would like to double-cross me in order to realize your hidden dreams of power and authority."

"As a method, not as a goal."

"Your heart is still sunk in bondage."

"Try me out if you wish."

"I am a believing genie and I never overstep the bounds."

"Then remove yourself in peace from my path," said Gamasa once more, in despair.

"The fact is that I thought tranquilly on top of the mountains of Qaf and was persuaded that you had rendered me a service that cannot be gainsaid, even though unintended. I have thus decided to return the favor with a like one and not to overstep the bounds."

"But you are doing the very opposite of what you intended."

"How stupid you are!"

"Explain your purpose to me," he pleaded.

"You have a mind, a will, and a soul."

He was about to plead more with him but the genie let out a scornful laugh, then quickly withdrew his presence and vanished.

Gamasa al-Bulti awoke to a knocking at the door. His deputy walked in to inform him he was summoned to meet the governor al-Hamadhani.

XI

He wished he had been left to himself to think things over, but he had no choice but to go. He expected no good at all to come from the meeting. The flashes of hope in the autumn sky disappeared and the drums of victory fell silent. He would seesaw for a long time between the governor and Singam's pranks. He plunged into a bottomless pool of speculation as he rode on his mule along the road to the house of government, the way filled with movement and sound. He was encompassed by life's demands, followed scornfully by people's eyes. No joys or delusions: the days of pride had come to an end. A despised person feeding off ignominy—that is what Singam had persuaded him he was. His sole consolation was that he was the sword of state. But the sword had become blunt and security had broken down, so of what consequence was he? A murderous robber, protector of criminals, torturer of innocent men. He had forgotten God until he had been reminded of Him by a genie.

XII

He found Khalil al-Hamadhani standing in the middle of the reception hall like a spear ready for battle.

"The peace of God be upon you, O Emir," said Gamasa gently, to which the governor shouted in a voice trembling with rage, "Peace with your presence is nonexistent!"

"I work myself to death."

"And so the jewels of my women are stolen from within my own house!"

This was more than he expected. He wondered what Singam had been up to. He was dumbstruck.

"You're nothing but a useless hashish addict, an associate of thieves."

"I'm the chief of police," he said in a gruff voice.

"We'll meet up in the evening," shouted the governor, "or I'll sack you and cut off your head."

XIII

What was the point of searching? What could his men do in the face of Singam's power? He would be dismissed and would lose his honor, also his head. It was a fate to which he had often dispatched other people, so how could he blame him? But Gamasa would not accept his fate without defending himself—and fiercely too. Here was his life spread out before his eyes like a page: a concrete and terrifying testimony. It had started with a pact with God and had ended with one with the Devil. He had to topple it before death. The thought of the sheikh came to him like a stray breeze on a scorching summer's day: it blew, borne along on pure thoughts of nostalgia. He said to himself, "This is his time." He drew him forth from his deepest depths when his sorrows had ripped apart the solid crust besmirched with blood.

He found him in the simple reception room, as though expecting him. He bent over his head, silently, then squatted down on a cushion in front of him. Memories were inhaled like the perfume of a wilted rose, and in the empty space there materialized before him the verses of the Quran and the Sayings of the Prophet and the remnants of good intentions, like drops of blood. He drank his fill from the immanence of the divinely inspired peace until he was overcome with a sense of shame.

"I can read your feelings toward me, master," he said sadly.

"The knowledge of that is with God alone," said Abdullah al-Balkhi with his immutable calm, "so do not claim that of which you have no knowledge."

"In people's opinion," he said sadly, "I am a bloodthirsty policeman."

"Why, I wonder, do shedders of blood visit me?"

"How pleasant you are, master," he said, having taken heart. "The fact is, I have a story I would like you to hear."

"I have no desire to hear it," he said haughtily.

"I must make a decision and in no way can its significance be understood without the story being told."

"The decision is sufficient for an understanding of the story."

"The matter requires taking counsel," he said uneasily.

"No, it's your decision alone."

"Listen to my extraordinary story," he pleaded.

"No. One sole thing concerns me," he said calmly.

"What is it, master?"

"That you take your decision for the sake of God alone."

"It's for this reason that I am in need of your opinion," he said helplessly.

The sheikh said with resolute calm, "The story is yours alone and the decision yours alone."

XIV

He left the sheikh's house divided between doubt and certainty. It was as if the sheikh knew his story and his decision, as though he were blessing his decision provided it were for the sake of God alone. Had not despair played a role? Had not self-defense played another role? Had not desire for revenge played a third role? Would it, he wondered, diminish repentance if it were preceded by a sin? The thing to be taken into consideration was the final intention and persisting in it to the end. He was, in any case, burying the old Gamasa and evoking another one.

When he had taken his decision he gave a deep sigh of relief. His energy was redoubled. He visited his home and sat down with Rasmiya, his wife, and his daughter Akraman. His heart was flooded with mysteriously fervent emotions that made him feel his solitude more and more. Even Singam left him to his solitude. Nevertheless his resolution was final and knew no wavering. He faced the most dangerous situation in his life with rare courage and unfaltering resolve.

Returning to his place of work he freed, at his own initiative, the Shiites and Kharijites. He did this in a complete daze, and both troops and victims too were astonished at this action of his. As soon as it was evening he went to the house of government. He turned his gaze from the faces and places he met on his way as though they no longer concerned him. Finally he saw Khalil al-Hamadhani waiting with calm resoluteness, and he did not doubt that he too had arrived at a decision. The reception hall embraced them, no one being present but the human sufferings accumulated behind the cushions and fine draperies, and witnesses from all bygone generations. Exchanging no greeting, the governor coldly asked him, "What have you got to say?"

"Everything's fine," said Gamasa al-Bulti confidently.

"You've arrested the thief?" he inquired with sudden optimism.

"I've come for that purpose."

The governor frowned questioningly. "Do you think he's in my household?"

Gamasa pointed at him. "There he is," he said, "talking unashamedly."

"By the Lord of the Kaaba, you've gone crazy!" shouted Khalil al-Hamadhani, aghast.

"It is the truth being spoken for the first time."

As the governor prepared to take action, Gamasa drew his sword. "You'll receive your true deserts."

"You've gone crazy, you don't know what you're doing."

"I am doing my duty," he said calmly.

"Come to your senses—you're throwing yourself into the executioner's hands," he said in utter confusion and terror.

Gamasa launched a lethal blow at the neck. The governor's terrified screams mingled with his strangled bellowing as his blood spouted like a fountain.

XV

Gamasa al-Bulti was arrested and the sword snatched from his hand. He did not try to escape. He did not resist: he believed that his task had been completed. And so a sense of calm and serenity came over him, and a wave of extraordinary courage rose up that made him feel as though he were treading on his executioners, that he was greater than he imagined and that the base actions he had committed were in no way worthy of him and that submitting to their influence was a degradation that had driven him to his downfall and to being alienated from his human nature. He told himself that he was now practicing a form of worship whose purity would wash clean the filth of long years of dissipation.

With the autumnal breeze was spread the news, which became the talk of the high-class and the common folk. Consternation brought forth countless questions. Predictions conflicted and the ravings of maniacs flared up, while disorder began to sweep over the quarter and the city, its false rumors rising up to the sultan's palace itself. The vizier Dandan soon moved to the house of government at the head of a squadron of cavalry.

XVI

In irons, Gamasa al-Bulti was brought before the throne in the Hall of Judgment. Shahriyar appeared in his red cloak which he wore when sitting in judgment, on his head a tall turban studded with rare jewels. To his right stood Dandan, to his left the men of state, while guards were ranged on both sides. Behind the throne was Rama the executioner.

The sultan's eyes had a heavy look burdened with thought. He scrutinized the face of the chief of police for a long time, then asked him, "Do you not admit that I showed you my favor, Gamasa?"

The man answered in a strong, stirring voice. "Certainly, O Sultan."

The sultan waited for some sign of defiance from the prisoner despite his being shackled in irons.

"Do you admit killing Khalil al-Hamadhani, my deputy in your quarter?" he asked with a frown.

"Yes, O Sultan."

"What made you commit your repugnant crime?"

"It was to fulfill the just will of God," he said clearly and without heed to the consequences.

"And do you know what God the Almighty wants?"

"This is what I was inspired with through an extraordinary story that changed the course of my life."

The sultan, drawn to the word "story," inquired, "And what was that?"

Gamasa related his tale: being born of ordinary folk; studying at the prayer room of Sheikh Abdullah al-Balkhi; leaving the sheikh after learning the rudiments of religion, reading, and writing; his strong physique that had qualified him for service in the police; being chosen to be chief of police because of his rare ability; and being corrupted step by step until with time he was the protector of the corrupt and an executioner of the people of sense and judgment; the appearance of Singam in his life; the crises he had been through; and—finally—his bloody act of repentance.

Shahriyar followed attentively, with clearly conflicting reactions to his words.

"Gamasa's Singam following on from Sanaan al-Gamali's Qumqam," he said coldly. "We've found ourselves in the age of genies who have nothing better to do than kill governors."

"I haven't—and God is my witness—added a single word to the facts," said Gamasa.

"Perhaps you are dreaming that that will save you from punishment."

"My boldness affirms that I don't care," he said scornfully.

At a loss, Shahriyar said, "So let your head be cut off and hung above the door of your house, and let your properties be confiscated."

XVII

In an underground prison, and in darkness, he fought his pains and clung to his courage. He had aroused the sultan's ire and had triumphed over him, leaving him on his throne mumbling in defeat. Sorrowfully, he remembered Rasmiya and Akraman, while Husniya too ranged through his thoughts. His family would endure the same ignominy as had Sanaan's, but God's mercy was stronger than the universe. He thought that he would remain sleepless, but in fact he slept deeply, only waking at a loud noise and light from torches. Perhaps it was the morning and these were the soldiers come to lead him off to execution. The square would be crammed with people who had come out of curiosity, and there would be a mass of conflicting emotions. So be it. But what was he seeing? He was seeing the soldiers falling upon Gamasa al-Bulti with kicks, while the man woke up moaning with terror. What was the meaning of this? Was he dreaming? If that was Gamasa al-Bulti, then who was he? How was it that no one was taking any notice of him, as though he wasn't there? Amazed, he feared he was losing his mind— perhaps he had already done so. He was seeing Gamasa al-Bulti right there in front of him. The soldiers were driving him outside. And he— unlike him—was in a state of extreme terror and collapse. He also found himself free of his bonds. Resolved to leave the prison, he followed after the others. No one paid him any attention.

The whole city was crammed into the square where the punishment was to take place—men, women, and children. In the forefront were the sultan and the men of state. The leather apron, on which the execution would be performed, lay in the middle, with, alongside it, Shabeeb Rama and a group of his assistants. Neither Rasmiya nor Akraman had come, which was good. How many of the faces he knew and had had dealings with! He moved from place to place, but no one heeded him. As for Gamasa al-Bulti, he was approaching the leather apron amid his guards. A single face often appeared to him and surprised him: it was the face of Sahloul the bric-a-brac merchant. When the moment of awesome silence took control, and the leather apron wrenched all eyes to itself, his heart beat fast and it seemed to him he would breathe his last after the other's head had fallen. In a moment heavy with silence Shabeeb Rama's sword was raised aloft, then brought down like a thunderbolt, the head fell, and the story of Gamasa al-Bulti was at an end.

Gamasa al-Bulti had expected death, yet he passed it by and went off. His bewilderment was redoubled as he moved among the flow of people leaving, until the square was completely empty. He asked himself, "Am I Gamasa al-Bulti?" at which the voice of Singam came in answer, "How could you doubt it?"

The man, in a state of extreme excitement, called out, "Singam, it's you who are responsible for this miracle!"

"You are alive—all they killed was a likeness of my making."

"I am indebted to you for my life, so don't abandon me."

"No," he said distinctly, "now we're all square. I commend you to the protection of God."

"But how can I appear before people?" he called out in alarm.

"It is quite impossible for people to recognize you. Look in the first mirror you come across."

The
Porter

I

From above the door hung the head of Gamasa al-Bulti. Passersby looked at it, stood for a while, then went on—and Gamasa al-Bulti was one of them. They looked out of curiosity, or in pity, or gloatingly. As for him, he looked in stupefaction. He had not yet recovered from his distress on witnessing the eviction of his wife and daughter from their house. They had both passed by him without paying any heed, for he had assumed the form of a slim Ethiopian with crimpy hair and a light beard. His astonishment at his appearance did not cease, neither did his sadness for his family. He would circle round the house and listen to the conflicting comments voiced under the suspended head. The top people, like Karam al-Aseel, the druggist, and the draper would curse him mercilessly, while the common folk would express pity for him.

The new governor Yusuf al-Tahir, his private secretary Buteisha Murgan, and the new chief of police Adnan Shouma, supervised the confiscation of his house. He wondered what had gone to the general exchequer and how much had found its way into their pockets. He stayed close by the suspended head, looking and pondering and listening. He saw Ugr the barber saying to Ibrahim the water-carrier, pointing at the head, "They killed him for the solitary good act he did in his life."

"Why didn't his Muslim genie save him?" inquired the water-carrier.

"Don't delve into what you don't know," warned the barber, and Ma'rouf the cobbler confirmed his words.

Gamasa saw Sahloul the bric-a-brac merchant looking at the head with little concern and remembered his extraordinary energy on the day of the execution. When the merchant was on his own, he approached him and asked, "Can you not enlighten a stranger with the story of whose head this was?"

Sahloul glared at him with a look that sent shivers through his body. He felt that it penetrated to his depths, and the man took on for him an even greater mystery. As he made off, Sahloul said, "I know no more about him than others do."

Gamasa followed him with his eyes until he disappeared, then said to himself, "Perhaps he thinks himself too big to talk to a foreign Ethiopian."

He recollected his long history as a former policeman knowledge-able about people's circumstances, and he acknowledged that Sahloul had been the only influential merchant not to have formed a suspect relationship with him or with the governor. But he soon forgot him in the crush of his reflections. Then he saw Ragab the porter joining the group of Ugr, Ibrahim, and Ma'rouf, and he went up to him, impelled by a plan he had already worked out. He greeted him and said, "I'm an émigré Ethiopian and I want to work as a porter."

Ragab was reminded of his first friend, Sindbad, and said, "Come along with me, for God is a generous provider."

II

In spirit and body he hovered around his family. What value would there have been in his life if he had been detached from both his family and his head? He went on following Rasmiya and Akraman until they settled themselves in a room in the residence building where Sanaan's family were living. Without hesitation, he rented himself a room in the same building and became known as Abdullah the porter. In the clouds of his unrest it pleased him that it had been Umm Saad who had led his family to their new home. It pleased him that Umm Saad had not forgotten the fact that they had been neighbors of old and had not forgotten Rasmiya's attempt to help her in her adversity. She would join with Rasmiya in making the sweetmeats, which Fadil Sanaan would peddle round to the advantage of both families. He was greatly pleased by that, as well as by having them as neighbors. He enjoyed seeing them and knowing they were well. He would express his love for them and carry out such duties of a husband and a father as he was able to from afar, his situation being known by no one. He expected that Fadil would marry his daughter Akraman, as agreed with Sanaan, just as he dreamed one day of marrying Husniya, Fadil's sister.

He went on in that strange life, at times feeling he was alive, at others that he was dead.

III

Indeed, he was both Abdullah the living and Gamasa the dead: a strange experience never before known to man. Working for his daily bread in the company of Ragab, he would remember that he was alive; then, crossing the street under his suspended head, or seeing Rasmiya and Akraman, he would remember that he was dead. Never losing sight of his miraculous escape from death, he resolved to walk along the path of godliness till the end. He would find his pleasure in worship and would take delight in his solitude through remembering God. He would inwardly address his suspended head with the words "May you remain a symbol of the death of a wicked man who long abused his soul," though his heart would continually be filled with nostalgia for his short-lived persona, that persona that had crowned its life with a sincere repentance, ever stirred by the thought that a man could die when alive or live when dead. Who was there who could believe he was Gamasa al-Bulti in his hidden essence? Was it conceivable that he alone would possess this secret forever? Even Rasmiya and Akraman looked at him as if he were some stranger from foreign parts. He would thus feel before their indifferent gaze a cruel sense of alienation and of tortured injustice. Not once had they become aware of that deep-rooted love that lay behind his furtive glances. They gave back no echo to his feelings of longing. In their eyes the scene of the execution was repeated every morning and evening, and their sorrow at the memory of him cut into his soul as they immersed themselves in the daily worries of life. They would never believe that life had been granted to him by a miracle, nor be able to accept this fact. They had swallowed the agonies of his death and had suffered the grief. They had experienced life without him, and leaving their new situation would be as difficult as it had been to enter it. He would not venture to raze the new structure, would not be able to. He who had died must continue in death as a mercy to those he loves. It was up to him to get used to his death in his new life—let him be Abdullah the porter, not Gamasa al-Bulti. Let his happiness lie in work and worship. Nonetheless, his work often led him to the houses of his former friends and to the mansions of those with influence and positions of power: the world of outward piety and latent corruption. All that brought him back to thinking about himself and the circumstances of people, and it spoiled the serenity of his spiritual peace. He was pursued by crookedness and deviation as though his limbs had been taken by storm and their functions negated. He told himself that just as the stars proceed on their way in splendid order, so too must the concerns of God's creatures.

"But have I stayed on in life by a miracle in order that I might work as a porter?" he asked himself uneasily.

IV

Shahriyar looked at the specters of the trees that whispered together in the night. The sultan reclined in his seat on the back balcony despite the fact that autumn was retreating before the harbingers of winter. He was more able to bear the cold than to dispute with the flood of his thoughts. Turning toward his vizier Dandan, he inquired, "Do you dislike the dark?"

"I like what Your Majesty likes," the vizier said loyally.

He was always asking himself whether the sultan had truly changed or whether it was a passing phase. But be patient. In the past he had been decisive, clear, cruel, and insensitive. Now a perplexed look was quick to flash in his eyes.

"The nation is happy and profuse in its thanks," said Dandan.

"Ali al-Salouli was murdered," muttered the sultan sharply, "and was quickly followed by Khalil al-Hamadhani."

"Good and evil are like day and night," said Dandan with compassion.

"And the genies?"

"When faced with the leather mat of execution a criminal makes up what story he can."

"But I remember the stories of Shahrzad," he said quietly.

Dandan's heart beat fast and he said, "A murderer must meet his punishment."

"The truth is that I was on the point of contenting myself with imprisoning Gamasa al-Bulti." Then wrathfully, "But I executed him as a penalty for his insolent way of addressing me."

Dandan told himself that his master had changed only superficially. However, he said, "The villain in any case received his due."

"And I got my share of depression," he said sharply.

"Your Majesty, no doubt it is a transitory indisposition."

"No, it is one of the conditions of being—and did Shahrzad's stories tell me of anything apart from death?"

"Death!" said the vizier uneasily.

"Peoples swallowed up by peoples, with a sole determined victor knocking finally at their door: the Destroyer of Pleasures."

"It is the will of God, may your continuance in life be long!"

"The heart is a place of secrets," he said in an even voice, "and melancholy is shy. The kings of old were cured at night by wandering round and investigating the circumstances of the people."

Grasping at the life buoy, Dandan said, "Wandering about and investigating people's circumstances—what an inspiration!"

He said to himself, "A being without limits to his power: he may show himself to be a flower or he may bring about an earthquake."

V

Abdullah the porter continues on his rounds without pause: in the culs-de-sac and winding alleys, in the merchants' and craftsmen's quarters, along the boat routes, through the squares for shooting practice, hunting, and executions, and under the huge gates that act as boundaries, with aromas diffused like signposts: the penetrating smell of the druggist's shop, the narcotic essences, the tickling cloths, the appetizing foods, the stinking hides. Rasmiya and Akraman pass by, and Umm Saad and Husniya. He extends a greeting with a tongue that is hesitant in this world and with a heart that has inhabited the other. In his wanderings he has got to know Fadil Sanaan and has cemented his relationship with him. Among the people are those who keep in touch, such as Hasan the druggist and Nur al-Din, while some avoid him like the Devil.

Abdullah was anxious that the story of the genie should not be spread abroad lest it put an end to the future of Akraman and Husniya, both of whom were well set up for successful marriages. He loved Fadil Sanaan for his seriousness, his piety, and his courage, so he chose the stairway to the public fountain as a place to rest during his day's work, and there they would meet and chat. Once he said to him, "You're a pious young man who performs all his prayers, so why do you not safeguard your virtue by marrying?"

"I cannot find the necessary expenses."

"Not much is needed."

"I have my self-esteem and pride."

"There's Akraman right in front of you," said Abdullah temptingly.

Their eyes met in a smile that revealed many secrets.

"And you, Uncle Abdullah, are forty or more and are not married," said Fadil.

"I'm a widower, and I too would like to safeguard my virtue."

"It seems that you are in no need of a matchmaker."

"The lady Rasmiya, the mother of Akraman," he said gently.

Fadil laughed and said, "Let's wait a little and we'll present our-selves together."

"Why wait?"

"So that the memory of Gamasa al-Bulti may be erased."

His heart contracted: he wanted Rasmiya on the strength of his loyalty and piety. But if he obeyed his desires he would choose none other than Husniya. The day that Rasmiya accepted him he would rejoice with half his heart, while the other half would be in mourning.

VI

Whenever he found himself alone he would ask, "Have I been kept in life by a miracle that I might work as a porter?" He would also wonder, "Why did Singam not desert me at the crucial moment, as Qumqam did with Sanaan al-Gamali?" Filled with perplexity, like a vessel open to the rain, he found his legs had brought him to the house of Sheikh Abdullah al-Balkhi. He kissed his hand and sat down cross-legged in front of him, saying, "I am a stranger."

"We are all strangers," the sheikh interrupted him.

"Your name is like a flower that draws to it the wandering bees."

"Good actions are better than good words."

"But what are good actions? This is my difficulty."

"Did you not, on your coming, happen upon a man at his wit's end?"

"Where, master?"

"Between the stations of worship and of blood?" he said gently.

He trembled in fear and realized that the sheikh could see that which was veiled.

"In the pitch-black night the full moon is not to be found," he said with a sigh.

"I have known three types of disciples," said the sheikh.

"In all cases, they are fortunate."

"People who learn the principles and strive in the world; people who penetrate deeply in learning and assume control of things; and

people who persevere in journeying right up to the spiritual station of
love—but how few they are!"

Abdullah the porter thought for a while, then said, "But mankind
is in need of supervision."

Without losing his composure, the sheikh said, "Each in proportion to his zeal."

Abdullah overcame his own hesitancy by saying, "Yet I have had
you as my goal, master." He stumbled in silence as though to collect his
thoughts, and the sheikh said, "Do not speak to me of your goal."

"Why not?"

"Each in proportion to his zeal." And he lowered his eyelids,
withdrawing into himself.

Abdullah waited for him to open them again, but he did not do so.
Bending over and kissing his hand, he made his departure.

VII

He told himself that the sheikh was privy to his apprehensions and had
brought him back to himself. This he must accept, since he had put his
trust in someone. Tomorrow the evildoers will meet their woe by the
resolve of a penitent man and the guile of an experienced policeman. He
continued in his work, earning serenity and concentration of thought,
and from a compassion that spread through his heart his mind provided
itself with thoughts that knew no compassion, thoughts as sharp as the
blade of a sword. All too quickly life had taken him by surprise with its
droll contradictions, gory outcomes, and promised happiness. He refused to retreat because he had refused to take the gift of life without
paying the price. Then Husniya would appear before him like a ray of
hope gleaming in the sky of another world. In the late afternoon he
would take himself off to the stairway of the public fountain, where Fadil
Sanaan met with him. It became evident that the young man had leapt
over time more quickly than he had reckoned.

"I am going to ask for the hand of Akraman," said Fadil.

"Were you not thinking it best to wait a while?" Abdullah said in
astonishment.

"No, I've changed my mind—and I shall ask on your behalf for the hand of the lady Rasmiya."

Abdullah stayed silent in thought. No doubt she was in need of a man in her ordeal, and she could not hope for someone better than him.

"How lovely for mother and daughter to marry on the same night," said Fadil joyfully.

Having come to like and trust him, Fadil began to recount to him the stories of Sanaan al-Gamali and Gamasa al-Bulti.

VIII

When Fadil had finished his exciting tale, Abdullah commented, "God honors those He wishes to honor and humbles those He wishes to humble."

"Each in accordance with his zeal," muttered Fadil Sanaan.

The sentence hit him like the smell of pepper, and he wondered whether Fadil had learned the words from the same source. Preparing the way for a new direction in the conversation, he said, "And part of the perfection of zeal is caution."

Each of them turned about in his mind his own thoughts for a while, then Abdullah said, "We are on the point of becoming one family, and so I tell you that a porter enters houses that are open only to the elite."

Fadil guessed that his friend was about to deliver himself of a confidence. He gave him an inquiring look and Abdullah said, "In the houses of Yusuf al-Tahir the governor and Adnan Shouma the chief of police there are sometimes whisperings about the enemies of the state."

"It's only to be expected," said Fadil, feigning indifference.

"No one imagines that I understand the meaning of what is going on or that I am paying any attention to it."

"You're an unusual man, Uncle Abdullah, and you continue to astonish me."

"There is nothing astonishing about the astuteness of a man who has moved about in different places and circumstances."

"I'm truly happy to be with you," said Fadil.

Abdullah continued with what he had to say. "They are people obsessed with delusions. The more they go to excesses of criminality, the more they conjure up the specters of Shiites and Kharijites."

"I know that only too well."

"So it was that I said that part of the perfection of zeal is caution."

Fadil gave him a questioning look and asked, "What do you mean?"

"You're intelligent enough to know."

"You seem to be warning me."

"There's no harm in that."

"I am nothing but a seller of sweets—is there anything about me to cause you disquiet?"

He gave an enigmatic smile and said, "I like caution as much as I like the Shiites and Kharijites."

"To which group do you belong?" Fadil asked him eagerly.

"Neither to these nor to those, but I am the enemy of evildoers." Abdullah found himself before an open invitation, but, as a former policeman, he preferred to proceed in his own fashion.

IX

Abdullah the porter darted out like an arrow into the sky of his perceived holy war. Calling upon his strength of former times, he subdued it on this occasion to his pure and firm will. Immediately, Buteisha Murgan, the private secretary, was felled, murdered. It happened as he was making his way among his guards from the house of government to his own house after midnight, when, from out of the darkness, an arrow struck him, lodging in his heart. He was sprawled across his mule among the lances and lanterns of his guards, who swooped down on the surrounding quarters, arresting every passerby they came across, the loafers and those sleeping about in corners. His house was consumed with grief and the house of government was rocked, with Yusuf al-Tahir going out like a madman at the head of his forces. The news reached the vizier Dandan, who was made sleepless with terror till morning. And with morning the news had spread through the quarter and the whole city.

People were in a state of agitation and rumors were rife. It was a new link in the chain of the violent deaths of al-Salouli and al-Hamadhani, a new confirmation of the mysterious world of genies. Or was it the Shiites or the Kharijites? Or perhaps it was an isolated incident behind which lay concealed a woman's jealousy or a man's envy?

The skies opened up with heavy rain, which continued for the whole day so that mud piled up and water covered with scum flowed in the alleys and lanes, spoiling the arrangements for Buteisha's funeral and burial, and warning of a cruel winter. Abdullah the porter slipped in among the common folk at the Café of the Emirs, his senses alert with concealed attention. The murder became the subject of all conversation, views differing between the declared thoughts of the elite and the whispered exchanges of the common folk. Abdullah spotted Sahloul the bric-a-brac merchant engaged in a long conversation with Karam al-Aseel the millionaire and his heart tightened. He did not forget the penetrating look Sahloul had given him under his suspended head and he remembered seeing him circling around the retinue of the private secretary when he, Abdullah, had been about to shoot the arrow. So how was it that he had not been arrested? How had he vanished from the sight of the guards? Abdullah's heart contracted with fear. He was surprised that, during the whole of his time as chief of police, the only man in the quarter about whom he had not come to know some secret was Sahloul. He was conversant with the circumstances of all the persons of position, with what was known and what was hidden, except for this man, who was a closed riddle.

X

The fever heat of those in positions of responsibility did not abate, nor the harsh measures taken by them. As for the rest of the people, they became used to the incident, grew bored with talking about it, then forgot about it. Soon the demands of life took over from the events of history, and Umm Saad, the widow of Sanaan, said to the lady Rasmiya, the widow of Gamasa al-Bulti, "With the blessing of God and His wisdom, my son Fadil would like to marry Akraman."

Amid general rejoicing agreement was reached. They were all living in the real world and did not let a bygone dream spoil it. Then Umm Saad said, "You too, Lady Rasmiya!" And she made known the wish of Abdullah the porter to marry her. Rasmiya gave a slight laugh of surprise; she was neither pleased with the news, nor did she welcome it.

"Marriage is for Akraman and Husniya, not for us," she said shyly. Then, after a silence, she continued, "Gamasa has not died, his memory is still alive in me."

Fadil and Abdullah were both happy, each with the news he had received. Yes, Abdullah was upset at having to bury his emotions, but the Gamasa who was hidden inside him was overjoyed.

XI

The wedding was celebrated in Umm Saad's room. The two families were in attendance. Abdullah the porter was invited, and he brought as a present for the couple some amber and incense with the money he had earned during the day sweeping the courtyard, which he did with the same ardor he had employed when he embarked upon killing Buteisha Murgan, being intoxicated with the burning fragrance of the family, which had transfused into his limbs a lasting state of drunkenness. His heart boiled with the emotions of being a father and a husband, while at the same time love was humbled under the control of piety and love of God the Merciful. He regained the riches of an old emotion and took delight in being so close, burying his secret in a well that overflowed with sadness.

Husniya volunteered to enliven her brother's wedding, relying on her mastery of poetry and singing and her fine voice. To handclapping she sang melodiously:

"My eye translates from my tongue for you to know,
 disclosing to you what my heart conceals.
 When we met and tears were shed
 I became dumb and my eye spoke of the worries of my secret love."

They were all moved. So moved was Abdullah that his heart filled with tears. Rising to put wood on the fire, he heard a knocking at the door. As he opened it there loomed up in the cold darkness three spectral figures.

"We're foreign merchants," said one of them. "We heard some beautiful singing and told ourselves that noble people don't turn away strangers."

Fadil motioned to the women, who hid themselves behind a screen that bisected the room.

"Enter in peace," he told the strangers. "It is just a wedding that is restricted to the simple people involved."

"We want only to enjoy a friendly atmosphere with good people," said one of the strangers.

"It's beautifully warm here," said another.

Fadil brought them a dish of the sweet *baseema* and another of *mushabbik* with the words: "We have nothing but this—it's what we make our living from."

"We praise God, Who has provided us with these delicious things to eat and has made our evening so enjoyable."

The leading man leaned over and said something into the ear of one of the others, who left the place in a hurry. Abdullah caught some glances from the leading man and it seemed to him that it was not the first time he had seen him. He tried to remember where and when it had been, but his memory failed him. Then the man came back loaded with fried and grilled fish. People's appetites were sharpened with the prospect of such delicious food.

"Our dwelling is not worthy of someone of your rank," said Fadil in thanks.

"A dwelling is known by those who live in it," said the man courteously, then made the request: "Let us hear some music, for it is this that has given us joy in making your acquaintance."

So Fadil went behind the screen and before he was seated again the voice of Husniya came to them as she sang:

> *"Had we known of your coming, we would have spread out*
> *our very hearts, the very blackness of our eyes;*

Spread out our cheeks that we might meet
through the exchange of glances.''

Everyone was moved and one of the strangers called out, "Praise be to
the Great Creator!"

The leading man asked Fadil, "How did you come to own this
slave-girl if you are as poor as you claim?"

"She's just my sister."

"She has a trained voice that bespeaks a noble origin."

Fadil was speechless, and it was Abdullah the porter who said, "He
is in fact of noble origin but his path was obstructed by the perfidy of
time."

"What's the story of that perfidy?"

"There is no one in our city," answered Abdullah the porter,
"who does not know the story of the merchant Sanaan al-Gamali."

The merchant was silent for a while, then said, "It is one of the
extraordinary tales we have heard of your city."

"But do you believe what is related of the genie?" inquired one of
his comrades.

"Why not," asked Fadil in his turn, "when such catastrophes have
been brought down upon us?"

"But the ruler cannot summon genies to give evidence or be
interrogated, so how can justice be done?"

"It is for the ruler to dispense justice from the beginning so that
genies don't intrude on our lives."

The leading man of the strangers asked him, "Do you suffer injustice in your lives?"

The caution he had acquired from his past experience in the police
force came to his aid.

"We have a just sultan, praise be to God, though life is not devoid
of ordeals."

The conversation continued for a while till the strangers rose and
left.

XII

The three of them plunged silently into the darkness. The second merchant turned toward the first and said, "Hopefully Your Majesty found the entertainment he had wished for?"

"A viewing of the afflictions of the heart," muttered the other.

Then, after a while, "The company of poets no longer exhilarates me, nor do the antics of Shamloul the hunchback make me laugh."

"May God keep you in His care, Your Majesty."

"A short and baffling dream," he said, addressing himself. "No truth shows itself but it vanishes."

The other waited for the sultan to throw some light on his words, but he kept silent.

XIII

Fadil and Akraman took a room, while a second room did for Rasmiya, Umm Saad, and Husniya. Despite the simplicity of their life, the two newlyweds enjoyed a serene happiness, and Fadil wished for Husniya the same sort of happy outcome as he had had.

He was more successful in forgetting the past than the women were, for he had things to occupy him, while for them the bygone days with their glory and bright lights were not erased from their memory.

He spent time alone with Abdullah the porter exchanging the thoughts of mind and heart. The man was made of sound metal and had a noble soul; his attention was drawn to the worries of mankind, as though he were a man of religion rather than a porter. Had a passerby listened in to the conversation that took place between them, he would have been taken aback and would have thought them to be men of consequence disguised as peddler and porter.

One day Fadil said, "I have opened my heart to you, but you have kept yours closed."

Abdullah denied this with a movement of his head.

"There's a secret in your life," he went on, "and you're no simple porter."

"I had a spiritual guide in my native land," Abdullah said, reassuring him. "There's no secret about that."

"That explains it."

"In any event we both quench our intellectual thirsts from one and the same source."

"And so I'd like to ask you one favor," said Fadil boldly.

Abdullah fixed him with an inquiring look and Fadil said significantly, "By reason of your work you come and go in all sorts of houses."

Abdullah gave a knowing smile and was silent while he waited for him to continue.

"Do you sometimes agree to carry messages?"

"There are people who find meaning to their lives by pursuing troubles," he said smiling, remembering Akraman affectionately.

"Do you accept?" he asked, ignoring what Abdullah had said.

"As you wish—and more," he said quietly.

XIV

He performed this subsidiary task with complete ease and assurance, for he did not reckon it to be a significant addition to his basic function. His personal worries—Rasmiya and Husniya, and his wavering between life and death—though not erased from the surface of his mind, no longer troubled him, while his general worries had disappeared, as the waves of a river disappear into the open sea. The second person in his program was Yusuf al-Tahir or Adnan Shouma, whichever was easier. But he gave precedence over them to Ibrahim al-Attar the druggist, for an anomalous slight that had not previously occurred to him: Abdullah had once carried for him certain goods; they had quarreled about payment, and the powerful merchant had cursed and insulted him.

The lethal arrow became embedded in Ibrahim al-Attar's heart as he was returning home after the evening session at the café. Terror erupted in the city and memories of the killings of al-Salouli, Buteisha Murgan, and al-Hamadhani were awakened.

Abdullah and Fadil met up on the steps of the drinking fountain at the height of the trouble. They exchanged alarmed looks while in vain trying to conceal their pleasure.

"What terrible happenings!" muttered Abdullah.

The other intuited his views and said in all innocence, "The assassination was not part of our plan."

Feigning dismay, Abdullah said, "Perhaps it was an act of personal revenge."

"I don't think so."

"But he was no more corrupt than anyone else."

"The upper class know that he was putting poison into the medicine of the governor's enemies."

Abdullah said to himself that his friend knew as many people's secrets as he knew himself—maybe more. "If the assassination was not part of our plan, then who was the perpetrator?"

"God knows," said Fadil irritably. "He kills and we pay the price."

XV

When he put out the candle and took himself to bed, he felt the strange presence crowding in on him. His heart quaked and he mumbled, "Singam!"

The voice asked him coldly, "What have you done?"

"I do in my own way what I believe is best."

"It was more a reaction to the insult inflicted on you."

"All I did was to give him precedence," he said hotly. "His turn would have come sooner or later."

"Your account is with Him Who is privy to what is in people's breasts. Beware, man."

Singam vanished, and Abdullah did not sleep a wink.

XVI

Above the dome of the mosque of the Tenth Imam, in a session replete with tranquillity and the cold of winter, Qumqam and Singam sat enveloped in the cloak of night, while underneath it swarmed the forces of the police, out for revenge, sparks flying from their blood-red eyes. Qumqam whispered scornfully, "O the suffering of mankind!"

"All I did," said Singam apologetically, "was to save Gamasa al-Bulti's soul from hellfire."

"We never once interfered in their lives with things turning out as we wanted."

"And to connive with them is more than we can bear."

At that moment there passed below them Sahloul the bric-a-brac merchant. Pointing to him, Qumqam said, "I am happy for him that he lives with them as though he too were a human."

Sharing his opinion, Singam said, "But he is an angel, the Angel of Death, Azrael's agent in the quarter. His duty requires of him that he mix with them night and day, and he is permitted to do things that we are not."

"Let us pray to God to inspire us to do what is right."

"Amen," replied Singam.

XVII

The activities of Abdullah the porter were obstructed by an incident that troubled him. He had made his way with a large weight of nuts and dried fruit to the house of Adnan Shouma, the chief of police. He had not stopped mulling over the killing of Ibrahim al-Attar the druggist: how much was genuine holy war and how much anger and a desire for revenge? The path of God was clear and it should not be fused with anger or pride, or else the whole structure would collapse from its foundations.

Adnan Shouma's house lay in Pageants and Festivals Street, a short distance from the house of government. It was a dignified street, on both sides of which were private mansions and large inns; it also had a garden and an open space where slave-girls were sold. As he entered the house he said to himself, "Your turn's coming soon, Adnan." Then, about to leave, he was stopped by a slave, who asked him to go and see the master of the house. He went to a reception room, his heart quivering with unease. The man looked at him with his small, round face and cruel, narrow eyes as he fingered his beard, then asked, "Where are you from?"

"Ethiopia," answered Abdullah humbly.

"I have been told that you have a good reputation and that you don't miss a single prayer."

"It is by God's kindness and His mercy," he said, having received the first breath of comfort.

"That is why my choice has fallen on you."

The intended meaning circulated in his head like a strong aroma in a closed room. How many times, when he was chief of police, had he spoken just such words to some man, foreshadowing his recruitment into the organization of spies, the man knowing that to try to slide out of the assignment was tantamount to a sentence of death, that there was no choice but to obey!

"In this way," said Adnan Shouma, "you gain honor in the service of the sultan and of religion."

Abdullah pretended to be delighted and proud. He gave him such indications as would reassure him, at which the other said, "Be careful of that which brings the traitor to ruin."

"It makes me happy to serve in the ranks of God," he muttered enigmatically.

"Houses are open to you by virtue of your work," said Adnan, "and all you lack are some directives, which have been set down in secret records since the time of Gamasa al-Bulti."

XVIII

He left Adnan Shouma's house bearing a new load, a load heavier than the one he had brought. On meeting Fadil Sanaan, he let him into his new secret. Fadil thought about the matter for a long time, then said, "You have become two-eyed: one for us and one against us."

But Abdullah was immersed in his worries.

"Don't you regard this," Fadil asked him, "as a gain for us?"

"It is demanded of me that I show my sincere devotion to the work," Abdullah said gloomily.

Fadil took refuge in his silent thoughts and Abdullah continued, "I wonder if he summoned me because he suspects me."

"They are men of violence," responded Fadil, "and they have no need of subterfuge."

"I agree, but how should I prove my loyalty?"

Fadil thought for a time, then said, "Circumstances sometimes require that we send some of our people abroad. I'll point one of them out to you, so you can report him—and he'll slip away at just the right moment, as though by chance."

"A happy solution, but not one that can be repeated," said Abdullah, his eyes shining at the prospect.

"It's truly a way of putting them in a fix, though," said Fadil, talking to himself.

"So at last you're thinking as I do." And he asked himself whether he would be able to go on carrying out his secret plan.

Suddenly his thoughts were dispersed as he saw Sahloul crossing the street in front of them, paying no attention to anything. As usual his heart tightened, and he nudged Fadil.

"What do you know about this man?" he asked.

"Sahloul the bric-a-brac merchant," said Fadil in a natural tone. "He was one of father's friends, and perhaps he's the one merchant who enjoys a blameless record."

"What else do you know about him?"

"Nothing."

"Doesn't his inscrutability arouse your curiosity?"

"His inscrutability? He's simplicity itself; an active, knowledgeable man who is not concerned with others. What makes you wonder about him?"

After a slight hesitation he said, "He has a penetrating gaze that makes me uneasy."

"There is no basis for your suspicions—he is a virtuous exception to a corrupt rule."

Abdullah hoped Fadil was right and that his own suspicions would be proved wrong.

XIX

From his previous experience he was certain that he would be placed under surveillance, as happened with all new plainclothesmen. It would be out of the question for him to undertake any new venture unless he removed Adnan Shouma himself from his path with a successful stroke.

And so he slipped into Adnan's house for a secret meeting and said to him, "Soon much fruit will fall. The quarter is full of infidels, but I think it best that I avoid coming to see you frequently."

"I shall appoint a go-between for you," said Adnan Shouma happily.

"That is sufficient for ordinary matters. But for important ones contact should be restricted to yourself."

"We'll arrange that later."

"The best kindness is the one soonest done," said Abdullah, quoting the proverb.

"I am sometimes to be found outside the wall of the quarter," said Adnan Shouma after some thought. "I think it is a suitable place."

His scheming had worked out better than he had hoped.

XX

With the assistance of Fadil Sanaan he forwarded a report about a young, unmarried man who lived on his own in a rooming house in the cul-de-sac of the tanners. When the force of troops swooped down on where he was living, it became apparent that he had left only minutes before to go on a journey. Adnan Shouma was furious and said to Abdullah, "You aroused his suspicion without realizing."

Abdullah assured him he was more crafty than he imagined, but Adnan sent him away, unhappy with him.

XXI

The governor's residence was rocked to its foundations, as was the quarter and the whole city, by the discovery of Adnan Shouma's body outside the walls. Shahriyar himself was enraged. Mysterious fears loomed up before the eyes of eminent people, who crept out of their lairs in the darkness. Abdullah learned from his sources that the investigation was concentrating on discovering why the chief of police had gone secretly beyond the quarter's wall. And Abdullah had been the first to know of his victim's secret of going to a private house to meet Gulnar and Zahriyar, the two sisters of Yusuf al-Tahir, governor of the quarter. In fact, he had known the way of life of the two women since he had first joined the service and before Yusuf al-Tahir had taken up his appointment. So it was that the chief of police had asked to meet him in a pavilion in the garden of the mansion and had then sent him away. He had not returned, though, to the quarter but had hung about for him in the dark until he left the mansion before dawn, when he had met him with the fatal arrow. Now his sense of security was vanishing and he did not think it unlikely that some of those close to Adnan Shouma, women and men, had known of the secret meeting between him and the man.

He decided to make his escape, if only for a while. He therefore left the whole quarter and took himself off behind the open space by the river, close by the green tongue of land where he used to practice his hobby of fishing, the same spot where he had met Singam. Finding a towering palm tree, he threw himself down beneath it and sank into thought. Night came, the stars twinkled gently and it grew cold. Had he planned things well, he wondered, or had his eagerness to carry out his plan thwarted his objective? When and how would he be given the chance to take action again? How could he avoid his enemies and make contact with his friend Fadil Sanaan?

In the silence of the night there came to him a voice saying, "O Abdullah!"

He looked in the direction of the voice, toward the river, and asked, "Who is calling?"

"Come closer," said the voice in a tone that diffused a sense of security, calm, and peace.

He approached the river, walking warily, until he saw its dark surface under the light of the stars. He saw too a spectral form, half in the water and half leaning with its arms against the shore.

"Are you in need of help?" he asked.

"It is you who need help, Abdullah."

"Who are you and what do you know of me?" he asked apprehensively.

"I am Abdullah of the Sea just as you are Abdullah of the Land, and the grip of evil is tightening around your neck."

"Sir, what keeps you in the water? What sort of living creature are you?"

"I am none but a worshiper in the never-ending kingdom of the water."

"You mean it's a kingdom that lives under the water?"

"Yes. In it perfection has been attained and oppositions have vanished, nothing disturbing its serenity but the misery of the people living on the land."

"Extraordinary are the things I hear but the power of God is without limit," said Abdullah in wonder.

"Likewise His mercy, so take off your clothes and plunge into the water."

"Why so, sir? Why ask this of me on a cold night?"

"Do as I say before the fatal grip closes around your throat."

In no time Abdullah of the Sea had plunged into the water of the river, leaving him to make his choice. Urged on by some crazy inspiration, he took off his clothes and plunged into the river until he had disappeared completely. Then he heard the voice saying to him, "Return safely to the land."

No sooner did he feel the ground underfoot than his heart settled itself between his ribs and he felt himself to be as one of the predators of the sky, the earth, and the night. He was conscious, too, of a warmth. Then sleep came over him. He slept deeply and peacefully, and it was as if the stars sparkled only that they might watch over him. He woke before daybreak. Looking into his mirror in the first rays of light, he saw before him a new face not known to him before.

"Blessed are wondrous things if of God's making!" he exclaimed.

It was neither the face of Gamasa al-Bulti nor that of Abdullah. It was a wheat-colored face with a clear complexion, a flowing black beard and thick hair with a parting that fell down to his shoulders, while the look in his eyes sparkled with the language of the stars. Abdullah had been overtaken by death, just as had previously happened to Gamasa al-Bulti. Fadil and Akraman had disappeared, Rasmiya and Husniya too, also Umm Saad. But new voices materialized and adventures that came with sunrise, and a new world that disclosed wondrous things.

XXII

He found life pleasant in the open space close to the green tongue of land that stretched out into the river. The date palm was his companion, and fishing in the river provided his food, while the pure air was constantly with him. The people who came for amorous diversion and music earned his displeasure yet gained his forgiveness. As for his heart's ease, he found it in conversing with Abdullah of the Sea.

People who crossed the river brought with them the news of the city. Among the things he learned was that the governor, Yusuf al-Tahir, had chosen Husam al-Fiqi as his private secretary and Bayumi al-Armal as his chief of police. He learned too that the security forces had stormed the quarter and were looking for Abdullah the porter. They had arrested his friends and had led Ragab the porter and Fadil Sanaan and his wife Akraman off to prison. Thus his feeling of security all too quickly came to an end and his heart became anxious. Once again he goaded himself into action.

XXIII

He did not go in order to kill but to present himself as a ransom for those he loved. He was not conscious of any feelings of fear or misgivings. His sense of enlightenment took him above his uneasiness. He went straight to Bayumi al-Armal at police headquarters and with calm composure said, "I have come to confess before you that I am the killer of Adnan Shouma."

The chief of police looked at him closely. "And who are you?" he asked.

"Abdullah of the Land, the fisherman."

From his appearance the chief of police reckoned him to be mad and ordered him to be put in fetters of iron in case he were dangerous, then asked him, "And why did you kill Adnan Shouma?"

"I am entrusted with the killing of evil people," he said simply.

"And who entrusted you?"

"Singam, a believing genie, and through his inspiration I killed Khalil al-Hamadhani, Buteisha Murgan, and Ibrahim al-Attar the druggist."

The man humored him, saying, "The previous chief of police, Gamasa al-Bulti, has already confessed to killing Khalil al-Hamadhani."

"Originally I was Gamasa al-Bulti," he exclaimed.

"His head's hanging at the door of his house."

"I've seen it with my own eyes."

"And you insist that the head is yours?"

"There's no doubt about it, and you'll believe me when you hear my story."

"But how and when did you fix yourself up with this new head?"

"Let me ask for Singam to come as a witness."

"You should be kept locked up forever in a lunatic asylum," the man bellowed, and he ordered him to be sent straight to the asylum.

"Help, Singam!" he shouted as he was being taken away. "Come to my rescue, Abdullah of the Sea!"

Fadil was tortured for a long time in prison, until the governor found no alternative but to release him, along with the others. At the same time he gave orders to discover the whereabouts of Abdullah the porter.

Nur al-Din
and
Dunyazad

I

Moonlight flooded the balkh trees in Shooting Square, making the smooth bezoar flowers glow, while it also immersed Qumqam and Singam. They were settled on one of the branches of the highest tree on a night when the breaths of departing winter were mingling with those of a spring that was ready to come into being.

"How good is time if it flows under the pleasure of Providence!" said Qumqam.

"When divine immanence abides, the whispering of the flowers is heard as they glorify and praise God."

"What does man lack for the enjoyment of the blessings of time and place?"

"That's what baffles me, brother: has he not been granted an intellect and a soul?"

Qumqam pricked up his ears warily, then asked, "Is there not some warning harbinger in the air?"

At this a male and a female genie alighted on a nearby branch, both shamelessly intoxicated.

"Sakhrabout and Zarmabaha," whispered Singam.

"Godlessness and evil," whispered Qumqam.

Sakhrabout laughed derisively and commented, "We enjoy existence without fear."

"There is no happiness for those whose hearts are empty of God," Qumqam shouted at him.

"Really?" said Zarmabaha sarcastically.

And she and her companion began making love, and sparks flew from their embrace. Qumqam and Singam disappeared, at which Sakhrabout and Zarmabaha let out a shout of triumph, and he said to her, "You've been away from me an age."

"I was playing a trick in a temple in India. And where were you?"

"I made a journey over the mountains."

"On my return," said Zarmabaha seductively, "I saw a girl whose beauty stunned me. It must be admitted . . ."

"I too saw a handsome young man in the Perfume Quarter, whose beauty has no equal among mankind."

"A glance at my girl would erase from your memory the picture of your young man."

"That's an unjustified exaggeration."

"Come and see with your own eyes."

"Where is your girl to be found?"

"In the sultan's palace itself."

In the twinkle of an eye the two of them were in the reception wing of the sultan's palace. A girl made her appearance: a prodigious beauty. She was taking off her cloak embroidered with threads of gold in order to put on her nightdress made of Damascene silk.

"Dunyazad, the sister of Shahrzad, wife of the sultan," said Zarmabaha.

"Her beauty is in truth greater than life itself. No fragile human being is favored with such beauty."

"You are right—it shines for just a few days, then time impairs it."

"So you take delight in gloating over them."

"They have an intellect but they live the life of imbeciles."

"How very immortal she appears!"

"Perhaps you will now concede that she is more beautiful than your young man?"

"I don't know," said Sakhrabout after some hesitation. "Come and see for yourself."

In less than an instant they were in the shop of the young man, a paragon of handsomeness. He was closing the shop and putting out the lamp before leaving.

"This is Nur al-Din the perfume-seller."

"His handsomeness is also outstanding. Where is your friend from?"

"As you see, he is a seller. What interest is it to us where he is from?"

"Of all males he is most suited to my young girl, and she of all females is most suited to him."

"They live in the same city but are as divided as the sky and the earth."

"This is indeed an irony—and yet it is we who are accused of playing jokes!"

"How is it that the matchmakers are not competing over this girl?"

"Steady! Many would like to have her, among them Yusuf al-Tahir, governor of the quarter, and Karam al-Aseel the millionaire, but who is worthy of the sister of the sultan's wife?"

"Zarmabaha, this world is weighed down with stupidity."

"I've an idea," exclaimed Zarmabaha joyfully.

"What is it?"

"An idea worthy of Satan himself."

"You've set my curiosity afire."

"Let's have some crafty fun and bring them together!"

II

The black eyes of Dunyazad were lit up. It was the wedding party at the sultan's palace, a marvel of luxurious splendor. The palace rippled with the lights of candles and lanterns, setting aglitter the jewels of those who had been invited, and resounded with the singing of the male and female performers. The sultan Shahriyar himself bestowed his blessing by giving her as a present the jewel of the wedding night.

"May your night be blessed, Dunyazad," he said to her.

She waited in the bedchamber at the end of the night in a dress decorated with gold, pearls, and emeralds. Her mother bade her farewell, also her sister Shahrzad, and alone she waited in the bedchamber, lost in thought, concerned only with her anxious waiting and beating heart. The door opened, and Nur al-Din, in all his Damascene finery, Iraqi turban, and Moroccan slippers, entered. Like the full moon he advanced toward her and removed the veil from her face. Kneeling down in front of her, he clasped her legs to his chest. With a sigh he said, "The night of a lifetime, my beloved."

He began stripping off her clothes piece by piece in the silence of the bedchamber that was filled with hidden melodies.

III

Dunyazad opened her eyes. The curtain was letting light through. She found herself immersed in the memories of the magic source from which she had sipped. Her lips were moist with kisses, her ears intoxicated with the sweetest words, her imagination replete with the warmth of sighs. The sensation of being embraced had not left her body, nor the tenderness. This was now the morning, but . . . Only too swiftly the harsh winds of consciousness blew over her. Where was the bridegroom? What was his name? When had the formalities of the marriage been carried out? O Lord, she had not been proposed to, she had not been given in marriage, and there had been no party at the palace. She was being snatched from her dream like someone being led to the execution mat. Was it really a dream? But the nature of dreams is for them to vanish, not to become so firmly established and corporeal that they can be touched and sensed. The room was still fragrant with his breathing. She jumped to the floor. She found that she was naked and had been despoiled of her innocence. A terrible penetrating trembling assailed her.

"It's madness!" she exclaimed in despair.

Gazing around her in stupefaction, she again exclaimed, "It's ruin!" And madness loomed like some pursuing beast.

IV

As for the awakening of Nur al-Din, he was angry and agitated on seeing his simple bedroom in the dwelling that lay above his shop in the Perfume Quarter. Had it been a dream? But what an extraordinary dream, with all the power and heaviness of reality. Here was the bride in all her beauty, a reality that could not be forgotten or erased from his heart. When and how had he been stripped of his clothes? He was still smelling that lovely fragrance that had no parallel among his scents. He could still see the sumptuous bedchamber with its curtains, its divans, and its fantastic bed.

"What's the point of playing a joke on a sincere believer like myself?"

He was tortured not by reality alone but also by love.

V

Zarmabaha guffawed with laughter and asked Sakhrabout, "What's your opinion of this hopeless love?"

"A truly unique jest."

"Mankind has never known such a thing."

"Not necessarily," said Sakhrabout. "They are keen on creating illusions."

"But how?"

"How many there are who imagine that they have intelligence or the ability to compose poetry, or are possessed of courage."

"What idiots they are!" she said, laughing.

"I am amazed at why they should have been given preference over us."

VI

Dunyazad resigned herself to the fact that her secret was too heavy for her to bear alone. She hastened to Shahrzad's wing of the palace just after Shahriyar had gone off to the Council of Justice. No sooner did Shahrzad see her than she asked anxiously, "What's wrong with you, sister?"

Seating herself on a cushion at the feet of the sultana, she raised her eyes with an appeal for help. Choking with sobs she said, "I wish it were illness or death."

"I take my refuge in God—don't say such a thing. We parted yesterday and you were fine."

"Then something happened that does not occur in the world of the sane."

"Tell me, for you have upset my peace of mind."

Lowering her eyes, she recounted to her the story that had begun with an imagined marriage and ended in real blood. Shahrzad followed the tale with doubt and anxiety, then said encouragingly, "Don't hide anything from your sister."

"I swear to you by the Lord of the Universe that in my story I have not added or taken away a single word."

"Would he be some scoundrel from among the palace men?" inquired Shahrzad.

"No, no, I have never set eyes on him."

"What man of sense would accept your story?"

"That is what I tell myself. It is a story like one of your amazing tales."

"My tales are derived from another world, Dunyazad."

"I have fallen prisoner to the truth of your mysterious world, but I do not want to be its victim."

Shahrzad said sadly, "I shall know the truth sooner or later, but I am frightened that disgrace will overtake us before that."

"That is what kills me with fear and worry."

"If the sultan gets to know your story, his doubts will once more be awakened and he will revert to his low opinion of our sex and will perhaps send me to the executioner and himself go back to his previous behavior.''

"God forbid that any harm should befall you on my account,'' exclaimed Dunyazad.

Shahrzad thought for a while, then said, "Let us keep our story a secret, with neither the sultan nor my father knowing it. I shall arrange with my mother what shall be done, but you must return to our house with the excuse of being homesick.''

"How wretched I am!" muttered Dunyazad.

VII

Nur al-Din asked his mother, Kalila al-Dumur to come to see him. The old woman came, moving her lips in a silent recital of verses from the Quran. Her emaciated face bore traces of an old beauty. He sat her down by his side on a sofa from Khurasan and asked her, "Were we visited by any strangers while I was asleep?"

"No one knocked at the door.''

"Was no voice heard coming from my room?"

"None. While I myself sleep, my senses don't—the faintest of sounds wakes me up. Why do you ask such strange questions?"

"Perhaps it was a dream, though quite unlike other dreams.''

"What did you see, my son?"

"I saw myself in the presence of a beautiful girl.''

"It is an invitation to marriage from the unseen,'' said Kalila with a smile.

"It was a reality both felt and sensed,'' he said sharply. "I don't know how to doubt it, but I am also unable to believe it.''

Said the old woman simply, "Don't worry yourself—get married.''

"Have you ever heard of a reality that disappears in a dream?"

"The Lord is omnipotent—you will forget everything before an hour is past.''

"Yes," he said with a sigh.

He knew he was lying and that he would not forget, that his heart was throbbing with real love and that his beloved was flesh and blood, a beloved who would not be forgotten, whose impression was ineffaceable.

VIII

Nur al-Din opened up his shop and looked at people with a new face. All his adolescent life he had been known for his pure good looks and quickness of mind. But that spring morning he looked distracted and confused. Those who used to rejoice at his appearance wondered what it was that had altered him and taken over his mind. He too was all the time wondering about the extraordinary dream which surpassed reality in its devastating effect. He had reached twenty years of age without marrying because of an old desire to marry Husniya, the sister of his friend Fadil Sanaan. Formerly he had hesitated because of his limited income and the great wealth of her father; after that he had hesitated because of his mother's objection to his marrying the daughter of a man whose life had been mixed up with a genie.

"Keep away from evil, for we do not know anything about such secrets," the old woman had said.

He had kept his friendship with Fadil, leaving Husniya to time. But where was Husniya now? Where, too, the world and everything in it? Nothing existed but that sparkling image, the sumptuous bedchamber, and the bed itself which was larger than the whole of his own bedroom. He had seen a vision of reality, had made real love, and here he was now loving in a way in comparison with which any actual love would be weak and feeble. Here he was suffering life's languor, its loneliness, its melancholy and everlasting sadness in being separated from her; it lingered in his nostrils. As for her whispered words, they repeated themselves with his every breath.

He recollected his youth spent under the wing of Sheikh Abdullah al-Balkhi learning to read and write and the rudiments of religion. When he had had his fill and was about to bid the sheikh farewell, the man had said to him, "How better suited you are to Love."

Understanding that the sheikh was inviting him to stay on with him, he said, "My father is ill and I must replace him in the shop."

"I don't accept in my company of disciples anyone who does not work."

"Let worship and devoutness be enough for me."

He did not fail to keep to his thoughts on this and did not turn aside from the straight path. Now he remembered the spontaneous words of the sheikh: "How better suited you are to Love!" Should he visit the sheikh to seek advice? But he was afraid and conceded that it was appropriate that the secret be kept within his heart.

He followed with his eyes the stream of veiled women. Could his beloved be one of them? She was to be found somewhere, of that he had no doubt: to be found somewhere, in this time now and no other. Maybe our yearnings roam about crazily as they strive after a meeting with the beloved. Maybe He Who had performed the miracle of the dream would work out, through some other dream, its interpretation and fulfillment. It wasn't possible that such a dream should simply vanish as though it had never been. It wasn't possible that yearnings so strong should blaze up without rhyme or reason. The lover must attain his goal —rationally or crazily, he must attain it. But how lost is he who searches without a guide!

IX

The vizier Dandan was happy at the return of Dunyazad to his spacious house. As for the mother, she alone suffered—together with Dunyazad —the pain of living with the secret.

"You did wrong, Dunyazad," she said to her daughter in sadness and anger.

"I resign myself to the will of the Lord of the Worlds," said Dunyazad, weeping.

"The outcome will not be good."

"I resign myself to the will of the Lord of the Worlds," she repeated meekly.

When the signs of her condition became apparent, the woman set about arranging her daughter's abortion, while asking forgiveness of her Lord.

"We are putting off the disaster, but what happens if a bridegroom presents himself?"

"I have no wish to marry," exclaimed Dunyazad.

"What shall we say to your father if he finds a suitable person?"

"I resign myself to the will of the Lord of the Worlds."

Once on her own, she forgot the dangers surrounding her and remembered only her departed lover. When she did so, death itself seemed of no account. Neither did she heed the disgrace, only asking herself agonizingly, "Where are you, my love? How did you find me? What's your secret? What's keeping you away from me? Has not my beauty taken you captive as yours has me? Has not the fire that burns in my soul seared you? Do you not take pity on my torment? Do you not miss my love and longing for you?"

X

An obstacle rose in the path of events and people's hearts were affected. The town crier had passed by on his mule calling out to the sultan's subjects, informing them of the attack of the king of Byzantium on one of the ports and of the army being put on alert for a holy war to repel the invaders. Anxiety spread and the mosques were crammed with worshipers; prayers were offered up for the sultan Shahriyar to be victorious. In the evening the habitués of the Café of the Emirs, the high and the low, congregated. One bench was shared by Hasan al-Attar the son of Ibrahim al-Attar, Fadil Sanaan, and Nur al-Din. No one had any subject of conversation except the war. The doctor Abdul Qadir al-Maheeni was heard to say, "You have not witnessed an attack by the enemy—it is a storm of destruction that sweeps over cities and their peoples."

"God's army is unconquerable," said Galil al-Bazzaz the draper.

"God, too, has His underlying reasons for things."

"Sindbad's ship may be captured," said Ragab the porter.

To which Aladdin the son of Ugr the barber said, "You think only of yourself and your friend."

At which Ugr the barber said, "I had an extraordinary dream."

But no one asked him about his dream as no one trusted him to speak the truth and because they knew he liked involving himself in other people's affairs.

Nur al-Din shuddered at the mention of a dream. He said to his friends Hasan and Fadil, "Nothing is more remarkable in the lives of men than dreams," and he heard a voice commenting on his last words: "You are right in what you've said, my son."

He turned to the adjacent platform and saw Sahloul the bric-a-brac merchant gazing at him with a smile.

"You're wise and experienced, sir."

"He who is master of dreams is master of tomorrow," said Sahloul.

He gave his whole heart to the conversation, but Fadil, recollecting what his absent friend Abdullah the porter had told him, quietly nudged him and whispered in his ear, "Stop talking to him."

"But is he not a man of experience?" asked Nur al-Din.

"He's also as inscrutable as a dream," whispered Fadil Sanaan.

And he heard the doctor Abdul Qadir al-Maheeni say, "In my estimation the sultan's army will be victorious, but the owl will screech in the ruins of the treasury."

XI

Nur al-Din sighed sadly and asked himself when this yearning of his would end. His eyes were languid, his heart oppressed. He went roaming about in the streets, sometimes by day, sometimes by night, drawn in particular to places where women congregated in their favored markets. More than once he passed the house of the vizier Dandan at the time when Dunyazad was standing behind the wooden latticework looking out, but he did not notice her, nor she him. The unique experience appeared to him as an irrational phenomenon lodged far distant from the domain of hope, or it would whisper to him at times like some extraordinary truth that would be unveiled to him at such time as God's mercy willed. On another occasion, at the end of the night, he saw a specter approaching which, when it could be seen in the light above a doorway,

turned out to be the face of a dwarf—that of Karam al-Aseel the millionaire. What had brought him out of his magnificent house at such a
late hour? What was keeping him awake? What was he searching for? He
wondered whether the man had fallen captive to some dream as he
himself had done and whether his wealth would be of help in discovering who had made him captive. His heart contracted at seeing him
abroad for no apparent reason.

XII

Karam al-Aseel liked to walk at night in the empty streets. He loved to
wander about the quarter, and there was no part of the quarter without a
house or a khan owned by him. In his spacious home he had a wife and
tens of slave-girls, but he did not own their hearts in the same way as he
owned human beings and things. It was in his power to change destinies,
yet not to alter his own shape or form. Thus the world would often
appear to him as drab as his own face. Business transactions forced him
to mix with people, yet he loved the solitude of the night. He did not
like singing and was bored by conversation, but he adored wealth and
worshiped power. He had had the pleasure of being accepted as a confi-
dant of the sultan. He would pay the alms tax but practiced no form of
charity. He took care of his beard and was proud of it, for it was the most
beautiful thing he possessed, with its luxuriant growth. He had produced twenty daughters, but had not been granted a single male child.
He owned millions and was the richest man in the quarter, in fact in the
whole city.

He was also a lover of women and it was perhaps this that had
made Nur al-Din follow his shadow with a dark and deeply agitated
heart.

XIII

Karam was overcome with passion when the veil slipped from Dunyazad's face as she rode in her howdah at the celebrations for Ashura, the

anniversary of the martyrdom of the Prophet's grandson. His heart, immersed in business worries, shook as when lightning strikes in the dark clouds. He leaned toward Bayumi al-Armal, the chief of police, who was one of those in slavery to his handouts.

"Who's the slave-girl?"

"Dunyazad," he answered, smiling, "the sister of the sultana."

His chest tightened as he told himself that she was not to be bought for any money.

Thus he was proceeding at night in the company of musings that were not pleasant. When he spotted Nur al-Din he ignored him. He envied him his good looks, while protesting to himself angrily for envying another human being. Passing by the house of Sahloul the bric-a-brac merchant, he said to himself, "That man will become my rival in wealth." He regarded him as belonging to that rare minority that obliges others to show them respect, so he hated him more than he hated the others. As he made his way home, he said, "Karam al-Aseel or Abdullah al-Balkhi, which will read for us the unknown? My wealth should give me many times more happiness than I have."

XIV

The doorman said to him, "Sir, Husam al-Fiqi, the private secretary, is awaiting your return in the reception hall."

What had brought him at this late hour? At once he went to him. They embraced. The private secretary said, "My master, Yusuf al-Tahir, governor of the quarter, awaits you now at his house."

"What urgent matter brings you?"

"I don't know, except that it's important."

They went off in a hurry. When he was alone with him, Yusuf al-Tahir began in mock pomposity, "Commensurate with people's efforts . . ."

Karam al-Aseel looked at him with interest, and the other continued, "Our army has been victorious. You are the first man to be informed of the good news."

He muttered in confusion, "A favor from the Lord of the Worlds."

The governor gave him a long look, then said, "The treasury has had expenses beyond its means."

His heart went cold as he grasped what it was all about.

"The sultan," continued Yusuf al-Tahir, "is in need of a loan to be paid after the land tax has been collected."

"And what," he inquired half in jest, "has this to do with me?"

"The sultan," said Yusuf al-Tahir with a laugh, "has singled you out for this honor."

"How much?" he asked without enthusiasm.

"Five million dinars."

There was no escape, no choice. Yet an idea flashed in his head that was so experienced at driving bargains.

"An opportunity to draw close to the sultan and to gain the reward of the Merciful."

"Well done!"

"But there's a request I have which I did not know how to express," he said quietly.

Yusuf al-Tahir kept smiling in silence, until Karam al-Aseel said, "The hand of Dunyazad, my ultimate hope of achieving the honor of being related."

Though astonished, Yusuf al-Tahir did not show it. He recollected how much he would have liked to have Dunyazad for himself. He felt unimaginably irritated at the other man, but said calmly, "I shall put forward the request as you wish."

XV

"What was to be feared has occurred!"

It was with these words that the mother expressed herself, in a state of great agitation. Dunyazad, on the other hand, had been expecting it.

"The bridegroom has come—he has obtained the sultan's compliance and your father's agreement."

Who could it be? Did fate have some new miracle stored up in which lay a remedy? Her eyes asked the question without her uttering a word.

"It's Karam al-Aseel the millionaire."

Dunyazad frowned, and desperation wrested the blood from her cheeks.

"Scandal, like thunder, knocks at the door," said the mother.

"I am innocent and God is my witness," said Dunyazad, weeping.

"No one will ever believe your story."

"God is sufficient for me."

"With Him is forgiveness and pardon."

"Do I not have the right of accepting or refusing?"

"It is the sultan's wish," said the mother, rejecting the suggestion.

"Oh, that I could escape from this world!" she groaned.

"That would be an even bigger scandal, and your sister might not be safe from the consequences."

As her weeping increased, her mother said, "Would that difficulties were solved with tears."

"But my tears are all I possess!" exclaimed Dunyazad.

XVI

Sakhrabout said to Zarmabaha as he laughed joyfully, "The trick we played has become excessively complicated and will have exciting consequences."

Zarmabaha, sharing his joy, said, "A rare entertainment!"

"Do you think the beautiful young girl will commit suicide, or be killed?"

"The best would be if she were to be killed and her father were to commit suicide."

"Is there further scope for having fun?"

"Let's just let things take their course, seeing that they don't require our intervention."

"The fact is that I'm afraid . . ."

"What are you afraid of, my darling?" she interrupted him.

"That goodness will sneak in from we know not where."

"Don't be so pessimistic!" she said scornfully.

Sakhrabout laughed and said nothing.

XVII

The news of Karam al-Aseel's engagement to Dunyazad spread through-out the quarter, dragging in its wake a trail of joy, curiosity, and mock-ing remarks. The poor dreamed of a generous windfall of charity from a man who did not even know the joy of being charitable, while the people of distinction rejoiced at this relationship by marriage between the sultan and their quarter, although warning whispers were abroad about a monkey marrying an angel. Dunyazad, in her solitude, la-mented, while communing with the unknown. "Where are you, my beloved? When are you coming to rescue me from ruin?"

Nur al-Din continued wandering about in the alleyways. The news of the marriage aroused his sadness as he too communed with the unknown. "Where are you, my beloved?" Meanwhile, Qumqam and Singam followed the whispered communings with deep sorrow.

"Look," said Singam to his companion, "what time and place do."

"The moans of mankind," Qumqam said to him, "from of old gush forth into the river of sorrows among the stars."

Under their tree Sahloul hurried by.

"He's off on some assignment," said Qumqam.

"Sometimes," said Sahloul in confusion, "I receive incomprehen-sible orders!" And off he went.

XVIII

Sahloul ended up at the wall of the lunatic asylum where he stood in the darkness.

"Were it not that I have faith, I might ask myself the meaning of all this."

He imposed his will on the ground between himself and the cell of Gamasa al-Bulti and a tunnel burst open which no humans could have cut through in less than a year. In seconds he was standing in the darkness above the head of Gamasa al-Bulti and listening to his regular breathing. He gently shook him until he woke up and asked, "Who is it?"

"That's not important," he said to him. "Release from suffering has come to you, so give me your hand for me to take you to freedom."

Not daring to believe, Gamasa al-Bulti nonetheless abandoned himself to Sahloul until he was steeped in a cool spring breeze.

"O mercy of God!" muttered Gamasa. "Who are you, stranger? Who has sent you?"

"To your old secluded spot on the riverbank!" said Sahloul, pushing him forward.

XIX

When the stranger had gone, Gamasa al-Bulti said to himself, "This is not the work of humans. Remember that, O Gamasa. Remember and ponder it."

He had lived among madmen until he had come to terms with madness. He had realized that it was a closed secret and an exciting revelation. He had hoped to plunge into its depths and face up to its challenges.

Refreshed by the breeze, his heart made its way to Akraman, Rasmiya, and Husniya. He wished he could visit the rooming house and mingle with his beloved. But who was he? They had shaved his head and beard and he had twice been flogged. Today there was no such thing as Gamasa, nor even Abdullah. Today he was without identity, without name, filled with worries and a striving toward piety.

He took himself to the date palm at the tongue of the river. He remembered his dream friend, Abdullah of the Sea. Once again he said, "A being without identity, his goal is beyond the cosmos, but remember and ponder, for release from suffering has not come to you without some reason."

XX

Dunyazad was conveyed to the palace so that her marriage might be celebrated under the aegis of the sultan in accordance with his sublime wish. Winds of terror swept over the heart of the bride and that of her sister, the lady of the stories. Shahrzad advised her sister to claim that she was ill and she asked the sultan to postpone the marriage until she had recovered. The doctor Abdul Qadir al-Maheeni was called and he undertook her treatment. He was very soon dubious. Being astute and resourceful, and with an experience of men's souls no less than his experience of their bodies, he thought it likely that the bride had an aversion to the monkey who was to be her husband. He nonetheless cleverly feigned ignorance in accordance with her wish, burying her secret deep down in the sacrosanct well of his profession and affirmed that treatment would take a long time. Karam al-Aseel, however, was annoyed at the decision and was also assailed by doubts, so he pleaded with the sultan to be allowed to make the marriage contract but for the wedding itself to be postponed till the bride was cured. The sultan agreed to this and the chief cadi was brought and the marriage contract made out. Thus Dunyazad became the lawful wife of Karam al-Aseel the millionaire. Some people awaited with impatience the splendor of the festivities, while others expected imminent catastrophe.

XXI

Nur al-Din's uncertain footsteps led him one evening to the river, where he sat on his own by the tongue of land. In a gentle solitude disturbed only by the breath of spring, ablaze with tongues of yearning, there came to him the sound of someone communing. He felt certain it was the voice of someone at worship. He was drawn to him in his search for ease and solace. He came upon an old man under the date palm and, reluctant to interrupt him, sat down and listened. When he had finished, the man asked him, "Who are you? And what has brought you?"

"I am in torment," answered Nur al-Din. "And you? Are you from this place?"

"Places are not important to those who have made worship their pleasure. But what is the secret of your torment?"

"I have a strange story."

He was moved by a strong desire to unburden himself, so he told him his dream in all its details and the madness that followed upon it, then asked, "Do you believe me?"

"Madmen don't lie," replied the man.

"Have you an explanation of the secret?"

"There is an angel or devil behind you, but it is a reality."

"And how shall I be rid of my yearnings?"

He said gently, "We suffer yearnings without number that they may lead us finally to the yearning after which there is no yearning, so love God and He will make everything superfluous for you."

After a silence Nur al-Din said, "I am a believer and am sincere in my worship, but I am still a lover of God's creatures."

"Then don't stop searching."

"I am tired out and sleepless."

"The lover does not tire."

"It seems to me that you are a person of experience."

"I knew a man who was deprived not only of those he loved but of existence itself."

"By death?"

"No, in life."

"Have you doubts about my state of mind?"

"It's veritable madness."

"And sanity too."

After a hesitation Nur al-Din said, "You are difficult to comprehend and grow more so."

With a smile the old man inquired, "Then what do you say about your dream?"

XXII

Nur al-Din returned to the city, plunging through seas of darkness. The worshiper had not quenched his burning thirst—or had only partly done so. He had urged him to search but had not promised him that he would be successful and had not warned him against despair. He had then made clear that he was one of those afflicted by God. Nur al-Din had not been made for asceticism in the world, but was made for loving God in the world. On this understanding he had parted from Sheikh Abdullah al-Balkhi that day. In that instant he could not but be certain that his beloved existed somewhere and that she was imprinted with the mark of his love. It was of that that the gentle night breezes spoke to him, in the same way as the twinkling of the stars dipping down between the domes and minarets spoke to him. In his solitude he called out in a loud voice, "Lighten my torment, O You Who are gentle with Your servants."

"Who complains at this hour of the night?" asked a deep voice.

He was conscious of the shape of two men blocking his path.

"Are you from the police?" he asked.

"We are strangers, merchants who are amusing ourselves in the long night by walking about in your ancient quarter."

"Welcome to you both."

"What is your complaint, young man?"

"People are there to help others," said his companion, "and complaints do not go unanswered among men of honor."

Moved by his noble sentiment, Nur al-Din said, "I invite you to my lowly house, which is nearby."

They were soon seated in an elegant room where he provided them with the doughnuts known as *zalabiya* and glasses of *karkadeh* made of the petals of the hibiscus flower. They ranged around the question of his complaint, while he asked them where they were from, to which they answered that they came from Samarkand. Again they hinted about his complaining, to which he replied, "He who is at a loss divulges his secret to a stranger."

"And he may well find in him something that was unexpected," said the man with the deep voice.

"So let the skies bring down unexpected rain upon us," said Nur al-Din with a sigh, and he started to recount to them the story of his extraordinary dream until his voice disappeared into an all-pervading silence and he was staring at them shyly. Then the man with the deep voice said, "We have become acquainted through our hearts, as is proper with high-minded people, but the time has come for us to know one another's names. I am Ezz al-Din al-Samarkandi, and this is my partner Kheir al-Din al-Unsi."

"Nur al-Din, seller of perfumes," said Nur al-Din.

"A trade as handsome as your face."

"God forbid! I am not handsome—God places His beauty only where He wants to place His approval." Then he asked, "Have you believed me?"

"Yes, young man," said Ezz al-Din. "I am much traveled and have heard stories of our forebears as would not occur to human hearts. Thus I do not doubt the truth of your dream."

Hopes revived in Nur al-Din's heart. "Can I attain my goal of finding my beloved?"

"I do not doubt it."

"But how and when?" he asked with a moan.

"By patience and perseverance attainment will be achieved."

Kheir al-Din al-Unsi asked him, "Are you in need of money?"

"I ask nothing of God except that I achieve my goal."

"Be of good cheer at God's release which is close at hand," said Ezz al-Din.

XXIII

Shahrzad had never seen the sultan so excited. They were on the balcony that overlooks the garden. He had finished his morning prayers and was having his breakfast of milk and an apple. Soon he would put on his official attire and go to the Council of Judgment, but at the moment he looked like a child who has made a new discovery.

"Last night," he said, "in my wandering I lit upon a story that was like one of yours, Shahrzad."

Despite her hidden sorrow, she said smiling, "The fact that stories repeat themselves is an indication of their truth, Your Majesty."

"Yes, yes—the secrets of existence are splendid and more delicious than wine."

"May God grant Your Majesty enjoyment of existence and its secrets."

After deliberation he said, "The truth is that I am ever on the move and my heart is never still—the brightness of day and the darkness of night contend for me."

"Ever thus is living man," she said gaily, concealing her listlessness of spirit.

"Don't be in a hurry. My turn has come to tell you a strange story." And he presented to her the dream of Nur al-Din the perfume-seller. He noticed the expression on her face and said in astonishment, "What an impression it has made on you, Shahrzad!"

"I woke this morning unwell," she said, as though excusing herself.

"The effect of humidity; it will soon wear off. The doctor will see you. As for me, I would like to charge the town criers to go round with the story so as to bring together the lovers."

"It is best for us to proceed slowly lest two innocent people be exposed to evil tongues," she said fervently.

He thought for a while, then asked, "Am I not capable of protecting them?"

Shahrzad told herself that this man used to occupy himself only with cutting people's heads off, and that the devil in him still had influence that was not to be underrated, though it no longer had total possession of him.

XXIV

Shahrzad said to her mother, who was staying at the palace on the pretext of looking after Dunyazad in her illness, "An unprecedented event demands of us even more wisdom."

"My heart," said the mother with a sigh, "is in no state to face any further events."

"Mother, the man of the dream has become a reality!"

The woman's mouth opened wide in astonishment. "Don't talk to me of dreams," she muttered.

"He is none other than Nur al-Din the perfume-seller." And she recounted to her in detail the sultan's adventure, at which the mother, in bewilderment, said, "It is not possible for someone like him to slip into the sultan's palace at night."

"If your doubts are correct, mother, it would have been easy for her to elope with him."

"But what would that have achieved? Your sister is a legal wife of Karam al-Aseel and the catastrophe draws nearer hour by hour."

"And the town criers will give out the story, and it is not unlikely that the truth about it will come out."

"Danger takes us unawares," groaned the mother.

"It's the awful truth."

"Shall we wait like the man who's been thrown down on the execution mat?"

"I'm frightened," said Shahrzad, distraught, "for Dunyazad and for myself too. There is no trusting the blood-shedder. The worst affliction a man can suffer is to be under the delusion he is a god."

"It's like death—it's inevitable."

"Sometimes it seems to me that he is changing."

"Your father says that too."

"But what goes on inside him? In my view he is still a mysterious riddle that cannot be trusted."

"The story may please him when it is far away, but when it beats at his door and concerns him, that's something else. His delusions may revert."

"And he goes back to being the devil he was, or something more ghastly."

"And what have *you* done wrong?"

"I think we should share our worries with Dunyazad."

"I am very apprehensive about that."

"Why should we flee from the truth when it is encircling us?"

The housekeeper Murgan sought permission to enter. "My mistress Dunyazad," she said fearfully, "has disappeared and has left this message."

Shahrzad read the following words: "I seek Your Majesty's pardon, but I am incapable of disobeying your order to marry Karam al-Aseel and yet it is not possible for me to marry him. I have therefore chosen to do away with myself, and God is the Forgiving, the Merciful."

The mother gave a sob and fainted.

XXV

The town criers began broadcasting the extraordinary dream and inviting the two lovers to meet under the protection of the sultan. It was then that the sultan received the news of Dunyazad's suicide, with sadness and displeasure. He issued an order that her body should be found wherever it was. Karam al-Aseel was so upset that he remained in seclusion far from those who were gloating or making fun of him, and left his house only in the middle of the night. As for Yusuf al-Tahir, the governor of the quarter, he had received the news with a mixture of deep sorrow and joy: joy at the fact that Dunyazad was released from the grip of the monkey-man and deep sorrow at the death of the young girl he had wanted for himself and for whose sake he had seriously thought of arranging a plot to assassinate Karam al-Aseel.

XXVI

The madman was meditating in the darkness of night under the date palm when his attention was drawn to a specter approaching in the light of the stars. He heard a female voice greeting him and saying, "In the name of God I ask you to direct me to a ship that will take me away from the city."

"Are you fleeing from some deed that angers God?" he asked her gently.

"I have never angered God in my life," she said gently.

Her voice reminded him of Akraman and Husniya, and the tenderness of the earth was blended with the cravings of the sky in his heart.

"You must wait," he told her amiably, "until daybreak, when God will in His mercy take charge of you."

"Can I wait here?"

He gave a smile which she did not see and said, "The open air has been created for fugitives! Where are you going?"

"I want to get far away from the city."

"But you are alone and perhaps beautiful."

When she kept silent, he said, "Perhaps God will help you through me, if you so wish."

"I want nothing except for you to make it possible for me to travel."

"Can you swear by God that you are not leaving behind some harm you have done to a human being?"

Reassured, she said in a shaking voice, "It is I who am unjustly wronged. I left my home to kill myself, then was afraid that God would meet me in anger."

"Why, daughter?"

When she burst into sobs, he called out to the heavens, "You are most knowing as to where to place Your mercy."

"I am innocent and wronged."

"I do not wish to intrude upon your heart's secret."

"You are one of God's good servants and to you I'll divulge my secret," she said, having decided to abandon herself. And she began to recount her story.

"Are you the person in the dream?" he interrupted her.

"How did you know that?" she exclaimed.

"I knew it from your partner at this same place, and after that I heard it from the town criers."

"I don't follow you—do you know my partner in the dream?"

"The town criers are repeating his name everywhere—it is Nur al-Din the perfume-seller."

"The town criers?" she said as though addressing herself. "Behind them is the sultan! How strange! Nur al-Din . . . Nur al-Din . . . But I am married—or rather dead."

When she had completed her story, the man said, "Go to your husband!"

"Death is easier," she exclaimed insistently.

"Go to your husband Nur al-Din!"

"But I am a lawful wife to Karam al-Aseel!"

"Go to Nur al-Din and let the dawn come up."

XXVII

"What do I see?" said Sakhrabout furiously. "Things are proceeding toward a happy solution."

Concealing her feelings of bitterness, Zarmabaha said, "Wait, the way is still strewn with thorns."

They spotted Sahloul under the tree hurrying along in the darkness.

"An unforeseen assignment, angel?" Sakhrabout asked himself.

"Let's hope it's for us rather than against us," said Zarmabaha.

Sahloul went on his way without paying them any heed.

XXVIII

Early in the morning Nur al-Din left his house to open his shop. By his shop he found a young veiled girl, who seemed to be waiting. She wore a dress of Damascene silk that bespoke lofty origins. She looked at him with interest, then gave a deep sigh. Amazed at her, he felt his heart throb, revealing obscure emotions. She soon unveiled her radiant face, while staring at him with submissive ardor. An age passed as, outside all existence, they were immersed in a dream that breathed passionate magic. Spring breezes blew and filled them with the fragrance of the sky's blue. Their happiness made them forget the memories of torment and confusion. Peace came down to earth and in a movement as spontaneous as the singing of birds they clasped hands.

"Human and alive!" he exclaimed. "Reality and not a dream, here at this moment!"

"Yes," she whispered in a trembling voice. "You, Nur al-Din— and I, Dunyazad!"

"What act of mercy led you to where I was?"

The words flowed from her mouth as she told him of the tragedy and the way it had been resolved.

"We should have been assured," he said deliriously, "that the miracle was not happening to no avail."

"But thunder is stronger than the cooing of pigeons."

"Together and forever," he said finally.

"It was fated."

"Let's go to the sultan."

The flame of her fervor was extinguished, "But I'm married to Karam al-Aseel," she said.

"The sultan's promise is stronger."

"False steps, too, possess their own power."

But he was in an utter state of intoxication.

XXIX

The sultan's council was held at noon and was attended by the eminent men of state. Before the throne stood Nur al-Din, seller of perfumes, and Dunyazad, sister of the sultana.

"We have been taken unawares by wondrous and inscrutable happenings," said the sultan, scowling. "The days and nights have taught us to pay attention to such wonders and to knock at the door of the inscrutable so that it may open wide and reveal light. This wondrous happening, disguised as a dream, has invaded my very home."

As the sultan fell silent, the heart of Dandan his minister trembled and the faces of Dunyazad and Nur al-Din paled. No doubt conflicting forces strove for ascendancy in the sultan's heart. The cruel demon had been bewitched by the stories, yet they had not altered his quintessence. Then, with a face more sullen, he said, "But the sultan's promise is valid!"

The feeling of distress left the hearts of many and faces brightened with the light of hope. Then the mufti, official expounder of the law, said, "But the lady Dunyazad is already married at law."

"Bring Karam al-Aseel," the sultan ordered Dandan.

Then rose Yusuf al-Tahir, governor of the ancient quarter.

"Your Majesty," he said, "Karam al-Aseel was found dead last night not far from his home."

The news struck at people's hearts, shaking them like an earthquake, and quickly brought to mind the violent deaths of the governors and leading citizens. Bayumi al-Armal, the chief of police in the quarter, rose to his feet and said, "Our men, after a long search, have found the escaped madman who was wandering aimlessly about at night in the quarter and they have arrested him."

"Are you accusing him of killing al-Aseel?" asked the sultan.

"He himself admits, proudly and boastfully, that it was he who committed all the crimes."

"Was he not the man who insisted he was Gamasa al-Bulti?"

"The very same, and he is still insistent."

Here Yusuf al-Tahir said, "We would ask Your Majesty's permission to behead him, which is safer than returning him to the madhouse."

"My vizier Dandan told me that the tunnel by which he made his escape could not have been made by human beings."

"That is so, Your Majesty," admitted Bayumi al-Armal.

The sultan hesitated for so long that his close companions felt that for the first time in his life he was being assailed by fear. When Dandan realized this, he said adroitly, "He's nothing but a madman, Your Majesty, yet he has a secret which is not to be underrated, so let him go—there is no kingdom that does not have a handful of the likes of him who are in divine care. I believe he should be released and that a search should be made for the killer among the Shiites and the Kharijites."

"You have given good advice, Dandan," said the sultan, inwardly thanking his vizier for his acumen. Then he looked at Dunyazad and Nur al-Din and said, "You have the promise, so get married. Dunyazad shall have all that she requires from the treasury."

The assembly was enveloped in an air of peace and happiness.

The Adventures of Ugr the Barber

I

Minds were confused by the death of Karam al-Aseel, but Ugr the barber was preoccupied with himself to the exclusion of the world and what it contained. In ordinary circumstances nothing distracted him from what was happening, for he was a deeply-rooted minder of other people's business, making mountains out of molehills and regarded in his shop as a spinner of tales before being a barber, deriving interest and pleasure from news and exaggerated rumors. However, a smile had restored his natural disposition, and hopes that had been long suppressed sprang up anew.

He was short and thin with bright eyes and of a dark brown complexion, not originally devoid of charm. He harbored an avidity as no one else did. The woman with the smile was middle-aged, older than he by a year or two. Why does she smile to a barber like him? Perhaps she liked men. Perhaps she was tempting him with femininity and liberality, for no one had any doubts about Ugr's poverty.

O Lord, how he loved women! Were it not for his poverty, Fattouha would not have remained his sole wife during all that life of his. Perhaps he dreamt of women as his adolescent son Aladdin did, dreamt too of affluence, food, and drink. She had persisted in passing by in front of his shop for days on end until he had gone up to her and she had made an appointment with him by the sultan's school just after sunset. He had waited, saying to himself, "Your turn for some luck has come, Ugr." For the first time he speaks appreciatively of luck and prostrates himself in prayer; for the first time he welcomes the coming of the setting of the sun; for the first time he feels at ease with the street as he prances about. The shops are closing their doors as he is filled with excitement and expectation.

When the street was empty, or almost so, the madman appeared in ample gown and flowing beard; unexpectedly he had appeared to pierce the night with his secrets, he who was always volunteering that he had committed great crimes and who claimed that he was Gamasa al–Bulti, the conqueror of death, who had invaded the sultan's stone heart and who had been set free. Ugr liked him like some mysterious plaything but he did not welcome his appearance at this fateful hour. Just as he feared, the madman approached, until he was standing right in front of him.

"Go home," he said in his loud voice, "for no one goes out at night unless he has an aim."

Overcoming his feeling of tension, Ugr laughed and said to him, "The hair on your head grows like a balkh tree, while your beard extends downward and outward like a curtain. Why don't you pay me a visit in my shop so that I can give you a good trim?"

"Your brain is rotted so you do not obey me," he chided him.

"What a delightful madman you are!"

"An ignorant fellow from ignorant progeny!" he said, passing on his way.

He remained alone for no more than a minute when the woman arrived.

II

A burning experience in which the unknown was held in contempt. After twenty years of daily married life, it led him in darkness diluted by the lanterns on doorways to an almost isolated house with a garden outside the walls. He believed that the person leading him was someone of rank, wealth, and a dissolute life, and he was increasingly happy about this. As he plunged into a dark place, fragrant smells wafted to him and he realized it was the garden. Then he found himself in a hallway lit by lamps in the corners, in the midst of which was a sumptuous couch and a sitting area of cushions arranged round a table heaped with food and drink. The woman left, then returned, unveiled and in a silken robe; she was compactly built with handsome features, older than he had reckoned but wantonly coquettish. His gaze moved across the woman, the food, and the drink and he said to himself, "Look at how dreams are fulfilled."

"Our night," he said, girding himself for action, "has no equal."

She filled two glasses and said, laughing, "Only an ingrate denies favors."

She clapped her hands and a slave-girl in her twenties came bearing a lute. She was so like the woman as to be her sister, though excelling her by her youth.

"Play to us," said the woman. "Happiness must be made complete."

The drink played with their minds, the lute with their hearts. With Ugr's accustomed abandon he applied himself to the drink, the food, and the woman. Many times he asked himself when their acquaintance would be consummated. But what did that matter? Let him beware of haste and play his part as he should. He did not doubt that he was in the presence of a loose woman—but a loose woman who was generous, who gave and did not exploit. It was a dream that did him no harm, except that it did not come true.

III

She set aside for him every Monday. He would have liked more, but she disregarded this. He advised himself to be content. She avoided indicating who she was and he became convinced that she was from a family of distinction. Why did she not settle down in a palace with some eminent person? Perhaps the reason was debauchery or vanity, so which of these should he take pleasure in? As for the young slave-girl, she was indisputably her sister—doubtless immersed in corruption, and wholly obedient and compliant to the woman, like some female attendant. She was enticing, as the two of them exchanged furtive glances. He would assuredly fall into the snare of the younger as he had done into that of the older, and it would not take too long. It was a party redolent with passion and betrayal, yet he was infinitely wary about the woman. He loved the food and the drink in the same way as he loved the woman, and with the passage of time he loved the food and the drink more. He would wildly and unashamedly launch himself at the table so that he became an amusing spectacle for the two women. Nevertheless he was careful lest his desire for the young slave-girl should compromise him, while she herself encouraged him, though hiding behind an excess of wariness. At the Café of the Emirs he felt himself to be of a higher order than the notables and happier than Yusuf al-Tahir. He felt he was another Shahriyar.

IV

He went one night and found no one there but the young slave-girl. The hall was the same as ever but the table was empty. He was perplexed but said nothing.

"She's ill and has charged me with making her excuses," the slave-girl said. His heart throbbed, his eyes sparkled and he smiled.

"I must hurry back quickly," she said.

"She's very trusting!" he said. He stepped forward and took her in his arms.

"Who knows?" she said without showing any real resistance.

"But the opportunity will not slip from our hands."

"What an adventure!"

"You're free, like her—you are doubtless her sister."

She removed herself gently from him and brought food and drink. They both set about the drink liberally so as to disperse the atmosphere of tension and speculation. They dissolved into a burning passion.

Mounting the summit of provocation, they withdrew from mere existence.

He woke early. He rose on unsteady feet with a heavy head. He drew the curtain and daylight flooded in. His mind turned to memories of the previous night. A gasp escaped him and his eyes goggled as he saw the beautiful young slave-girl butchered. Her blood had drained away completely as death lodged itself in her. When? Who? How? Should he flee? How heavy his head was! It was as though he had drunk some narcotic in his wine. The charge lay over his head. He thought quickly, illogically: the garden, burying the corpse, removing the traces of blood. Was there anyone in the house observing him? He must act or give himself up to the fates. There was no time for reflection. The whole structure had collapsed and there was no recalling the past. The specter of the other woman was constantly with him.

When he gave the place a final look, he saw a necklace with a diamond that had fallen under the bed. He gathered it up, not knowing what to do with it. He thrust it into his pocket and went out stealthily.

"It will be a miracle if I escape," he told himself.

V

Ugr went on groping about in the prison cell of his enduring torment. The crime beleaguered him and spread its convulsive grip to suffocate him. "O Lord, I pledge myself to repent if You save me."

His son Aladdin saw him and was delighted at his return, while Fattouha, his wife, bared her teeth.

"I was overcome by sleep in a hashish den," he said, showing little concern.

She swore at him: life between them was full of ups and downs. He opened his shop later than usual and received the heads and beards with a mind that was distracted and wandering in the valleys of terror. There was some third person who was without doubt the murderer. But why had the young girl been killed? Out of jealousy? The jealousy of some unknown man, or the jealousy of a woman? Always he was pursued by the form of the elder sister: strong, dissolute, and capable of committing atrocious crimes. Would she discover the body? Did anyone know he had crept out at night? Would he one day be led off to the executioner to be beheaded? "O Lord, I pledge myself to repent if You save me." He thought for several moments about taking flight. The necklace that was lodged over his stomach would bring fortune, but to offer it for sale would be to bring about his downfall. No, he had not murdered and he would not flee, and divine providence was not sleeping. Yes, divine providence was not asleep, but who was this? He looked in dejection at the madman as he entered the shop and sat down on the ground without ceremony, eating an apricot. Ugr was trimming the beard of the doctor Abdul Qadir al-Maheeni.

"What has brought you so unusually during daytime?" he asked the madman.

"Your daytime has become night, Ugr," said the madman plainly.

"I take refuge in God from such evil words."

"Don't mislead us, man, for madness is the acme of intelligence," said the doctor, laughing.

"I was once a policeman," said the madman.

"You still insist you are Gamasa al-Bulti?"

"And the policeman, when he turns to God, does not give up his old profession."

"Spare me your madness," said Ugr testily, "for I am not in a good mood."

"Only the likes of you," said the madman gently, "call upon me, you ignorant one."

The doctor laughed loudly and said, "He is usually called in when our knowledge fails to do the job."

The madman rose to his feet and went off, saying, "God is the refuge of the living and the dead and of the living-dead."

When the door had closed behind him, Ugr said to the doctor, "My heart now tells me that this madman is a dangerous killer."

Abdul Qadir al-Maheeni muttered, "How many killers there are, Ugr!"

Ugr felt that the madman knew his secret. Could it be that he had butchered the beautiful girl? When, O Lord of the Heavens and the Earth, would his affliction be removed?

VI

Monday night came—the appointment with Gulnar that gave warning of mysterious possibilities. If he went, he would be going to hellfire. And if he did not go, evidence would be put forward about a crime he did not commit. He went to the house of the crime and of terror. He submitted himself to the fates, his body trembling with fright. He hid the garden from existence by averting his gaze. As for the head that had been torn from the beautiful body, it stayed with him step by step. He saw Gulnar and the table and took in the first breath of summer weather heavy with humidity. He should curb his confusion lest it give him away. He must perform the act of love on the bed of blood. The body seemed to fill the place and to obscure the voracious woman. How sweet was escape! He applied himself to the drink in despair. The woman was calm and smiling. Should he ask about Zahriyar or should he wait? Which would arouse more suspicion? But it was Gulnar herself who broached the subject with the inquiry "Where is Zahriyar?"

"Did she not come with you?" he inquired.

She stared at him in confusion as she drank with him, then said, "I sent her to you with my excuses."

"We exchanged a couple of words and then parted," he said with pounding heart.

"She has disappeared as though into thin air. Those who have been diligently searching for her have given up. The house is up in arms."

He clapped his hands together in a gesture of despair and muttered, "A truly extraordinary thing to happen—is there any reason for her disappearing?"

"I can't imagine any! The house is up in arms."

"What house, Gulnar?"

"Our house, Ugr. Do you think we have no family?"

"And this house, what is it?"

"It's only a place to relax in—a place we have set apart for entertainment."

He hesitated, then asked, his head heavy, though not with elation, "Who are your family, Gulnar?"

"Some people," she said, smiling. "What are they to you?"

He became more deeply immersed in his worries and inquired sadly, "I wonder where you are, Zahriyar?"

"The news has doubtless saddened you?"

"I am only human, Gulnar," he said dejectedly.

"And a good human, Ugr," she said, playing with his beard.

Drunk with wine, she drew close to him. Depression closed in around him. A lack of appetite for the food and drink came over him and the wells of passion dried up. He was put off by the woman because he felt frightened of her. It was a long and heavy nightmare which must come to an end.

VII

On the next appointment he went as though going to the executioner's leather mat, but no one answered his knock at the door. When it was not opened to him, he felt at ease for the first time since his discovery of the crime. Perhaps her family had at last become aware of her secret behavior. Perhaps she was avoiding him. Perhaps she had joined her sister. Whatever had happened to her, a not inconsiderable part of his torment had ended. He would not again approach the scene of the crime. He would fight against the color of blood that pursued him and would not fail to remind himself that he had not, during the whole of his lifetime, ever committed a murder. He wasn't even able to kill a chicken. The memories of the food and drink and of making love all withdrew themselves, and he told his defeated self that maybe they had never been a reality. Every day that passed made him a gift of peace of mind. Fear is the due of the guilty, not of the innocent. And he was, without doubt, innocent. Whenever peace of mind permeated him, life gained vitality with suppressed desire and he went back to recollecting the nights of lovemaking and food, and he would sigh nostalgically. He would remember, too, the valuable necklace that lay above his stomach and which he could not offer for sale, and he would feel sad. He was carrying about him a futile fortune, and he had had an unforgettable experience with happiness, and greed and lascivious yearnings would well up in him and he would ask in confusion, "Isn't it best for me to repent?"

But the nights with Gulnar had lit up within him a craze for women. His eyes roved stealthily among beautiful women, darting glances of fire. On one of his wanderings his gaze alighted upon Husniya the daughter of Sanaan and sister of Fadil; her poverty and the reputation of her deceased father encouraged him to have designs on her. He took his opportunity when Fadil came to his shop to have his beard and mustaches trimmed. He was excessive in his greeting of him and asked with remarkable straightforwardness, "Mr. Fadil Sanaan, there is someone who is asking to be related to you by marriage."

"Who's that, Ugr?" asked Fadil with an unencumbered mind.

"My humble self," he said with the same straightforwardness.

Fadil was taken aback and hid his reaction. He told himself: perhaps Ugr is in better circumstances than myself, but he is Ugr and I am Fadil, and Husniya is no less well brought up than Shahrzad herself. In order to gain time in which to think, he asked, "My sister?"

"Yes."

In an apologetic tone he said, "It seems that someone has beaten you to it."

Ugr took refuge in silence, without believing it. If someone had beaten him to it he would have known of it, for was anything that happened in the whole quarter ever hidden from him? Ugr was angry. How was it that Fadil did not consider his request a favor, when he was asking to form a relationship with a house upon which the Devil's curse had fallen?

VIII

His desire for love increased and he did not cease to crave for affluence. Like an adolescent, and despite the fact that his son Aladdin had not yet married, he became absorbed in dreams of virgin girls. He had visions of himself lolling about among cushions in magical houses like those he would sometimes enter to give his services. Just as he had fallen in love with Husniya, so too did he lose his heart to Qamar the sister of Hasan al-Attar the druggist. This was a love stronger than the first, and made stronger still by its hopelessness: a love that was condemned by secrecy, sorrow, and pain.

One day he had gone to the druggist's house to trim the beard of Hasan al-Attar and had had a glimpse of the beautiful girl and had lost his peace of mind forever. But he did not lose the dream and would rove about among the great houses like those of al-Attar, Galil al-Bazzaz the draper, and Nur al-Din. And Nur al-Din—what a happy young man he was! He had gone from being a simple seller of perfumes, whose rank was no higher than that of Ugr, and who was perhaps less endowed than his son Aladdin in handsomeness and qualities, to being one of the notables and a son-in-law of the sultan, the husband of Dunyazad, sister of Shahrzad. Was not God capable of everything?

IX

In the Café of the Emirs he would habitually sit every night. After a hot summer's day the night would bestow a welcome breeze. One night, he found himself sitting as close as could be to the platform of Master Sahloul the bric-a-brac merchant. The storyteller had finished a section of the legendary story of Antar, the rebab was silent, and conversation had started up.

"You haven't honored us with a visit for a long time," said Ugr to Master Sahloul, who was one of his customers.

"One day I'll pay you an unexpected visit," said the man, smiling. Along came Hasan al-Attar the druggist and Galil al-Bazzaz the draper, and with them Fadil Sanaan. They took their places and Ugr greeted them effusively. They returned his salutation with aloofness. He forced himself on the gentlemen but they answered without any encouragement, wary of his intrusion. Now he was more important than Fadil, but they were keeping to how things were in former times. His constant dream was that he might be allowed to give his services in exchange for being able to listen at their tables. He would succeed the once and fail tens of times, and his greedy appetite would be fired. Today Fadil was his adversary, after refusing his proposal of marriage to his sister. As for Hasan, he was gaining the favor that Ugr had no hope of. He directed his hearing toward where they were sitting, while pretending to be relaxed and sleepy. They were talking about a delightful evening party that was to be held in celebration of the arrival of the draper's ship with a cargo from India. There would be food, even better than Gulnar's, and there would be plenty to drink. The seller of sweetmeats would fill his belly like in the days of old.

"The weather's hot—we need some place out of doors."

The vagabond was making known his wishes as though he were one of the notables, and Galil answered him, "The green tongue—it's an island of greenness."

"And I have invited Shamloul the hunchback," said Hasan al-Attar.

"What fun to have the sultan's jester playing the buffoon for us!"

Even the jester! As for you Ugr, no sooner does luck smile on you than it is swept away by human blood. He looked toward Master Sahloul and said sorrowfully, "Master Sahloul, you are a species on your own in your abstention from frivolity."

"That's true," said the master quietly.

"You are a noble and modest man, and you would not have refused for me to be your drinking companion."

He smiled and did not reply. Ugr thought for a while as to how to induce him to indulge in frivolity. He looked toward him again and found his seat empty. His eyes roved around the café but saw no trace of him. Thus would he disappear all of a sudden and in a trice. What a strange person! But Ugr was determined that he would take part in the evening at the green tongue, whatever the cost—even if the adventure ended up with his being thrown out.

X

The green tongue stretching out into the middle of the river was like a narrow island, with no light but the faint glow of the stars. Not far away stood the dark form of the date palm, its base the home of the madman. They had to lay down rugs, make ready a cloth with food, and light a fire for grilling. Unfortunately, a specter forced its way in among them, volunteering to serve them, saying, "The attendant of the gentlemen!"

The voice won no encouragement and Galil al-Bazzaz called out, "Ugr! What a disagreeable hanger-on you are!"

He said resolutely, his hands never ceasing to work, "A hanger-on, yes, but I'm not disagreeable. How can a party like this be right without a servant?"

"On condition you close your mouth with glue!" threatened Hasan.

"I shall not open it unless urged to."

The voice of Shamloul the hunchback was raised, as high-pitched as that of a child, saying, "How can a tramp like you thrust yourself among important people!"

Though he felt enraged, Ugr nonetheless immersed himself in his work, putting the bottles and glasses in place and beginning to light the fire. They all set about drinking. Shamloul took up a lute, which was almost as big as himself, and began softly humming in a voice that merely provoked laughter. Despite his diminutive size, his heart seethed with a basic pride.

Following the first glass to find its way into Ugr's stomach, he forgot his pledge and asked, "Have you heard the latest anecdote about Husam al-Fiqi, secretary to the governor, Yusuf al-Tahir?"

"We don't want to hear it, so shut your mouth," Hasan al-Attar shouted at him.

While they were drinking, an unseen voice came to them, murmuring, "The One," and all heads turned toward the shadow of the date palm.

"It's the madman," said Fadil.

"Didn't he find any place other than that to spoil the green tongue for its visitors?" questioned Galil.

"He claims he's your father-in-law, Gamasa al-Bulti," said Hasan al-Attar, addressing Fadil.

"That's what he claims, but Gamasa's hanging head says otherwise."

"Everything is possible in this crazy city," said Shamloul the hunchback.

At which Ugr the barber said, "If you want the truth . . ."

"We don't want the truth and we don't like it," Galil interrupted him.

"Don't remind us of death," called out Shamloul. "That's what the sultan has ordered."

"How do you spend the evenings with the sultan, Shamloul?" asked Galil.

"I am not one to give away secrets, you most despicable fellow!" said Shamloul haughtily.

They all laughed, with the exception of Hasan al-Attar, whose drunkenness exploded into anger. "You vermin!" he shouted at him.

The hunchback was enraged and threw down the lute and jumped to his feet. All of a sudden he was urinating over the cloth with the food and drink. They were speechless as they realized that their evening had been ruined. Drink roused their anger, which they vented on the hunchback.

Fadil sprang at him and pushed him onto his back, then took him up by his two small feet and went with him to the edge of the green tongue of land and plunged him into the waters of the river, then took him out again and let him fall to the grassy ground, where he lay in terror and ire. Staggering to his feet, he took up the brazier and threw it at them, the live coals scattering about and burning some of them. They were now so angry that in drunken fury they bore down on him and kicked and beat him until he fell unconscious.

In dismay Ugr followed what they were doing and protested, "Enough, gentlemen—he's the sultan's jester."

Silently he bent down over him in the darkness. Raising his head, he said, "Gentlemen, you have killed the hunchback."

"Are you sure of what you're saying?" asked Galil.

"See for yourself, master."

The silence was charged with fear. Ugr gloated over them and said, "A crime for nothing knocks at the sultan's door."

"It's madness!" shouted Hasan al-Attar.

"What wretched bad luck!"

"Are we to be ruined without rhyme or reason?"

Ugr's head was full of extraordinary imaginings, jumping from dream to dream. Finally, feeling a sense of being in control for the first time, he said quietly, "Take your things and go."

"How can we go, leaving this crime behind us?" said Galil.

"Go," said Ugr in a commanding tone. "The body will disappear and the jinn themselves won't find a trace of it."

"Are you sure you can manage?"

"Completely sure, and my success is through God alone!"

"Expect a commensurate reward, the like of which no one has ever heard of," said Galil in a trembling voice.

"It's the least I expect," he said coldly.

"But perhaps many in the café heard us inviting him to our party."

"Yes, they did, but I joined you without an invitation and I can bear witness to the fact that he stayed with us for only a while then went off on his own, excusing himself by saying he wasn't feeling well. Get it right and remember."

XI

Once alone with the body of the hunchback, he remembered Zahriyar and the blood, and his whole body trembled. But there was no time for frustrating thoughts. He had to move away from the cultivated land. He had to search for some hole in the desert, for some safe place to keep the body until he had fulfilled his desires. One corpse had thwarted his good luck and here was another one that promised to restore what he had lost. Speed and secrecy were needed.

A voice came to him that rent the silence: "O you who walk in the darkness, free yourself of burdens."

His body shook as never before. The madman. Always he was interrupting his solitude. All he had to do was wrap up the small corpse in the end of his cloak. He stretched out his hand, then drew it back as though he had been stung. There had been a movement, perhaps a pulse. Some breathing like a moaning. O Lord, the hunchback had not died. Once again the voice reached him, "Free yourself."

Curses! He was still pursuing him, the killer of beautiful Zahriyar. Why had he killed her? Why had he not killed Gulnar? He slung Shamloul onto his left shoulder and covered him with the right side of his cloak.

"Be reassured, Shamloul," he whispered. "I am your friend. I shall take you to a place of safety."

Would the reward be lost? Would his desires vanish into thin air? Ah, if only he had the ability to kill! An idea occurred to him: to hide Shamloul in his house until he got what he craved. The idea took hold of him, and he was not one to consider ideas from different viewpoints.

XII

Fattouha looked at the motionless minuscule hunchback with wonder.

"Listen and do what I say," Ugr said to her.

"He wouldn't make much of a meal," she said scornfully.

"We'll prepare him a comfortable place in the upstairs room," he said enthusiastically, "and he can stay there for a few days till he recovers his health."

"Why not take him to his family?"

"He's a lucky star which will bring us happiness and improve our lot. Give him what he requires and bolt the door of the upstairs room. It won't take long, and I'll tell you all you should know."

XIII

He scarcely slept a wink that night and went off to work early in the morning. It was the most decisive day in his whole life and all the miracles had to happen in it without delay. Let him be bold and daring and without shame—though he had never had any sense of shame. It was but a single chance, one that would never recur, and everything is as God wills it.

Having decided to start with the most valuable quarry, he went to the house of Hasan al-Attar before the time he went to his shop. The young man came to him in the comfortably-furnished reception room.

"How are things with you, Ugr?" he asked eagerly.

"Everything's fine, master," he answered in a tone full of confidence. "You're safe for the rest of your life."

"It will turn out all right, with God's permission," he said, pressing his arm. "Have you met up with Master Galil?"

"Not yet—I wanted to start with the top man."

"Here's a thousand dinars—good luck to you."

"You should make it ten thousand, master," he said gently.

Hasan frowned in dismay. "What did you say?"

"Ten thousand dinars."

"But that's a fortune which would weigh heavily on the most generous of rich persons."

"It's a mere drop from your ocean," he said in the same quiet voice, "and your life is worth more than the wealth of Qarun himself."

"Be content with five thousand and Galil al-Bazzaz will make it up to ten."

"I shall not waive a single dirham."

Hasan lost himself in thought for a while, then rose to his feet sluggishly. He was away for a time, then returned with the money that had been demanded.

"You have no pity," he muttered.

"May God forgive you," said Ugr in protest, stuffing the money into his pocket. "Have I not saved your necks from the sword of Shabeeb Rama?"

"But your greed is deadlier than his sword."

"With God's favor," he said, ignoring the remark, "Ugr will become one of the prominent people and will invest his money with the elite of the likes of Master Sahloul. He will thus become able to fulfill his real dreams."

"And what are your real dreams?" he asked with a hidden sarcasm to relieve his feelings of rancor.

"To seek the honor of being related to you by asking for the hand of your honorable sister."

"What?" he exclaimed, jumping to his feet.

"Don't make me aware of your contempt, to which you are not entitled. We are all from Adam's loins. Previously there was no difference between us other than in wealth, and today there is no such difference."

Hasan suppressed his feelings of rage to avoid any unpleasant consequence. Ridding himself of his annoyance, he said, "But, as you know, she must give her consent."

"She will consent to save the neck of her beloved brother," he replied with a meaningful look.

"Your request is not a noble one," he said with a deep sigh.

"Love believes only in love," he said with conviction.

Silence reigned and the two of them were immersed in the day's mounting heat. Then Hasan said, "Let's put this off for a while."

"We'll meet at noon," he said forcibly.

"Noon!"

"Today at noon for the contract and we'll have the wedding later." He rose and bowed to him in greeting. As he walked away he could feel the burning look of hatred directed at his back.

XIV

Before the morning was over he had obtained another ten thousand dinars from Galil al-Bazzaz. He left him stifled with anger. Ugr told himself that he must strengthen his relationship with the chief of police, Bayumi al-Armal, in case of any treachery in the future. He ought, too, to make his mark with the governor of the quarter and with the personal secretary, as the wealthy do, and in so doing gain prestige and security. As for Fadil Sanaan, he went into his shop, where he found him alone. As he passed by him he looked at him with contempt and asked, "What have you for me as a reward for saving your head, Fadil?"

Fadil laughed in confusion and said, "I have my head, which is the most precious thing I possess."

"You previously refused in disdain to take my hand," said Ugr bitterly.

"It is your right that I make it up to you," said Fadil in apology.

Ugr was silent for some moments, then said, "God has granted me someone who is better than her, but keep in mind that in view of your poverty I saved your head for nothing."

XV

At noon that day the legal ceremonies were carried out for Ugr to marry Qamar al-Attar in an atmosphere more reminiscent of a funeral. Ugr's concern was concentrated on keeping Shamloul the hunchback in his house until the bride was given in marriage to him. Meanwhile, he had rented a beautiful house and had begun to prepare it for receiving the bride. He was not wholly confident about the future, for his deception would sooner or later be exposed. In addition to which, Fattouha would learn of his marriage to Qamar and clouds of troubles and worries would gather. Yet he might be saved from ruin if he embraced his bride to himself and was in some manner embraced into the al-Attar family, and if he invested his money and was granted an ample and lasting revenue.

He went to the marketplace, where he met Master Sahloul and said to him, "I have some money that I would like to invest with you, for you are the best person to invest with."

"Where did you get this money from, Ugr?" asked Sahloul, who never expressed his astonishment.

"God bestows upon whomever He wishes."

"I don't go into business with anybody," he said brusquely.

"Teach me," he entreated, "for teaching is a reward in itself!"

Sahloul laughed as he said, "My profession is not learned, Ugr. Wait until Sindbad returns."

He proceeded immediately to Nur al-Din, the brother-in-law of the sultan. The young man asked him with a certain suspicion, "Do you swear that the money came to you lawfully?"

Though his heart was troubled he nevertheless swore to it.

"A ship will set sail this month—come to me at the end of the week."

Ugr went off in fear at the outcome of the false oath he had given, but he pledged himself in his conscience to expiate his sins by making the pilgrimage, by giving alms, and by repentance.

XVI

Ugr realized that the march of time was giving warning of the destruction of his hopes and that he was not able to bring it to a halt. It was impossible to keep the hunchback in his prison forever, and he would never find a secure place in the city for him. Nothing remained but to take possession of his bride and flee with her on the earliest ship. In far-off countries he could begin a new life, a life of wealth, love, and repentance. He defended himself by saying he was not wicked and had done what he had done only through deprivation and weakness—God had given him the lot of the poor and the tastes of the rich, so what was his fault? In the evening he went to the Café of the Emirs and immediately and with a firm step he made his way to where Hasan al-Attar, Galil al-Bazzaz, and Fadil Sanaan were ensconced. Reluctantly they made room for him. He said to himself, "Yesterday I was despised and today I am utterly loathed." But his situation with al-Attar would be resolved at the end of the evening gathering and as of tomorrow he would set forth into the world of beautiful dreams. Then he saw Fadil staring at the entrance to the café aghast and motioning to his companions to look. He himself directed his gaze toward the entrance and saw Shamloul the hunchback glaring at them with blazing eyes and trembling all over with agitation.

XVII

Despair and terror wrenched at his soul as the hunchback drew toward them with short, quick steps until he was standing in front of them defiantly. In a voice as high-pitched as a whistle he shouted, "Woe to you, you gypsies!"

He first turned on Ugr, "So you imprison me in your house claiming that I was receiving hospitality I hadn't asked for!"

Ugr said not a word and the hunchback continued, "Your wife freed me when she heard the news of your marriage, so expect to hear some thunder in your house."

He then turned to the three others, "You strike the sultan's man, you villains! Every strong man has someone stronger and deadlier than he, and you'll get your true deserts."

He marched out of the café with short, quick steps, yellow in the face with rage, as a storm of laughter erupted. The faces of the three men had set, then they were overcome with fear and anger. They glared at Ugr with looks of loathing.

"Deceiving villain," Hasan al-Attar hissed at him. "Return the money and revoke the contract."

"Return the money or we'll break your bones," said Galil al-Bazzaz.

"I thought first of all he was dead—and God is my witness."

"Then you turned into a swindling criminal—return the money and revoke the contract."

With death-defying bravado he said, "Beware of the scandal. The secret of drinking, riotous behavior, and aggression will be made public. You are better off trying to placate the hunchback before he takes his complaint to the sultan. As for the money you gave me, consider it as an atonement for your life's sins."

"Woe to you, you will not get away with a single dirham, you swindler."

All of a sudden Ugr jumped to his feet and left the place as though in flight.

XVIII

All sense of security had vanished from his world and hope's lamp had been extinguished. Though he was Qamar's husband, she was more distant from him than the stars. He was rich and yet he was threatened with death. He knew more than anyone about the secret cooperation between al-Attar and al-Bazzaz on the one hand and Yusuf al-Tahir the governor and Husam al-Fiqi the private secretary on the other. Meanwhile, too, Fattouha was lurking at home, impatient for his return so that she might fasten her fangs in his throat. How narrow was the world! He wandered about, slumbering for hours on the steps of the public fountain. For the whole of the day he withdrew into the farthest corner of the quarter. No doubt his enemies had won over the hunchback and were now engrossed in planning their revenge on him. In the evening he found himself in the Shooting Square, when suddenly his gaze was drawn to the light of torches and an unusual clamor.

XIX

What was happening in the square? A force of police were surrounding a large number of vagabonds and violently driving them to some unknown place. He heard a man nearby say aloud, "What an extraordinary decision!"

The man was in truth none other than the genie Sakhrabout in human guise, strutting about in a gown that bespoke high rank.

"What decision, sir?"

Sakhrabout was delighted at having attracted Ugr's attention.

"May God honor His Majesty the Sultan, for the palace astrologer has indicated that the state of the kingdom will not thrive unless its affairs are taken over by vagabonds. So His Majesty has ordered that the vagabonds be apprehended so that he may choose from among them those to fill the various commands."

In amazement Ugr asked, "Are you quite certain of what you're saying?"

"Have you not heard the town criers?" said Sakhrabout in surprise.

His heart jumped with joy. This wave of humans would sweep away all sorrows at a single burst. They would be his saviors from torment and despair, messengers of glad tidings of deliverance and mastery. What could his enemies do if he were to look down on them tomorrow from the rulers' balcony? Without hesitating a single moment, he crept in among those who had been arrested and allowed himself to be carried along.

XX

The stream of men proceeded toward the house of the governor, Yusuf al-Tahir, where they were gathered in the courtyard under guard and in the light of torches. Yusuf al-Tahir came, followed by Husam al-Fiqi. They were greeted by the chief of police, Bayumi al-Armal, who then said, "These are the ones we were able to apprehend this evening, and others will come in due course."

Yusuf al-Tahir inquired, "By this do you really guarantee that crimes of burglary and brigandage will be wiped out?"

"That is what is hoped, Lord," said Bayumi al-Armal.

At a gesture from the governor the soldiers stripped the men of their ragged clothes. All this time Ugr was flabbergasted and became convinced that he had led himself into a calamity compared to which his true troubles were insignificant. Whiplashes rained down upon them and his screaming rent the air even before his turn came—which it did. When they began taking them off to prison, Ugr screamed at the governor, "O representative of the sultan, I beseech you by God Almighty to look at me, for I am not one of them. I am Ugr the barber. The chief of police knows me, as does the private secretary. I am a friend of Nur al-Din, the son-in-law of the sultan."

Bayumi al-Armal listened to all this and said in astonishment, "But I didn't arrest you, Ugr."

"Things got muddled up—the work of the Devil."

Yusuf al-Tahir ordered him to be released and his clothes to be returned to him. Then suddenly the governor looked intently at the package around his middle. Ugr trembled and hid it with his arms. The governor, though, was suspicious and ordered that he be stripped of it and that it be examined. When he saw the necklace with all the precious stones he called out, "Zahriyar's necklace! You're nothing but a thieving murderer. Arrest him!"

XXI

The following day began with Ugr's interrogation. He told his story and swore by all that was holy that it was the truth. Hasan al-Attar and Galil al-Bazzaz came forward and gave evidence of his lying and deceit. Yusuf al-Tahir ordered that he be beheaded, and the whole quarter gathered to watch in the square. But before they had begun to carry out the sentence, the vizier Dandan arrived in an awe-inspiring procession.

XXII

Soon the courtroom was assembled at the house of the governor, with Dandan, Yusuf al-Tahir, Husam al-Fiqi, Bayumi al-Armal, and Ugr the barber all present.

"His Majesty," said Dandan, "has ordered me to conduct a retrial."

"To hear is to obey, minister," said Yusuf al-Tahir.

"The madman," said Dandan, "has supplied him with news that he wishes to verify."

"That madman," said Yusuf al-Tahir in astonishment, "who insists he is Gamasa al-Bulti?"

"The very same."

"And did His Majesty believe him?"

"I am here to interrogate you, not for you to interrogate me," said Dandan roughly.

The fearful silence was broken by Dandan asking Yusuf al-Tahir, "Have you two sisters, one of whom is alive and the other missing?"

"Yes, minister," said Yusuf al-Tahir.

"And have they led a dissolute and immoral life?"

"Had I known that," said Yusuf al-Tahir in a trembling voice, "I would not have remained silent about it."

"Rather it is they who silenced you before you took up your position by showering you with money earned immorally."

"These are but the imaginings of a crazy man," said the governor.

Dandan turned toward Husam al-Fiqi, the private secretary, and said, "It is said that you know everything about this matter, so—by order of the sultan—make a statement of the information you have, and be careful not to tell any lies which could result in having your head cut off!"

Husam al-Fiqi collapsed utterly. Doing what he could to save himself, he said, "Everything that has been said is the truth and not open to doubt."

"What do you know about the disappearance of Zahriyar?" Dandan asked him, frowning.

"I myself investigated that and it appeared that it was her sister Gulnar who killed her, motivated by jealousy."

Ugr was called upon to speak and he told his story from the time when he fell in love with Gulnar until the moment he slipped in among the vagabonds who had been apprehended.

The whole case was referred to the sultan Shahriyar, who ordered that Yusuf al-Tahir, being no longer fit to hold office, should be dismissed, as well as Husam al-Fiqi for having shielded his superior; that Hasan al-Attar, Galil al-Bazzaz, and Fadil Sanaan be flogged for drunkenness and riotous behavior; and that Ugr's money be confiscated and he be released.

When Dandan was alone with his daughter Shahrzad he said to her, "The sultan has changed and has become a new person full of piety and a sense of justice."

But Shahrzad said, "There is still a side of him that is unreliable, and his hands are still stained with the blood of innocent people."

As for Ugr, he became oblivious to his loss in the joy of escaping. He quickly revoked the contract between himself and Qamar and made his way to the date palm not far from the green tongue of land. He bowed down before the madman who was sitting cross-legged underneath it.

"I am indebted to you," he said in gratitude, "for my life, O kindly holy man."

Anees al-Galees

I

Shahriyar and Dandan plunged into the night followed by Shabeeb Rama. All human movement had come to rest. By the light of widely separated lamps, houses, shops, and mosques at slumber loomed into sight. Summer's heat had lessened and stars sparkled in the heavens.

"What is your view of what has been done?" inquired Shahriyar.

"Suleiman al-Zeini is a man who it was hoped would be governor, also his private secretary al-Fadl ibn Khaqan."

"When the citizens are asleep, good and evil sleeps. All are infatuated with happiness, but it is as if the moon is obscured by winter clouds. Thus if the new governor of the quarter, Suleiman al-Zeini, is successful, raindrops will fall from the sky, cleansing the atmosphere of some of the dust that floats about."

"That will be due to Almighty God and at the hand of His Majesty the Sultan and his wisdom."

"But severity," said Shahriyar after some thought, "must remain one of the means at the disposal of the sultan."

Dandan, in his turn, gave the matter some thought, then replied cautiously. "Wisdom, not severity, is what Your Majesty aspires to."

The sultan gave a laugh that rent the silence of the night.

"You are nothing but a hypocrite, Dandan," he said. "What did the madman say? He said that if the head was sound, the whole body was sound, for soundness and corruptness come down from above. He winked at me with a boldness possessed only by madmen, but he knew all the secrets of the case. How did he come by this knowledge?"

"How would I know, Your Majesty, what goes on in the heads of madmen?"

"He claimed that he had got to know the secrets from the time he had been chief of police."

"He is still insisting that he is Gamasa al-Bulti, a claim that is given the lie by Gamasa al-Bulti's head hanging over the door of his house. Perhaps he really is one of those who know the supernatural."

"Shahrzad has taught me to believe what man's logic gives the lie to," said Shahriyar as though communing with himself, "and to plunge into a sea of contradictions. Whenever night comes it seems to me that I am a poor man."

II

"I fear that boredom pursues us," said Zarmabaha to Sakhrabout.

"No, opportunities will be afforded us and opportunities will be created, O crown of intelligence," said Sakhrabout encouragingly.

The voice of Qumqam came to them from high up in the tree. "If grumbling rings out between you, it's glad tidings of contentment."

"You're just an impotent old man," Zarmabaha jeered at him.

"The earth glows with the light of its Lord," said Singam from his place alongside Qumqam, "and toward the light Gamasa al-Bulti and Nur al-Din the lover look night and day. Even Ugr is settled in his shop and has repented of his venturings. As for the bloodthirsty Shahriyar, some throb of guidance moves his frame that is so filled with spilt blood."

"You see nothing of things but their dumb shadow," said Sakhrabout in mockery. "Under the ashes there are live coals, and the morrow will take you from the slumber of blindness."

III

The movement started with a sound as soft as silk, then exploded into the rumble of thunder. That night, at the Café of the Emirs, Ibrahim the water-carrier deviated from his normal good manners and said in a loud voice full of agitation and excitement, "Very early in the day I carried water to the Red House."

"And what's new about that, you idiot?" Shamloul the hunchback asked him in his high-pitched voice.

Drunk with excitement, the water-carrier said, "I had a glimpse of the lady of the house—blessed be the Great Creator."

Both those seated on the ground and those who sat cross-legged on the couches laughed.

"Look at the madness of old age," said Ma'rouf the cobbler.

"A glance from her," said Ibrahim sadly, "fills the stomach with ten jugs of the wine of madness."

"Describe her to us, Ibrahim," said the doctor Abdul Qadir al-Maheeni.

"She is not to be described, sir," exclaimed the water-carrier, "but I ask God for mercy and forgiveness."

Two nights later Ragab the porter said, "I was asked today to carry a load to the Red House."

He at once attracted attention and appeared to become prey to an overwhelming emotion.

"I saw the lady of the house—I take refuge in God from the violence of beauty when it dominates."

It was no joking matter. Men of passionate natures hurried off to inquire. They hurried off to the Weapons Market where the Red House stood: a large house that had been deserted for a long time after its owners had perished in a plague. It had been left bare and its garden had died, until it had been rented by an unknown lady from abroad accompanied by a single slave. In the dead of night, from behind its walls, could be heard magical music and singing. They said that she was a woman of easy virtue.

And so Ugr found himself madly talking about her to every client he went to.

"She has completely disrupted my vow to repent and pierced me with an arrow of everlasting torment," he would say.

And he would say, "She summoned me to trim her locks and to pare her nails. Were she a decorous woman she would have called in a lady's maid, but she is a veritable firebrand from the Almighty."

He had learned that her name was Anees al-Galees. So many contradictory things were said of her that doubt was stirred up even in those describing her. Some said she was fair-skinned and blonde; some that she was golden brown; some described her as plump, while others lauded her slender build. All this so inflamed the secret wells of passion that the well-to-do and the notables rushed off to take the unknown by storm.

IV

It was Yusuf al-Tahir who was the first to start something. Since being dismissed, being a wealthy man, he had suffered from the boredom of having no work. Thus comfort and ease had come to him. At night he had gone to the Red House and knocked at the door. It had been opened to him by the slave.

"What do you want?" he asked.

"I am a stranger who is seeking shelter at the house of generous people," boldly answered the man who had for a time ruled the quarter.

The slave disappeared for a while, then returned and stood aside for him, saying, "Welcome to the stranger in the house of strangers."

He showed him into a reception room whose walls were decorated with arabesque, the floors spread with Persian carpets, and sofas from Antioch, the whole embellished with objets d'art from India, China, and Andalusia: luxury not to be found outside the homes of princes.

A veiled woman made her appearance; her form, concealed by her Damascene garment, giving her an air of splendor.

"From what country are you, stranger?" she asked, sitting down.

"The fact is that I am a lover of life," he said, drawing upon his vitality as though it were wine.

"By the sultan, you have deceived us."

"My excuse," he said with fervor, "is that a palmist has informed me that I live for beauty and will die in its cause."

"I am a married woman," she said in a serious tone.

"Really?" he asked anxiously.

"But I don't know when my husband will join me," she added.

"What strange words!"

"No less strange than yours," she muttered sarcastically.

Coyly she drew the veil from her face and there shone forth a beauty that had been created as though for him alone and which brought into being his most fugitive dreams. His mind no longer his own, he knelt down. From his pocket he took out a small ivory box; he placed it between her feet. It held a jewel that gave out a light like that of the sun. In a trembling voice he whispered, "Even the jewel of the crown is not good enough for your feet."

He awaited the judgment that would decide his fate.

"Your greeting is accepted," she said softly.

Rejoicing in his hope, he trembled all over. With his arms he embraced her legs, while he lowered his head and kissed her feet.

V

The start made by Yusuf al-Tahir was like an opening of doors to surging waves of madness that poured forth and engulfed the quarter like a deluge, striking at its richest sons. As for the poor, they were afflicted with sorrow and regret. The Red House in the Weapons Market became a focus of attention for Husam al-Fiqi, Hasan al-Attar, Galil al-Bazzaz, and others. Presents and more presents were taken there, hearts were lost and minds were led astray; extravagance and foolishness took control; possible consequences were brushed aside; the concept of time having vanished, nothing remained but the present moment, while the world, following in the footsteps of religion, became lost.

Anees al-Galees was a fascinating sorceress, loving love, loving wealth, and loving men. No object of desire slaked her thirst and she was ever demanding more. The men vied madly with one another through love and jealousy. No single one appropriated her, no single one renounced her. All were, with one single force, descending to ruin.

VI

Master Sahloul had not known such activity as in those days. He was the man of auctions and the first to make his appearance when bankruptcy overtook anyone. The first to fall was Husam al-Fiqi. He was concerned not so much by the loss of money as by the loss of Anees al-Galees. He was less distressed by the fate of his women and children than by being deprived of her.

"Nothing destroys a man like his own self," he said to Master Sahloul.

"And no one can save him like his own self," said Sahloul enigmatically.

"Exhortations were long ago bankrupt," said al-Fiqi derisively. In his fall he was joined by Galil al-Bazzaz, then Hasan al-Attar. As for Yusuf al-Tahir, he reeled on the very edge of the abyss. Commenting on Sahloul's increasing activity, Ugr the barber said to him, "Some people benefit from the misfortunes of others."

"It is they who are the perpetrators and they the victims," said Sahloul with little concern.

"If only you'd seen her, master, your soul would have fretted itself to madness," sighed Ugr sadly.

"She is nothing but the smile of a devil."

"I am amazed at how you didn't fall in love with her."

"The fates have ordered that in every crazy city there is to be found a single sensible man," said Sahloul, smiling.

One night, while Sahloul was plunging leisurely through the darkness, his path was blocked by Qumqam and Singam, and they exchanged a sacred greeting.

"See the foolhardiness that is raging through the city," said Qumqam.

"I have lived millions of years and nothing astonishes me," said Sahloul.

"Their souls will be seized one day when they are oozing sin," said Singam.

"Repentance may precede the coming of the hour of death."

"Why is it not permitted to us to assist the weak?"

"God has granted them something better than you possess: a mind and a soul," said Sahloul simply.

VII

Husam al-Fiqi reeled drunkenly to the Red House and knocked at the large door. The cup of his madness had flowed over and had led him to the door of deliverance, but no one opened to him.

"Open, O Opener of Doors," he shouted out angrily into the night. But no one heeded his call, so he withdrew into a corner under the wall in troubled obduracy. Soon he saw a shape approaching. Then he saw the face under the light of a hanging lamp and recognized it as that of his former chief, Yusuf al-Tahir, and he blazed up into angry wakefulness. The man knocked at the door and it was quickly opened to him. Husam al-Fiqi rushed forward in his wake, but the slave barred his way, saying, "I'm sorry, Master Husam."

Furious, he slapped him on the face, at which Yusuf al-Tahir said to him calmly, "Bestir yourself and behave as you should."

"Wealth and faith have been lost, so what is left to me?" he asked in anguish.

Yusuf al-Tahir turned aside to go in but the other leapt on him like a tiger, stabbing him in the heart with a poisoned dagger. At this the slave let out a scream that roused people from their sleep.

VIII

Husam al-Fiqi made no effort to flee and was arrested. Bayumi al-Armal regarded him with pity and said, "I am sorry for you, my old friend."

"Do not be sorry, Bayumi," Husam said quietly. "It is only an old story with which the elderly warm themselves: the story of love, madness, and blood."

IX

The slave said to Anees al-Galees, "My beloved Zarmabaha, soon Bayumi al-Armal, the chief of police, will honor our house with a visit."

"As we have planned, Sakhrabout," the woman said, "and we are awaiting him."

"Allow me to kiss the head that contains such genius."

X

The trial of Husam al-Fiqi took only moments, after which he was beheaded. The governor Suleiman al-Zeini was meeting with the chief of police. The private secretary al-Fadl ibn Khaqan and the chamberlain al-Mu'in ibn Sawi were also present. Addressing himself to Bayumi al-Armal, al-Zeini said, "What is this that the witnesses have said? Dozens of men are going bankrupt and two men lose their lives, all because of a strange and debauched woman? Where were you, chief of police?"

"Debauchery is a secret sin, while we are engaged in pursuit of the Shiites and the Kharijites," said Bayumi al-Armal.

"No, no, you are the eye of the law of Islam. Investigate the woman. Confiscate her illegal wealth. Make good what you have failed to do before you are asked about it in front of the sultan."

XI

Bayumi al-Armal stood among a selected group of his men in the reception hall at the Red House looking around him and wondering. Did the sultan's palace excel this house in anything? The woman, her face veiled and her form modestly clothed, appeared.

"Welcome to the chief of police in our humble house."

"You have no doubt learned of the crime that was committed at the entrance to your house," he said roughly.

"Don't remind me of it. I have not slept a wink since it was committed," she replied with feeling.

"I am not taken in by your act," he said sharply. "Answer my questions truthfully. What is your name?"

"Anees al-Galees."

"A suspect name. From what country do you come?"

"My mother is from India, my father from Persia, and my husband from Andalusia."

"You're married?"

"Yes, and I have just received a letter from my husband informing me that he will be coming shortly."

"Is it with his knowledge that you practice debauchery?"

"God forbid! I am an honorable woman."

"And what are the men doing who so frequently visit you?"

"Friends from among the gentlemen of the town who enjoy discussing canonical law and literature."

"God's curse be upon you—is that why they go bankrupt and fight among themselves?"

"They are generous, and that is not my fault. It is not a part of good manners for me to refuse their gifts. I do not know how it was that the Devil crept in among them."

"I have an order to confiscate your illegal wealth," he said, his patience exhausted.

He motioned to his men, who spread out through the house searching for pieces of jewelry, precious stones, and money. During all this time the two of them remained alone and silent. He sent inquiring glances through her veil, but without effect. She showed no concern. She resigned herself to fate—or so it appeared.

"Shall I, as from today, live from selling off my furniture?" she asked in rebuke.

He shrugged his shoulders disdainfully as she removed the veil from her face, saying, "I'm sorry, but the summer heat is unbearable."

Bayumi looked at her and was stupefied. Though not believing his eyes, he was thunderstruck. He gazed at her intently, unable to avert his eyes. He swam in a tumultuous sea of madness. He lost power, function, hope. With his own hands he buried the chief of police and from his grave there emerged a hundred and one genies. Thousands of hands pushed at him and he would have collapsed had it not been for the noise of his assistants as they roamed round the rooms. The observers and spies were arriving as well. But Bayumi al-Armal was lost forever.

"I ask you to behave generously, chief of police," she once again pleaded.

He wanted to give her a rough answer, an answer that would be suitable to the situation. At the same time he wanted to give her an answer that was gentle. However, he sank into silence.

XII

At midnight he lost his self-control and rushed secretly to the Red House. He appeared before her submissively, telling himself it was a question of fate, against which one could take no precautions and for which there was no precedent. Pretending not to see the state he was in, she said sadly, "O chief of police, I have nothing further for you to confiscate."

"I have done my duty," he said humbly, "but there is a part of me that is merciful." And he threw at her feet a bulging purse. She smiled sweetly and muttered, "What a gallant man you are!"

He knelt down in humility, wrapped her legs in his arms, then prostrated himself and kissed her feet.

XIII

Complaints began to rise from those who were claiming money from the treasury. Its clerks whispered among themselves that the money was not being spent on its lawful purposes as al-Zeini had ordered. The news reached the governor, who sent out spies and tightened control. He charged the private secretary, al-Fadl ibn Khaqan, and his chamberlain, al-Mu'in ibn Sawi, to undertake a secret investigation. Finally he decided to call in the chief of police and faced him with reliable reports. Bayumi al-Armal appeared submissive and indifferent. Surprised at him, the governor said, "I see in you someone else, someone I don't know."

"The old structure, sir, has been demolished."

"I did not imagine that you would make off with the money of Muslims."

"It is the madman who has taken up residence in me who has made off with them," he said in an even tone.

Sentence was passed on Bayumi al-Armal and he was beheaded. His place was taken by al-Mu'in ibn Sawi, and once again the wealth of Anees al-Galees was confiscated and a guard mounted permanently at her door to prevent any man from entering.

XIV

Her case was referred to the mufti, but he gave a judgment to the effect that there was no legal evidence of her moral depravity. Al-Mu'in ibn Sawi was performing his job at police headquarters when a woman sought permission to see him. He looked at her heavy veil without interest and asked, "Who are you and what do you want?"

"I am Anees al-Galees, who has been wronged," she answered with spirit.

The man turned his attention to her. "What do you want?" he asked brusquely.

She removed her veil and said, "You have confiscated my money and I have become entitled to alms and charity, so include me among those who are so entitled."

The man comprehended nothing of what she said. He forgot countless things, including himself. In vain he tried to find some strength in his conscience. His foot slipped and he tumbled into the abyss. He heard her voice repeating what she had said but again without understanding it.

"What did you say?" he finally asked her, breathing heavily.

"Include me among those entitled to alms and charity," she said, ignoring the state he was in.

"When shall I send you your needs?" he asked, hurling his reputation through the window.

"I'll be waiting for you," she said coquettishly, "just before the noon prayer."

XV

She burned with energy and vitality, saying that it was the day of decision and victory. She laughed at length, just as Sakhrabout did. At once she went to see the private secretary, al-Fadl ibn Khaqan. The same game and tragedy were repeated. She made an appointment with him for before the sunset prayer. As for Suleiman al-Zeini, his appointment was for before the evening prayer. Nur al-Din, the spirit-loving man and son-in-law of the sultan, agreed to go two hours after the evening prayer; he had also penned for her a note requesting a meeting with the vizier Dandan and another with the sultan Shahriyar, on the plea that with either of them she would achieve justice and fair treatment. All men toppled and each awaited his appointment, deprived of all good sense—even Dandan and Shahriyar.

XVI

Al-Mu'in ibn Sawi came to his appointment with cosmic accuracy, his eyes reflecting the preoccupation of an old lover. He threw down the purse with the zest of a happy young child, seeing nothing in splendid existence but his own brilliant star. He was drunk with rapture when he came to rest at her feet. There was nothing but the false flashes of happy promises, and no place for consequences. Sometimes he would drink from the hand of the slave, at others from her own hand. He reached such heights of passion that he tore off his clothes, reverting to a primitive state. But as he was rushing with her toward the bed, the slave hurried in and whispered—it would seem—some dread secret in her ear. She jumped up and covered her voluptuous body with her flowing robe.

"My husband has arrived," she whispered in fevered tones.

The man awoke from his drunken state in an instant. She pulled him by the hand into an adjoining room and let him into a cupboard, which she firmly locked.

"You will leave safely at the appropriate time," she told him, trembling with agitation and terror.

"Bring me my clothes," the man called out.

"They are quite safe," she told him, as she moved off. "Now be quiet—not a sound or a movement or we're done for!"

XVII

The men followed one after the other: al-Fadl ibn Khaqan, Suleiman al-Zeini, Nur al-Din, Dandan, Shahriyar. They all submitted to the captivating call. Drunk with boisterous frenzy, they were led off naked to cupboards. The voice of Anees al-Galees came to them as she laughed scornfully, and they realized that they had fallen into a well-contrived snare.

"Tomorrow, in the marketplace," she told them, "I shall put the cupboards up for sale—with their contents."

Once again she laughed, and continued, "The people of the marketplace will witness their sultan and his men of state being sold naked."

XVIII

When she returned to the reception hall she saw before her the madman, standing there quietly. She trembled in alarm. What had brought him? How had he invaded her house? Had he heard what she had said to the men?

"How did you enter my house without invitation or permission?" she demanded.

"I saw the men following one after another, and my curiosity was aroused."

She clapped her hands to call the slave, but he said, "He has gone."

"Where to?" she demanded angrily.

"Let's not worry about him, but be hospitable to your guest."

His long hair was parted and he was heavily bearded; barefoot, he was dressed in a flowing white gown which was open at the neck and revealed the hair of his chest. Should she lure him into her snare? She moved forward, but listlessly. For the first time her face could make no impression. It was a temptation, but only to the sane, not to madmen. She approached the table with a gliding motion.

"If you want food," she said, "then eat."

"I am not a beggar," he said with disdain.

"There's drink for you," she said, refusing to admit defeat.

"My head is full with jugs of it."

"You don't look drunk."

"You're merely blind."

"What do you want?" she asked him, frowning in distress.

"How is it that you live in a deserted palace devoid of all the comforts of life?" he asked in his turn.

She looked around with a dejected heart.

"Does not all this beauty please you?" she asked.

"I see nothing but walls between which the breaths of the ancient plague rebound."

Her turn came to strip naked like the others. Weakly she submitted before his defiant madness. All wiles and ruses had come to naught. She turned her back on him in order to think. His lips uttered some faint words. Desperate resistance did not come to her aid. Something like heavy slumber swept over her. Her nerves grew slack. She let the forward movement of change sweep on. The features of her face began to melt and spread out until they became a mass of swollen dough. The svelte figure collapsed, the grace and elegance were wrenched from her. With extraordinary speed there was nothing left of her but disparate parts, which themselves were transformed into smoke that simply disappeared and left no trace. Then the couches, the cushions, the rugs, the objets d'art—all were obliterated. The lamps were extinguished then ceased to exist, and darkness reigned. He took up the heap of men's clothes and threw them from the window. Then he went toward the room where the cupboards were.

XIX

The madman, addressing the men in the cupboards, said, "I shall not exempt you from punishment, but I have chosen for you a punishment that will profit you and will not harm God's servants."

He quickly opened the locks, then left the place.

XX

The men warily crept out of the cupboards, staggering with exhaustion. With feelings of subjection and shame not one of them opened his mouth; naked in body and in self-esteem, they stumbled about in the darkness. They were looking for their clothes—for any clothes, anything with which to cover their nakedness. Time was passing, merciless time, the light of day was drawing nearer, and scandal flashed in the darkness. They wandered about searching the place with arms outstretched. No sign of anything. No sign of a life, an illusion, or a nightmare. As for the scandal, that was real enough. It meant humiliation and despair. They guided themselves along the walls toward the outer door, time creeping behind them. As soon as they breathed in the air of the street they muttered a prayer, and some of them broke into tears. The city was empty. What a great relief! They rushed off naked and barefoot into the darkness of the night. Honor had spat them out and ignominy overwhelmed them, while sin cloaked their faces with a layer of pallid grayness.

Qut al-Quloub

I

Toward the beginning of autumn the madman was intoning the dawn Quranic verses under the date palm, when he heard the voice of the water-dweller calling. He hurried to the riverbank, saying, "Greetings to my brother, Abdullah of the Sea."

"I am amazed at you," said the voice.

"Why?"

"How often have you killed the deviant for his deviation—so why is it you spare sinners scandal?"

Said the madman sorrowfully, "I was sorry that morning should come and the citizens should not find a sultan or a vizier or a governor or a private secretary or a chief of police. They would have been taken by the strongest of the wicked."

"And has your wisdom been of use?"

"I see them with their hearts full of shame and having experienced the weakness of man."

"In our watery kingdom," whispered Abdullah of the Sea, "we regard a sense of shame as one of ten conditions that must be present in our rulers."

"Woe to people under a ruler without a sense of shame," said the madman with a sigh.

II

It was late for Ragab the porter as he stood outside the gate. On returning in the darkness he had seen shadows of people opening up a burial place and going inside. He wondered what would induce them to do this before dawn and his heart had tempted him into intruding on no easy mystery. He had soon scaled the wall, and, stretched out flat on his stomach, was looking toward the courtyard of the burial place, which showed up in the dim light of a candle held by one of the spectral figures. He saw a group of slaves opening a grave that stood on its own, as though made for servants. Then he saw them carrying a box and placing it in the grave and piling earth over it. He waited until they left. He too thought of leaving, but the box urged him to investigate. What did it contain? Why had they buried it at this late hour? Sparing himself no pains, he jumped down into the courtyard. With eager determination he opened up the grave and took out the box. Were it not for his strength and his experience in carrying weights, he would not have been able to do it. He applied himself to the box until he was able to open it. He then lit the candle that he always had with him on his trips. Casting a glance, he shuddered in pity and terror. It was a young girl, as beautiful as a full moon, her face uncovered and dressed in a robe rather than a shroud—dead, no doubt, but looking as if she were asleep. He realized that the circumstances of the burial indicated some sort of crime; he also realized that he had involved himself in a predicament that he could well do without. At once he prepared to flee without even thinking of returning the box to its grave or of closing it.

III

When he jumped down into the empty space outside the burial ground he found a form in front of him and his heart contracted. However, he heard the voice of Master Sahloul the bric-a-brac merchant, inquiring, "Who's there?"

Concealing his confusion as much as he could, he answered simply, "Ragab the porter, Master Sahloul."

"What were you doing inside?" he asked, laughing.

"Our Lord ordered that one should be discreet, master," he answered him spontaneously. He wanted to give the impression that there was some woman behind the wall. Sahloul laughed and asked scornfully, "Is there not a single upright man in this city?"

IV

Fear held him in thrall. He had not had previous experience of dangerous situations. The leather execution mat loomed up as a gloomy outcome. Though performing the dawn prayer with his body, his mind was taken up with misgivings. The corpse would be discovered. Sahloul would give witness to the fact that he had seen him jumping over the wall of the cemetery, and he was a porter who had been trained to carry such boxes. It was a question of either fleeing or confessing to the truth before it was revealed. He was tied to people and to place; he was not like his companion Sindbad, who was away at sea. Besides which, he was one of those to whom al-Mu'in ibn Sawi, the chief of police, was favorably disposed. He should therefore go to him and confess everything.

V

After prayers he decided to meet al-Mu'in ibn Sawi. However, he saw him hurrying along on his mule among his guard. He followed after him and found him going toward the house of the governor. Suleiman al-Zeini was in a rage and his house was in utter disorder. The governor met the chief of police in a bad mood and said angrily, "See what's happened at the residence of the governor? Have we returned to the days of chaos?"

Al-Mu'in was speechless and asked what had happened, to which the governor answered, "There's not a trace of my slave-girl, Qut al-Quloub—it's as if the earth had swallowed her up."

"When did this happen?" asked al-Mu'in in shock.

"I saw her yesterday and now she's nowhere to be found."

"What do the people living in the house say?"

"Like me, they wonder and are overcome by fear."

Al-Mu'in thought a while, then said, "Perhaps she has fled."

The face of Suleiman al-Zeini flushed angrily and he shouted, "She was the happiest of girls—you had better find her!"

He uttered the words in a fit of rage that was clearly threatening.

VI

In front of the door of the house al-Mu'in ibn Sawi found Ragab the porter waiting for him. With lowered head he advanced toward him.

"Sir," he said, "I have something to say."

"Get out of my sight," he interrupted sharply. "Is this the time for words, you fool?"

"Please have patience, sir," insisted the porter. "There's been a murder—the body is outside the gateway and it wouldn't be right to put off burying it."

The man took note of his words and asked, "What murder and what have you to do with it?"

Ragab hurriedly related the story, while the other followed it with increasing interest.

VII

With the first rays of light the box was carried to the reception hall of the governor's residence. Suleiman al-Zeini, al-Mu'in ibn Sawi, and Ragab the porter stood round it.

"I was led to the whereabouts of Qut al-Quloub and have brought her here," said the chief of police. "But I am sorry to say she is a lifeless corpse."

Under the pressure of his emotions Suleiman al-Zeini trembled in spite of himself. Al-Mu'in ibn Sawi opened the box. Al-Zeini bent over it with a face that overflowed with sorrow, mumbling, "Verily we are God's and to Him do we return." Al-Mu'in closed the box as he muttered, "May God lengthen your survival and lessen your sorrows."

"Woe to the criminal," Suleiman shouted. "Uncover for me the secrets that have swept away my happiness."

"Sir, it is still a mystery. How did she leave the house? Where was she killed? Who killed her? Here, sir, is a testimony that this porter volunteered."

He told him the testimony and al-Zeini glared fiercely at Ragab. "You filthy creature," he said. "It is you who are the murderer, or else you know who it is."

"By the Lord of the Heavens and the Earth," exclaimed the porter, trembling with fear, "I have not kept from you a single word."

"You have invented a tale with which to shield your deed."

"Had I not been telling the truth I would not have gone of my own volition to the chief of police and admitted what I had witnessed."

Al-Mu'in ibn Sawi, however, gave him an unexpected surprise. "In that, you have lied, man." Then, turning to the governor, "He was arrested at the scene of the crime."

Ragab was amazed and could not believe his ears. "What did you say?"

"You were arrested and did not come of your own accord," al-Mu'in repeated.

"How can you say that?"

"Duty comes before mercy," he said with feigned scorn.

"You shall not escape God, you liar," Ragab shouted.

"Confess and spare yourself the horrors of torture."

"The chief of police is a liar," said Ragab in despair. "I have no knowledge of anything beyond what I have told you."

Remembering the sole circumstance that he had not revealed, he continued, "Bring Master Sahloul the bric-a-brac merchant, for I saw him close by the cemetery."

VIII

Master Sahloul was brought. Nothing was changed in his habitual calm. Asked what had induced him to go so close to the cemetery at that hour of the night, he said, "By reason of my work, all times and places are the same for me." And he related to them the story of having come across Ragab by chance as he was jumping from on top of the wall.

"Do you believe he is the killer?" al-Mu'in asked him.

"I have no evidence of that," he said quietly. "Also there can be no killer unless someone has been killed, and where is that person?"

"In this box."

He gave a mysterious smile and said, "Allow me to see him."

Al-Mu'in opened the box and Sahloul looked at the corpse for some time, then said, "The girl is still breathing."

Hope gleamed in the eyes of al-Zeini and Ragab, but al-Mu'in shouted, "Are you making fun of us, you criminal?"

Addressing al-Zeini, the man said, "Hurry and bring a doctor or the chance will be lost."

IX

The doctor Abdul Qadir al-Maheeni came and at once proceeded to examine the "corpse."

"She's still alive," he said, raising his head.

A sigh of joy came from al-Zeini, while al-Mu'in ibn Sawi's face became as pale as a ghost's.

"She was given enough sleeping-draft to kill an elephant," went on Abdul Qadir.

He continued to attend to her until she brought up all the contents of her stomach. When she moved her head the porter shouted, "Thanks be to God, Lord of the wronged."

Receiving a furtive glance from the chief of police, Sahloul said, "She will reveal to us the secret of the story."

X

A tense period charged with silence and agitation passed until Qut al-Quloub regained consciousness. The first thing she saw was al-Zeini's face and she stretched out her hand to him in an appeal for help.

"Fear nothing, Qut," he said to her gently.

"I am frightened," she whispered.

"You are in safe hands, so smile."

Spotting al-Mu'in ibn Sawi, she became agitated and called out, "That monster!"

There was an astonished silence.

"I do not know," she said, "how it was that he took me to an empty house, where he threatened to kill me unless I gave in to his base desires. Then, from that moment on, I remember nothing."

All eyes were fixed on the chief of police.

"You treacherous dog!" al-Zeini shouted. He stripped him of his sword and dagger. "How quickly corruption spreads anew!"

He ordered al-Mu'in to be imprisoned so that he might question him himself, and he declared the porter's innocence and that of the bric-a-brac merchant. Asking Master Sahloul to stay behind for a while, he said to him, "I am much indebted to you, Master Sahloul, but tell me: have you any experience of medicine?"

"No, sir," he answered, smiling, "but I have experience of death."

XI

Suleiman al-Zeini spoke to al-Mu'in ibn Sawi. "I never imagined you would be a traitor. I thought that the ordeal we all went through had cleansed us and that our life would be founded upon justice and purity, and yet you betray trust, treat generosity with disdain, and plunge recklessly into debauchery and crime."

"I do not deny any of what you say," said al-Mu'in. "We announced our repentance, but the Devil has not yet repented."

"You have no excuse and I shall make an example of you for everyone who needs a warning."

"Not so fast—I am not such easy prey. The evil emanated from your house."

"Curse you!"

"I have an accomplice—Lady Gamila, your wife."

"What are you saying?" he shouted, shaking with anger.

"She called upon me through jealousy and urged me to get rid of your favorite slave-girl, Qut al-Quloub."

"Traitor and liar!"

"You should first of all check with your wife."

"A false allegation will not save you from being beheaded."

"I shall demand a fair investigation," said the man defiantly. "And I demand that the punishment I receive be meted out to her too. No one is above the law."

XII

Between one day and the next Suleiman al-Zeini became an old and broken man. He did not waver about forcing his wife Gamila to confess. She admitted to plotting the crime. He resisted facing up to the truth and was utterly bewildered. To announce the truth meant bringing about the ruin of the mother of his children; it also meant ruining his own position. The truth was evident but it seemed to him that he was too weak to take the right decision. He found himself inclining toward pardoning the two of them so that Gamila might remain in his house and al-Mu'in in his post. Taking the easy decision, however, he lost his honor.

Qut al-Quloub also let it be known that she would not remain in his house from that day on, that she was not safe in it. He was forced to set her free and to provide her with money. He allowed her to go and to take his heart with her.

XIII

Hearts beat with sorrow. Qumqam and Singam communed together, while the madman and Abdullah of the Sea were saddened at the downfall of those who had repented. As for Qut al-Quloub, she went to live on her own in a beautiful house; she lived in want of nothing but was wrapped by loneliness. Though her master had granted her request and been generous to her she had not freed him from the blame of his excessive treatment of her, and the bitterness of solitude set a hellfire ablaze with frustrated love. Many were those who came seeking marriage, out of love and greed, but she refused them all. She refused Hasan al-Attar, just as she refused Galil al-Bazzaz. Others, like al-Mu'in ibn Sawi, desired her from afar, while Ragab the porter inquired of himself, "Is it not the right of someone who has brought a corpse to life to own that person?"

XIV

Simple incidents occurred at which the eyes of the city did not blink, but which shook the hearts of those concerned. Ibrahim the water-carrier married Lady Rasmiya, the widow of Gamasa al-Bulti. The treasury put the house of Gamasa al-Bulti up for sale and Suleiman al-Zeini ordered that al-Bulti's head be buried in a pauper's grave. The madman made a point of witnessing the burying of his head, telling himself that he was the first human being to accompany himself on the way to the Hereafter. He was happy at the marriage of his widow to Ibrahim the water-carrier because her loneliness had begun to spoil his peace of mind. Al-Mu'in ibn Sawi found the feeling of rejection oppressive, so he began a new chapter of suspect cooperation with the merchants and the rich. Unusually, the skies rained that autumn.

XV

Three ghostly figures were cutting through the darkness in silence. Under Qut al-Quloub's house the strings of a lute called to them and a melodious voice communed with the cool autumn dampness:

> *"Advance and retreat is time's custom.*
> *Among mankind no single state persists.*
> *Yet sadly what hardship and horror do I bear,*
> *in a life that is all hardship and horror."*

Their steps slowed until they came to a stop.

"This is the place we want, Dandan," one of them whispered.

Shabeeb Rama the executioner knocked at the door. A slave-girl opened it and inquired who it was.

"Dervishes from the men of God," said Shahriyar, "who are seeking honorable conviviality."

The slave-girl disappeared for a while, then returned and led them to a reception room with soft cushions and rugs. A curtain had been let down in the main hall that separated them from the lady of the house.

"Would you like some food?" asked Qut al-Quloub.

"No, we would like to have more singing," said Shahriyar.

The voice sang again in a new mode, sending the men into an ecstasy of delight.

"Are you a professional singer?" said Shahriyar.

"No, O man of God," she whispered.

"Your voice has a buried sadness," said the sultan.

"And what living creature is devoid of sadness?"

"And what saddens you when your house speaks of happiness?" he asked gently.

She took refuge in silence, so Shahriyar went on speaking. "Tell us your story, for our vocation in life is the curing of wounded hearts."

She thanked him and then said, "My secret is not to be divulged, O men of God."

She insisted on keeping silent and they asked permission to depart, with the sultan upset at her silence.

"Bring me the secret of this taciturn woman," said the sultan, leaning over Dandan's ear.

XVI

The demands of the sultan were as heavy as mountains, not to be lifted from Dandan's shoulders until he had fulfilled them.

And Dandan knew best the sultan's ire if his demands were thwarted. The sultan was still veering between right guidance and error and his anger could not be trusted. So it was that Dandan summoned the governor of the quarter, Suleiman al-Zeini, and described to him the location of Qut al-Quloub's house.

"In the house," he said, "is a mysterious woman with a melodious voice and a secret sorrow. His Majesty the Sultan wishes her heart to be like an open sheet of paper with nothing of it hidden."

Al-Zeini was shaken, realizing that he was being led to confess. Dandan would search out the truth at the hands of anyone he sensed had an ability to expose the secrets of men; and at the head of these was al-Fadl ibn Khaqan. The truth would find its way to him sooner or later, so let him at least have the merit of confessing and thus getting close to the sultan. He was, after all, a moral man and his heart had not been at peace for a moment because of his behavior, which he preferred to repent in any fashion.

He told the vizier the hidden details of his secret.

XVII

When Shahriyar learned the truth from his vizier he was furious and exclaimed angrily, "Al-Mu'in and Gamila the wife of al-Zeini, must both be beheaded."

However, his anger suddenly cooled off. Perhaps he remembered the way in which he had made his escape at night, naked, with his sin in pursuit; perhaps he remembered that al-Zeini and al-Mu'in had both been among the best of men. Nevertheless, he dismissed the two from their posts and confiscated their property; he also ordered that Gamila and al-Mu'in be flogged. To Qut al-Quloub he made a grant of ten thousand dinars, while asking her kindly, "And what else would you like to have, young lady."

"O Majesty, I would ask you to pardon al-Zeini," said Qut al-Quloub.

"It seems that you still love him," said the sultan, smiling.

She lowered her head shyly and he said firmly, "We have issued an order to the effect that the new men should be appointed and there is no going back on that. Thus al-Fadl ibn Khaqan will become governor, Haikal al-Zafarani private secretary, and Darwish Omran the chief of police."

Her eyes revealed a tear about to burst forth, at which Shahriyar said, "It is in your hands to pardon him, and perhaps that would be better for him than any official appointment."

She kissed the ground at his feet and was about to depart when he asked her, "What do you intend to do, young lady?"

"To pardon him, Your Majesty," she answered simply, her eyes welling with tears.

Aladdin with the Moles on His Cheeks

I

In the quietness of the night Gamasa al-Bulti called out from under the date palm, "O God, free me from yesterday. O God, free me from tomorrow."

Then Singam's voice was heard: "We love what you love, but between us and people is a barrier of destinies."

The laughter of Zarmabaha rang out. "Why were honey and wine created?"

Shahriyar was going about his nightly peregrinations with his two men.

"Continuous whisperings pass through me, but my head spins in a state of bewilderment," he said to Dandan.

II

He was sparely built, radiant of countenance, sleepy-eyed, and with a mole on each cheek, about to penetrate shyly the age of adolescence. Ugr the barber looked at him and said, "You have learned what you need to, so take the tools of your trade and move off—God will provide for you."

"May God spare you the evil of wicked men," muttered Fattouha.

The young man went off, spirited and happy.

"He has the handsomeness of Nur al-Din," said Ugr as though talking to himself, "so may God bestow His good fortune amply upon him."

"The amulet of mine that he wears on his chest will deter him from the path his father took," said Fattouha.

Ugr cast a poisonous look at her but said not a word.

III

He went on his way, working in the street and in shops, and everyone whose eyes alighted upon him would say, "May the Great Creator be praised!"

When the time came for a rest he chose the stairway of the public fountain, and a quick friendship grew up between him and Fadil Sanaan, the seller of sweetmeats. Once he invited him to where he was living in the rooming house, where he saw Fadil's wife Akraman, his mother Umm Saad, and his sister Husniya. His adolescent state stirred him secretly and clashed with his piety and the religious upbringing he had received at the Quranic school, so he began to make excuses whenever Fadil invited him to his home. Fadil perceived his piety and said to him, "You are a young man who is worthy of God's words that are concealed in your heart."

"It is through my Lord's grace," muttered Aladdin.

"What is your feeling," he asked cautiously, "when you see sins carrying people away?"

"Sadness and sorrow," he murmured.

"And what good does that do?"

"What more do you want?" he asked, bewilderment in his eyes.

"Anger!"

He repeated it, then said, "A lion deserves the best."

IV

The quarter was honoring the birth of the saint Sidi al-Warraq. Processions marched out, flags fluttered, drums and pipes answered one another. The good and the bad gathered round the bowls of sopped bread, meat, and broth. In the parties of the elite were Hasan al-Attar, Galil al-Bazzaz, Suleiman al-Zeini, al-Mu'in ibn Sawi, and Shamloul the hunchback. Fadil Sanaan, Ugr the barber, Ma'rouf the cobbler, Ibrahim the water-carrier, and Ragab the porter were also there. Alone, and for the first time, Aladdin of the Moles put in an appearance. Fadil had him sit alongside him.

"If al-Warraq were to be resurrected he would draw his sword!" said Fadil.

Aladdin gave the smile of someone who was gaining more experience in coming to know his friend. Then Fadil said in a significant tone, "Since the good do not draw their swords, then I shall do so."

"They speak a lot about the repentance of His Majesty the Sultan," said Aladdin innocently.

"Sometimes," said Fadil sarcastically, "he repents of his repentance, and for sure he is not the most deserving of the Muslims to be in sovereign power."

Aladdin's eyes were drawn toward the right and he detached himself, for a time, from what his companion was saying. Over there was a thin old man of joyous face and arresting appearance. Aladdin felt he had not looked toward him just by chance: he found the old man's eyes awaiting his own. There was a secret invitation from the man, an answering from Aladdin. He felt at ease, the delight of the sane at heart at the splendor of an opening rose. Fadil, noticing Aladdin's attention drawn to the old man, said, "Sheikh Abdullah al-Balkhi is the principal holy man."

"Why does he look at me?" Aladdin inquired naively.

"Why do you look at him?" asked Fadil cryptically.

"The fact is that I love him," he whispered.

Fadil frowned and found nothing to say.

V

Aladdin left the anniversary festivities with his heart overflowing with the echoes of the songs. He was floating in the darkness under the faint light of the stars, with the autumnal breeze playing against him, when a deep and resonant voice called to him: "Aladdin!"

He stopped and his heart told him that the voice was that of the sheikh. The sheikh caught up with him and said, "You are invited to be my friend."

"What a wonderful invitation, sir!" he said shyly. "But how did you know my name?"

"My house is known," said the old man, not replying to his question, "to those who want it."

"My work takes up my whole day," he said, as though excusing himself.

"You do not know what your work is."

"But I am a barber, sir."

Again, the old man did not concern himself with Aladdin's answer, but queried, "Why did you attend the festivities of al-Warraq?"

"I have loved such festivities since I was small."

"What do you know about al-Warraq?"

"He was a godly saint."

"Here is a story he used to relate. He said, 'My sheikh gave me some small scraps of paper, with the instruction that I should throw them into the river. But my heart did not allow me to do this and I placed them in my house. I went to him and said, "I have undertaken what you ordered." So he asked, "And what did you see?" I said, "I saw nothing." He said, "You didn't do as I ordered. Return and throw them into the river." So I returned, being in doubt about the sign he had promised me, and threw them into the river, and the water parted and a box appeared. Its lid opened so that the pieces of paper fell into it, at which it closed and the waters flowed over it. So I returned and informed him of what had happened and he said, "Now you have truly thrown them." So I asked him to explain the secret of this, and he said, "I wrote a book about Sufism which only the perfect could aspire to, and my brother the Khidr★ asked it of me, and God ordered that the waters should take it to him.' ' "

Aladdin was amazed and took refuge in silence. They went off together leisurely with the sheikh saying, "One of the Sayings of the Prophet that has been handed down is: 'The corruption of scholars is through heedlessness, and the corruption of princes is through injustice, and the corruption of the Sufis is through hypocrisy.' "

"How delightful are his words!" muttered Aladdin with joy.

The sheikh said in a voice that was slightly raised in the calm of the night, "So be not one of the associates of devils."

Spurred on by a feverish yearning, Aladdin asked, "Who are the associates of devils?"

"A prince without learning, a scholar without virtue, a Sufi without trust in God, and the corruption of the world lies in their corruption."

"I want to understand," said Aladdin fervently.

"Patience, Aladdin. It is only the beginning of a mutual acquaintance under a starlit scene—and my house is known to those who want it."

VI

That night Aladdin dreamed that the madman had come to him in his gown, which hung down over his naked body, and said to him, "Let your beard grow."

He was amazed at this request, and the madman said, "It is only a snare for hunting."

"But I am a barber not a hunter," said Aladdin.

"Man was created to be a hunter," shouted the madman.

★ A legendary figure in Islam.

VII

At the breakfast table Aladdin told his parents the story of Sheikh Abdullah al-Balkhi. Fattouha was delighted and said, "A blessing from our
Lord."

As for Ugr, he listened to it without interest, saying, "You're
nothing but a barber and you are sufficiently religious, so be careful not
to overdo it."

With this difference of opinion the husband and wife quarreled
and exchanged bitter words.

VIII

Above the stairway of the public fountain he went on listening to what
Fadil had to say with astonishment.

"You are annoyed at our exalted men."

"Have you known them well?" Fadil asked him.

"Sometimes my father takes me with him to their houses as his
assistant and I see at close range al-Fadl ibn Khaqan the governor of our
quarter, also Haikal al-Zafarani the private secretary, and Darwish
Omran the chief of police."

"This does not mean that you have known them."

"Great men. With only one of them did my heart contract on
seeing him—that was Habazlam Bazaza, the son of Darwish Omran. It
seemed to me that he resembled the Devil."

"Have you seen the Devil?"

"Don't make fun of me, it was only a feeling."

Fadil Sanaan gave a deep sigh and said, as though talking to himself, "Scoundrels!"

"How is it that you have formed such a low opinion of them?"

"There is no smoke without fire."

"God is present," he said, after thinking a while.

"But we are among His instruments with which He brings goodness into effect or eradicates evil."

"What do you mean, Fadil?" he asked, looking him in the eyes.

"I aspire to make you into a friend and a companion," he said enigmatically.

IX

Early in the evening he sat in the simple reception room at al-Balkhi's house waiting for him to come in. It was his first visit. He had heard his father, Ugr, relating a story about the sheikh that had distressed and saddened him. He had said that Darwish Omran the chief of police had asked for the hand of the sheikh's only daughter for his son Habazlam Bazaza. She was a pure and pious girl who had taken after her father and was of outstanding beauty. He remembered the devilish image of Habazlam Bazaza and what was said about his conduct and he had been upset and further saddened. His father had gone on with the story and said that the sheikh had thanked Darwish Omran and excused himself. But the chief of police was doubtless angry, and if the chief of police is angry then the person against whom his venom is directed is not safe from harm.

He had asked his father, "Does Sheikh al-Balkhi not realize this fact?"

"It is known of the sheikh," answered Ugr, "that he fears no one but God. But does the chief of police fear God?"

He came to visit the sheikh with a heart heavy with sadness for him. But no sooner did he see him coming cheerfully toward him than he forgot his sadness and realized that he really did not fear anyone but God.

The sheikh sat down cross-legged on a cushion in front of him.

"What is your feeling," he asked, "as you visit me for the first time?"

"I feel as though I have known you since I was born," Aladdin said truthfully.

"Each of us has another father and the happy one among us is he who discovers Him," he said smiling.

"And what you said on the night of the festivities captivated my heart."

"We draw the blind who are astray to the Path. What did your father say?"

"He wants me to dedicate my heart to my work," Aladdin said, perturbed.

"He is sleeping and refuses to wake up," he said seriously. "But how do you assess yourself, Aladdin?"

Finding that he did not know how to answer, the sheikh asked him without formality, "What sort of a Muslim are you?"

"I'm a sincere Muslim."

"Do you pray?" he asked.

"I do, thanks be to God."

"I don't think you have ever prayed!"

He looked in amazement at the sheikh, who said, "With us prayer is performed in depth, and the person praying feels nothing if touched and burnt by fire."

Aladdin, helpless, kept silent.

"You should accept Islam anew," said the sheikh, "so as to become a true believer. When belief is effected in you, you start off on the Path from its beginning, if you so wish."

Aladdin remained silent and the sheikh said, "I do not belittle the hardship of the Path with honeyed words, for the light of salvation is a fruit that is withheld from all but its followers. God accepts from you less than that—to each one in proportion to his zeal."

Silence reigned until it was broken by Aladdin asking, "Does that require that I should give up my work?"

"Each sheikh has a Way of his own," the other answered forcefully, "and as for me I accept only those who work."

"I shall come quickly and eagerly."

"Do not come," he said, "unless you are driven by an irresistible desire."

X

He came up to Fadil Sanaan at the public fountain as a new person. Fadil was dubious and muttered impatiently, "How long are you going to leave me in a state of hope?"

"I," said Aladdin, "am in the state of confusion."

"Did you find the way to the sheikh's house?"

"Yes—how did you know that?"

"I know his tracks." Then he added, "I moved around with him for a long time."

"You!"

"Yes."

"He is a righteous sheikh."

"That, and more," he conceded, bending his head.

"Perhaps patience failed you and you discontinued?"

"I received at his hands an upbringing whose effects do not abate, yet I preferred permanence to the obliteration of self."

"I do not understand, friend."

"Be patient, understanding is not made possible except with time. I would like to see you as one of God's soldiers, not one of his dervishes."

"I am truly confused."

"The logic of faith is everlasting and eternal," said Fadil. "The Path is one at first, then it splits inevitably into two. One of these leads to love and to obliteration of self, the other to holy war. As for the people of obliteration of self, they are dedicated to themselves, and as for the people of holy war, they dedicate themselves to God's servants."

At this Aladdin sank into deep thought that caused him to forget time.

XI

Darwish Omran the chief of police and his son Habazlam Bazaza were trotting along on two mules from the police station to their house with the sun about to set. At the turning into Shooting Square the madman suddenly fixed them with a stare. Blocking their way, he cried out at Darwish Omran, "Visit your friend al-Mu'in ibn Sawi and convey my greetings."

The man then went on his way and Habazlam asked, "What does madman want?"

"A madman is not held answerable for his words or actions."

He nevertheless realized that he was reminding him of the fate of the chief of police and that he was referring to his digressions. His son too realized this despite his question, especially as he normally acted as intermediary between his father and the merchants.

"Madmen have a place they do not depart from," Habazlam retorted.

"He enjoys the affection of His Majesty the Sultan," said Darwish Omran.

"As I see it," Habazlam said derisively, "he is afraid of him."

"Mind your tongue, Habazlam."

"What ignominy, father," exclaimed the young man. "Isn't it enough that the deviant sheikh refused to accept me as a husband for his daughter?"

Darwish Omran frowned without uttering a word.

XII

"For him whose happiness is not valid, that happiness bequeaths troubles; and for him whose sociability is not in the service of his Lord, that sociability bequeaths alienation."

Among the lessons in religion that the sheikh would give Aladdin, his cup brimmed over with fragments of enlightening aphorisms. It was as though he was communing with himself, but the young man would receive them in a daze.

"Everyone thereon is transitory, except His face, and he who delights in the transitory will be beset by sorrow when that which delights him comes to an end. Everything is vanity except the worship of Him; sorrow and alienation throughout the world ensue from looking at everything but God."

Aladdin remembered his dreams, his conversations, and his actions and the world appeared to him like a covering of mysteries. He remembered his father and his mother and he was overcome with sadness.

"He who has been endowed with three things alongside three other things has escaped from the banes of life: an empty stomach on a contented heart; continued poverty with present abstinence; and total patience with constant invocation of His name."

Aladdin said to himself: We pray to the Merciful, the Compassionate in the name of the Merciful, the Compassionate.

At this the sheikh asked him, "What are you thinking about, my son?"

With reddened cheeks he emerged from his momentary daze. "Nothing will take me out of my state of confusion except the benevolence of the Merciful."

"You must, before receiving the wine, cleanse the container, removing from it all elements of dirt."

"What a good spiritual guide you are!" he said joyfully.

"But 'the other' forces himself upon us while that guide is absent."

Realizing that he was referring to Fadil Sanaan, Aladdin inquired, "What do you think of him, master?"

"A noble youth who knew what suited him and was satisfied with it."

"Is he straying from the right path?"

"He is waging war against error to the extent of his ability."

"Now my heart is at peace," said Aladdin happily.

"But you must know yourself."

"He is poor, but rich in bearing the worries of mankind."

"A creed for the sword and a creed for love."

Aladdin was silent and the sheikh said, "Blessed are those who have accomplished the transfer of the heart from things to the Lord of things. The world does not come to my mind, so how should it come to the minds of those who know not the world?"

After this the sheikh continued with his lesson.

XIII

One night the sheikh received him in the same room but he saw that a curtain had been let down at its right-hand corner. He was beset by youthful notions.

"Listen, Aladdin," said the sheikh.

The strings of a lute were struck behind the curtains and a melodious voice sang:

> *"My night is resplendent with your face*
> *with darkness in force among people.*
> *While people are in the depths of darkness,*
> *we are in the brightness of daylight."*

The voice was silent but its echo continued to penetrate the depths.

"This is Zubeida, my daughter," said the sheikh. "She is a sincere disciple."

"I am happy and honored," mumbled Aladdin in rapture.

"I have refused to give her to the son of the chief of police." Then, continuing after a silence, "But I make of her a gift to you, Aladdin."

"But I am nothing but an itinerant barber," he said in a voice that trembled with emotion.

And the sheikh recited:

> *"A visitor whose handsomeness was revealed—*
> *how hides the night a full moon that comes forth?"*

Then he said, "He who is humble about himself, God raises his worth; and he who exults in himself, God humbles him in the eyes of His servants."

XIV

A marriage contract was made between Aladdin and Zubeida. The young man transferred himself to the house of the great sheikh. Ugr, Fattouha, and Fadil Sanaan, Master Sahloul and Abdul Qadir al-Maheeni attended the simple wedding feast. And, without an invitation, the madman came along and sat to the right of the bridegroom. After the feast Ugr went off to his house in the company of a group of his special friends, where glasses of wine made the rounds and he went on dancing and singing until dawn.

XV

Only a few days after the night of the wedding the peaceful atmosphere of the quarter was troubled by painful events when the epidemic of evil, with its somber face, advanced once more upon it. A rare and valuable jewel had been lost from the residence of the governor, al-Fadl ibn Khaqan, and his wife was greatly upset. This had reminded the governor of those unruly incidents that had beset the quarter from time to time in the shape of assassinations and robberies that revealed the ugliest of conspiracies and ended up with the killing of the governor or his dismissal. The man poured out his anger against Darwish Omran, the chief of police, who denied that his organization had been negligent and promised that the perpetrator would be arrested and the jewel found.

The chief of police dispatched his plainclothesmen throughout the quarter. On the basis of reports received he made a raid on the house of Sheikh Abdullah al-Balkhi, paying no heed to the murmurings of the people. He searched it thoroughly and came across the jewel in Aladdin's cupboard, where he also found some letters that showed conclusively that he was cooperating with the Kharijites. Thus Aladdin was arrested and thrown into prison and it was decided that he should be put on trial immediately.

XVI

With this a pall of sadness fell upon the hearts of the people. It burned not only at Zubeida, Fattouha, and Ugr, but hearts generally were pained at the fate of the handsome young man. They were determined that he should be freed and pointed to the chief of police and his son Habazlam Bazaza as being those who had planned the crime. What increased people's suspicions was the appearance of a sudden favor granted to al-Mu'in ibn Sawi, which led them to believe that the planners had had recourse to his previous experience as chief of police in carrying out what they had plotted. Ugr went to solicit compassion from al-Fadl ibn Khaqan and Haikal al-Zafarani, but he found himself rebuffed by them. He urged Sheikh Abdullah al-Balkhi to exert himself, making use of the veneration in which he was held, but no word or movement issued from the sheikh. Events moved with startling speed and Aladdin was tried and sentenced to be beheaded.

XVII

On the morning of a cold autumnal day Aladdin was led off to execution under close guard amid a vast crowd of the inhabitants of the quarter that included both officials and working men. Aladdin himself could not believe what was taking place and was calling out, "I am innocent—God is my witness."

His gaze roamed among the faces that stared at him, some pitying, some crowing over his fate, and he raised his face toward the heavens behind the clouds, submitting himself to his Creator. The screams of his mother and his wife came to him and his heart quaked. Despite his state of bewilderment he was able to recall how he had hoped to emerge from his confusion to the sword of holy war or to divine love. It had never occurred to him that his fate would instead be the executioner's sword.

Many expected that some miracle might occur at the last moment, as had happened to Ugr, but the sword was raised high before their eyes amid the atmosphere of gloom; then in its falling it scattered all hopes: the handsome and noble head was severed from the body.

XVIII

In the sheikh's house Ugr moaned, "My son is innocent."

"Innocent and blameless," wailed Zubeida. "God is sufficient for me."

The sheikh sat cross-legged, calm and silent. He did nothing; even sadness he did not express. His daughter said to him, "Father, I am racked with pain."

"You haven't made the least movement," Ugr said to him sharply. "It's as if the matter didn't concern you."

He looked at his daughter without paying any attention to Ugr and said, "Patience, Zubeida."

Then, after a silence, he went on: "Here is the story of a venerable sheikh who said, 'I fell into a hole and after three days there passed by a caravan of travelers. I told myself that I should call out to them. Then I went back on my decision, saying that no, it was not proper that I should seek help other than from Almighty God. When they approached the hole they found that it was in the middle of the road and they said, "Let's fill this hole lest someone fall into it." I was so exceedingly perturbed that I lost all hope. After they had filled it in and gone on their way, I prayed to Almighty God and gave myself over to death, relinquishing all hope in human beings. When night fell I heard a movement at the surface of the hole. As I listened to it the mouth of the hole was opened and I saw a large animal like a dragon. It let down its tail to me and I knew that God had sent it to rescue me. I clung on to its tail and it drew me up. Then a voice from the heavens called out to me, "We have saved you from death with death." ' "

The Sultan

I

The three men carved their way through the darkness in the garb of foreign merchants: Shahriyar, Dandan, and Shabeeb Rama. Three specters approached them and when they faced each other, one of the specters asked, "What are you doing at this hour of the night?"

"We are foreign merchants," answered Shahriyar, "alleviating our boredom with the breezes of spring."

"You are to be my guests, strangers," said the man who had spoken.

Calling blessings upon him, they went off as one group, with Shahriyar asking, "I wonder who our generous host can be?"

"Patience, O noble gentlemen," said the man.

II

They walked until they arrived at the riverbank and made their way toward a waiting ship, its lights shining from it like stars.

"We are linked with the market—are you wishing to travel?"

Another voice answered, "O strangers, you are in the presence of His Majesty Sultan Shahriyar, so give him the greetings due to the ruler and give praise to God for your good fortune."

Astonishment silenced the tongues of the three men. What sultan? Which Shahriyar? In their bewilderment they were rooted to the spot.

"Greetings, strangers," said the second voice.

Shahriyar recovered from his state of shock and determined to embark upon the experience and see it through to the end. He quickly bowed down in front of the alleged sultan and was immediately followed by Dandan and Shabeeb Rama.

"May God make victorious the face of the Commander of the Faithful and give him long life and perpetuate his reign."

Within the retinue they followed him until he had seated himself on a throne under an awning in the bow of the ship. They took their seats on cushions that had been laid down on an empty space extending in front of the throne. In spring weather, under the smiles of wakeful stars, the ship set sail.

III

The ship anchored by the shore of an island, where it was met by guards with torches.

"It's a new kingdom, with us asleep!" whispered the real Shahriyar in Dandan's ear.

"Maybe it's hashish, Your Majesty?"

"But from where are they getting the money to pay for these luxuries?"

"Soon," said the vizier uneasily, "the truth will speak with its hidden tongue."

They entered a fine pavilion and found a tablecloth spread out with all sorts of food and drink. Surrounding it was a gathering of the men of the kingdom, who partook of the food till they were sated, and of the drink till their spirits were aglow with rapturous joy. From behind a curtain a slave-girl sang:

"The tongue of passion in my innermost self to you is speaking,
telling you that I am in love with you."

"What a royal banquet it is, and we are nothing but subjects," whispered the true Shahriyar in Dandan's ear.

Then, at a prescribed moment, the other sultan called out, "The time has come for us to hold the divine tribunal."

"Should we not excuse ourselves," Dandan asked his master, "so that we may send troops to surround them before they are scattered?"

"Let us rather remain so that I may see with my own eyes what is happening—things that have not happened to me even in my thoughts."

Quickly some people took up the cloths on which the food had been spread. A dais for the court was brought and set up in the center of the pavilion. The other sultan seated himself, with his vizier standing to his right and on his left the executioner. Guards with unsheathed swords were stationed in the corners. The real Shahriyar sat down, together with his two followers, amid a few of the elite who were permitted to follow the tribunal of divine justice.

IV

From above the dais and addressing the elite who were present, the other sultan said, "I thank God, Who has helped me to repent after I had become immersed in the shedding of innocent blood and in plundering the property of Muslims. In truth He is generous in mercy and forgiveness."

The face of the real Shahriyar turned pale, yet he remained motionless. The other sultan continued what he had to say:

"This tribunal is being held in order to investigate a complaint raised by a simple man. If what he reports is correct, then a terrible crime has been brought to light in which innocence has been done to death to the advantage of baseness, villainy, and oppression. It is of God, first and last, that help is asked, so let the complainant, Ugr the barber, enter."

The man entered and stood before the dais, humble and wary.

"What is your complaint, Ugr?" the sultan said to him.

"My only son Aladdin," said the man in a quavering voice, "died as the victim of a savage and treacherous plot."

"What was the charge for which he was beheaded?"

"Plotting against the sultan and stealing the jewel of the lady Qamar al-Zaman, the wife of the governor al-Fadl ibn Khaqan."

"Who, in your opinion, devised the plot?"

"Habazlam Bazaza and his father Darwish Omran the chief of police, and they sought the help of al-Mu'in ibn Sawi, who had been sacked because of his wrongdoings. He succeeded in stealing the jewel and in placing it in Aladdin's cupboard, together with forged letters that told of his treachery to His Majesty the Sultan."

"And what in your opinion was the motive behind the plot?"

"To revenge themselves on Aladdin because he had married Zubeida the daughter of God's saint, al-Balkhi, who had refused to give her in marriage to Habazlam Bazaza because of his evil character and behavior."

"Have you any evidence for what you are saying?"

"Aladdin's innocent nature is beyond any evidence. Ask all the people living in the quarter about him. The plot is a reality and everyone believes in it. Had I any clear evidence I would have saved the neck of the innocent and blameless young man, but I place my hope in the sultan's justice and his unequaled influence."

Immediately the sultan had Ugr taken away and called for the governor of the quarter, al-Fadl ibn Khaqan. The man was brought before him, the lineaments of his face expressing fear and contrition. The sultan said to him, "Governor, I have no doubt that you are a virtuous man. I chose you for the post after you had been educated for it and as you had the experience for it. I command you by Almighty God to reveal to me the secret behind this affair, for I have no doubt that you are knowledgeable about it."

"O God, I bear witness that I shall speak the truth," mumbled the governor as he spread out the palms of his hands. Then, addressing his master, he said, "After the death of Aladdin I got to know about the whisperings of people regarding his innocence and the guilt of the others. I was alarmed as a man would be who has been brought up steeped with the ideologies of the true faith. I sent off my spies to all quarters and they were able to obtain the truth from the mouth of al-Mu'in ibn Sawi himself when he was drunk. I there and then determined to bring down the culprits. However, I . . ."

The governor fell silent, then said meekly, "However, I weakened, Your Majesty, for it was I who had tried Aladdin and sentenced him to be beheaded. I was frightened of the consequences of the truth being revealed and made known, for he who has killed a single soul has killed all people."

"You feared the consequences for your reputation and your position as governor," said the sultan.

The man lowered his head and remained silent.

"Did your private secretary know of the truth?" the sultan asked him.

"Yes, Your Majesty," he said sadly.

"God has His own wisdom in His creation, and as for us we have the canonical law. Thus we give sentence that al-Mu'in ibn Sawi, Darwish Omran, and Habazlam Bazaza be beheaded; we also give sentence that al-Fadl ibn Khaqan and Haikal al-Zafarani be dismissed from their posts and their properties be confiscated."

V

The leather execution mat was brought, together with the culprits. The executioner moved forward. At this the real Shahriyar could not stop himself from rising to his feet and saying in a loud voice, "Stop this farce!"

The guards leapt forward and the sultan called out from his dais, "Who has given you permission to talk, you mad stranger?"

"Wake up from your state of madness," chided the sultan firmly. "You are addressing the sultan Shahriyar."

The surprise silenced all tongues. Dandan and Shabeeb Rama took their positions alongside the sultan, their swords drawn. As for the sultan, he took from his pocket the ring of kingship and waved it in the other's face. The false sultan, recovering from his amazement, jumped down from the dais, then prostrated himself before the sultan.

"Your slave, Ibrahim the water-carrier," he said in a trembling voice.

"What's the meaning of this farce?"

Quaking with terror, the man said, "Your pardon, Majesty! Give me permission to relate my story and forgive me my stupidity."

VI

Ibrahim the water-carrier told his story to the sultan at the meeting chamber of the summer council in the palace.

"Since my childhood, Majesty," he said, "I have been one of those who put their trust in God. I toil from dawn till dusk and though my earnings are limited, my heart is content and I get my pleasure from a pipe of hashish. God presented me with a great blessing when I married the widow of Gamasa al-Bulti and I never dreamt of eating meat other than on the feast of Greater Bairam. When the son of my friend Ugr the barber was killed my balance was disturbed and I heard people whispering. I was overcome by a sadness I had not known previously and I told myself that we poor had no one other than God. Destiny was concealing from me a surprise that I had never imagined, and I found a treasure outside the gate and became one of the richest of men. I thought—and this is the usual thing—to enjoy the wealth on my own, but my love for the poor pushed me to another path and I decided to set up an imaginary kingdom in which we could all be on an equal footing."

"Hashish has consumed your mind," said Shahriyar, smiling.

"I don't deny that, for the idea would occur only to the mind of a hashish smoker. The vagabonds were very enthusiastic about the idea. Our choice fell on this deserted island where I crowned myself sultan and chose viziers, commanders, and men of state from among the bare-footed hungry. We did not come together to act out our game other than at night, when we would be transformed from down-and-out vagabonds into great men of state, each in accordance with his situation and rank. The plot that brought about the death of Aladdin was the inspiration for us to hold each night a tribunal at which justice would take its course after it had been unable to do so in the world."

"And you squandered the treasure, you hashish addict?" scoffed the sultan.

"There is only a little left, but we bought with it a happiness that cannot be reckoned in terms of money."

VII

Though greatly delighted at the story of Ibrahim the water-carrier, Shahriyar said to Dandan, "Bring me up to date on what is being said about the death of Aladdin the son of Ugr the barber."

"You will find the key, Your Majesty," said the vizier, "with al-Fadl ibn Khaqan, so summon him and you can bring great influence to bear on him."

"Do you think we should be guided by what the sultan Ibrahim the water-carrier did?" asked the sultan.

"In truth, Your Majesty," said Dandan, "it was an extraordinary trial which affirms that hashish did not consume the whole of his mind."

"I won't hide from you the fact that I was also delighted at the judgment," said Shahriyar.

Thus events proceeded: the transgressors fell and al-Mu'in ibn Sawi, Darwish Omran, and Habazlam Bazaza were beheaded and al-Fadl ibn Khaqan and Haikal al-Zafarani were dismissed from their posts and their property confiscated.

The Cap of Invisibility

I

"Abbas al-Khaligi the governor of the quarter, Sami Shukri the private secretary, Khalil Faris the chief of police—no depravity is to be expected from them in the near future," said Sakhrabout listlessly.

"Why not?" asked Zarmabaha scornfully.

"They came to their positions following bitter experiences that toppled those who had transgressed."

"Let us leave the rulers till ruling corrupts them, and look at that active young man Fadil Sanaan."

"He is a living epitome of work that spoils our intentions and plans," said Sakhrabout indignantly.

"What a target truly worthy of our skill and our wiles!"

Mirth crept into his voice as he said, "You're an inexhaustible treasure, Zarmabaha."

"Let's think up together some delightful sport that is worthy of us."

II

Fadil Sanaan was relaxing on the stairway of the public fountain after a hot summer's day. He was always missing Aladdin and mourning him with a wounded heart, and he would ask himself angrily, "When will release from suffering come?"

He became aware of a man of radiant appearance and smiling countenance coming toward him and sitting down alongside him. They exchanged a greeting, but the man displayed toward him such attention that it was as though he had come there because of him. Fadil waited for him to give expression to his thoughts. When he did not do so, he said, "You are not, I believe, from our quarter?"

"Your instinct is right," said the man in a friendly manner, "but I have chosen you to speak to."

He stared at him with a wariness that he had learned from being pursued by plainclothesmen.

"Who are you?" he asked.

"That's of no importance. What really matters is that I am a man of destiny and I have a gift for you."

Fadil frowned, even more wary, and inquired, "Who has sent you? Speak openly, for I do not like riddles."

"Nor do I," he said, smiling. "Here is the gift—it makes anything else unnecessary."

He extracted from the pocket of his gown a cap decorated with colored embellishments, the like of which he had never seen. He fitted it onto his head and in the twinkling of an eye he was invisible. Fadil was amazed and looked around him anxiously.

"Is it a dream?" he asked.

He heard the man's voice asking with a laugh, "Have you not heard of the cap of invisibility? That's what this is."

The man took off the cap and he again assumed concrete form where he had been sitting. Fadil's heart beat faster.

"Who are you?" he asked nervously.

"The gift is both real and tangible and any question beyond that is unimportant."

"Do you really intend to give it to me?"

"It is for this reason that I have sought you out rather than anyone else."

"And why me in particular?"

"And why did Ibrahim the water-carrier find the treasure? But do not squander your treasure as he did his."

Fadil said to himself that the world was being created anew and that it behoved him to be careful of this present for saving mankind. Quickly his heart was filled with noble aspirations.

"What are you thinking about?" the man asked him.

"About beautiful things that will please you."

"Tell me what you'll do with it," he asked cautiously.

"I shall do with it as my conscience dictates," he said, his face radiant.

"Do anything except what your conscience dictates," said the man.

The look in his eyes cooled and he was overcome by a sense of disappointment and disquiet as he inquired, "What did you say?"

"Do anything except what your conscience dictates—this is the condition. You are free in what you accept or refuse, but be careful not to be deceitful, for then you will lose the cap and you might well lose your life as well."

"Then you are pushing me toward evil, you knave!"

"My condition is clear—don't do what your conscience dictates to you. You must also not commit any evil."

"Then what shall I do with it?"

"Between this and that are many things that bring neither profit nor harm. You are free."

"I have lived an honorable life."

"Continue it as you will, but in your turban and not with the cap. What, after all, did you reap from it?—poverty and prison from time to time."

"That is my affair."

"The time has come for me to go," said the man, rising to his feet. "What do you say?"

His heart beat anxiously: it was a chance that did not present itself twice. He could not refuse. He said confidently, "An acceptable present and there's nothing for me to fear from it."

III

Right away the next morning Fadil Sanaan went off like the breeze that is present everywhere but which is not seen. The new magical experience took control of him. He tried to be a hidden moving spirit, so happiness made him forget everything, even his daily toil in search of a living. By being hidden he felt that he was rising up and taking charge, that he was reaching equal terms with the hidden powers, that he was in control of the reins of affairs, and that the scope for action stretched out without limit before him. It was a unique period during which he was at rest from his body, from the eyes of men, and from human laws. He pondered that it might all have been made possible for some scoundrel and he thanked the good luck that had singled him out for attention. Because of his great happiness he was not really aware of himself till evening came. Then he remembered that Akraman and Umm Saad were waiting for his limited amount of dirhams so they could prepare supper and buy the ingredients for making the sweetmeats. Worried, he realized that he could not return to his home in the rooming house empty-handed. He passed by a butcher's shop; the man was calculating his day's earnings, while his young lad had moved to one side. He decided to take three dirhams, that being the amount of his daily earnings, telling himself that he would return them when things were easier. He found himself entering the shop and taking the money. He came out into the street again feeling down at heart, guilty for the first time in his life of stealing. He looked toward the shop and saw the butcher raining down blows on his young assistant, then driving him out, accusing him of theft.

IV

After supper he thought of cheering himself up by visiting the Café of
the Emirs while wearing his cap. It would afford chances for some
innocent pranks, though he would have to be careful not to involve
himself in any dishonorable action as he had done at the butcher's shop.

For the first time he saw familiar faces without their being able to
see him. His gaze passed scornfully over Hasan al-Attar, Galil the draper,
Ugr the barber, Shamloul the hunchback, Master Sahloul, Ibrahim the
water-carrier, Suleiman al-Zeini, Abdul Qadir al-Maheeni, Ragab the
porter, and Ma'rouf the cobbler. He heard Ugr asking, "What has kept
Fadil Sanaan?"

Shamloul the hunchback answered in his high-pitched voice,
laughing, "Perhaps some catastrophe has befallen him."

He determined to punish the buffoon. The waiter came bearing
glasses of *karkadeh,* prepared from the petals of hibiscus flowers, and
suddenly the tray was spilt over the hunchback's head. With the drink all
over him, the hunchback jumped up shouting, while the waiter stood
there dumbfounded. The men laughed mockingly. The owner of the
café gave the waiter a slap and began apologizing to the sultan's jester.
Ingratiating himself in an exaggerated way, the owner himself brought
some fresh glasses of *karkadeh,* which this time were spilt over the head of
Suleiman al-Zeini. Wonderment and secret delight took over, with
more than one voice calling out, "It must be the hashish!"

Ugr, freed of constraints and forgetting his sorrows, laughed out-
right, but he was not allowed to enjoy his laughter, for he received a
resounding slap on the back of his neck. Turning round angrily, he
found Ma'rouf the cobbler behind him and struck him in the face with
his fist, and the two of them were soon locked in battle. Darkness fell
when a stone struck the lamp. In the gloom blows were exchanged,
tempers rose, and they shouted and fought until all were strewn about
the street in an ugly state of madness and fear.

V

Fadil practiced his normal life and hid the cap in his pocket until such time as he should need it. He told himself that he had derived nothing from it up to now except that it had caused him to steal and to commit some meaningless pranks. He was anxious and depressed. He told himself that he could not ignore a rare opportunity like this. He had not had the chance of thinking things over, but what was the advantage of doing so? If it was impossible for him to do good with the cap, then what could he do with it?

He was resting on the stairway of the public fountain after sunset a short distance from a peddler selling watermelons. He saw someone going toward the man to buy one. His limbs trembled when he saw that it was a prison warder well known for torturing his fellow creatures. He saw him making his way with the watermelon toward a nearby alley where it seemed that he was living, so he followed him. When he was sure there were no passersby he put on the cap and vanished from sight. Having forgotten the pledge to himself, he drew out the knife which he used for cutting the sweetmeats. Let him at least find out how the man who had given him the cap would prevent him from doing what he wanted. He came up to the jailer, who was not aware of his presence, and aimed a deadly blow at his neck. The man fell down covered in blood.

The feeling of victory exhilarated him. He could do what he wanted! He did not leave the scene but stayed on to see what would happen. He saw the people gathering in the light of lanterns; he saw the police come and heard the jailer utter the name of the watermelon-seller before breathing his last; he saw the police arresting the innocent vendor. Fadil was shocked and disturbed. What was there between the jailer and the vendor that had made him bring him down? His unease became impossible to bear.

"There is no choice," he told himself, "but to save this innocent man."

At this he saw the owner of the cap in front of him, saying, "Be careful that you don't break the pact."

"Did you not let me kill the criminal?" said Fadil in panic.

"Not at all," said the other. "You did not kill the criminal but his twin, who is a good and blameless man."

VI

From stealing, to committing stupid pranks, to murder. He had fallen into the abyss. When the watermelon-seller was beheaded the following day, he found himself overcome by a state of complete despair. He roved around aimlessly in the lanes like a madman. He hated himself so profoundly that he hated the world itself and his everlasting dreams.

"To confess and to face the penalty, that is all that is left to me," he whispered to himself.

Then he saw the owner of the cap in front of him, saying, "Beware!"

"May you be accursed!" he shouted angrily.

The other disappeared, saying, "Is this the recompense for someone who has handed you the key to power and pleasure?"

Bitterness enveloped him, mixed with heated madness, and he began to drink, summoning the devils from their hiding-places. He brought to mind thoughts that were heavy with lust, thoughts that tempted him and were driven off by piety. They manifested themselves through radiations of red-hot madness in two shapes: that of Qamar the sister of Hasan al-Attar and that of Qut al-Quloub the wife of Suleiman al-Zeini. He told himself: "Seeing that the wine is lodged in my stomach, why should I fear being drunk? Nothing remains for me but to submit gracefully to the curse, so let me raise myself to the skies, let the devils burst forth from their bottles, and let punishment come crowned with victims."

VII

"Why Fadil Sanaan?" Qamar al-Attar asked herself. "What a dream!" But she realized that the dream had left behind it signs that could not be denied. She was bewildered and said to herself, "It's as though he were the Devil." Terror took hold of her and death appeared before her eyes.

"It's a nightmare," said Qut al-Quloub to herself. "But why Fadil Sanaan, whom I had never thought of in that way?"

Yet from a nightmare signs had been left and a state of terror exploded within her. Suleiman al-Zeini discovered that money of his had been stolen. Khalil Faris the chief of police came along. Qut al-Quloub concealed the story of her nightmare, and the thought of death closed in on her.

VIII

He kept to his daily life during the daytime and did not fail to show up at the Café of the Emirs. He would often repeat to himself, "God have mercy upon you, Fadil Sanaan—you were a good young man, like Aladdin and better."

He was met by the madman in his wanderings and as usual he offered him some sweets, but the madman this time did not hold out his hand, and went on his way as though he had not seen him.

He was dismayed and fears hovered around him like flies. The madman had not changed without reason. Perhaps he had sensed the devil that lay behind his skin.

"I should be frightened of the madman," he muttered to himself.

He saw the owner of the cap smiling at him encouragingly and saying, "You are right, and he is not the only one you should be frightened of."

He frowned and felt humiliated.

"Let me alone," he said sharply.

"Kill the madman—that won't be difficult for you," he said calmly.

"Don't suggest things to me—that was not part of the bargain."

"We must become friends. Thus I also counsel you to kill al-Balkhi, that charlatan of a sheikh."

"We are not friends and I shall do nothing except by my own free will."

"I concede that wholly, but you will not regret it. You are suffering by reason of the change of habit, but you will achieve dazzling wisdom and will understand life as it must be for you."

"You're making fun of me," shouted Fadil.

"Not at all. I am urging you to kill your enemies before they kill you."

"Let me alone," he said with loathing.

IX

Disturbing events occurred: a strange disease attacked, almost at one and the same time, two distinguished and beautiful women, Qamar al-Attar and Qut al-Quloub the wife of Suleiman al-Zeini. Neither the sincere devotion nor the experience of Abdul Qadir al-Maheeni was of any use in saving them. With their deaths the doctor realized he had a secret worry he did not know how to ignore. Should he keep silent to protect the reputation of his friends? Should he be afraid that his silence might be covering up some crime or criminal? He thought for a long time, then went off to see Khalil Faris the chief of police.

"I shall tell you of my concern in the hope that God may guide us to the right path," he said. He gave a deep sigh, then went on: "It was not an illness that afflicted the sister of Hasan al-Attar and Qut al-Quloub. It is clear to me that they both died of a poison that slowly killed them!"

"Suicide?" muttered the chief of police with concern. "But why? And why should anyone want to murder them?"

"Before each one died she uttered the name of Fadil Sanaan with terror and abhorrence."

The man nodded his head with growing interest and the doctor said, "The substance of what I understood was that they had both dreamt that night that he had assaulted them, then it became clear to them that there were certain traces left behind that showed conclusively that the dream had been a reality."

"This is astounding. Had he drugged them?"

"I don't know."

"Where did the dream occur?"

"In their own beds in their own homes."

"This is truly astounding. How did he steal into their houses? And how did he drug them so that he could have his way with them? Had he accomplices in both houses?"

"I don't know."

"Have you broached the subject with Hasan and al-Zeini?"

"I hadn't the courage to do so."

"What do you know of Fadil Sanaan?"

"A blameless young man."

"There was a suspicion, which has not as yet been supported by any evidence, that he is a Kharijite."

"I know nothing about that."

"I shall arrest him immediately," said the chief of police resolutely, "and shall interrogate him closely."

"I trust that your investigation will be carried out in secret so as to spare the reputations of the two women."

With a shrug Khalil Faris said, "Uncovering the truth is my primary concern."

X

Fadil was arrested and immediately taken off to prison. The governor of the quarter, Abbas al-Khaligi, interested himself in the matter and asked to see Hasan al-Attar and Suleiman al-Zeini and surprised them with the secret that the doctor had been loath to divulge. It was like a violent blow aimed at their heads, death itself being easier to bear. Al-Khaligi then ordered that Fadil Sanaan should be brought from prison so that he himself might question him. Khalil Faris, however, came to him on his own, saying with great embarrassment, "The criminal has escaped—there is no sign of him in the prison."

The governor stormed and raged and hurled rebuke and accusations at the chief of police.

"His escape is a mystery," the man said with utter helplessness. "It is as though it were an act of black magic."

"It's more like a scandal that will rock the very foundations of confidence."

The plainclothesmen spread abroad like locusts. Akraman the wife of Fadil Sanaan, Husniya his sister, and Umm Saad his mother were brought in. Their interrogation revealed nothing.

"My husband," said Akraman weeping, "is the noblest of men and I do not believe a single word said against him."

XI

Fadil Sanaan realized that he had become as good as dead—after today he could have no life other than under the cap, the life of some accursed spirit wandering in the darkness, a spirit who could move only in the spheres of frivolous pastimes or evil, deprived of repentance or of doing good; he had become a Satan who was damned. As he groaned in his desolation the owner of the cap appeared before him.

"Perhaps you are in need of me?" he asked.

Fadil glared at him balefully and the other said to him in friendly fashion, "There is no limit to your authority and you will not lack for anything."

"It is a state of nonbeing!" he exclaimed.

"Wipe out old notions and be aware of your great luck," he said mockingly.

"Loneliness. Loneliness and darkness. Wife, sister, and mother are lost to me, as are my friends."

"Listen to the advice of someone of experience," the other said quietly. "It is in your power to enjoy every day with some event that will rock mankind."

XII

Mysterious events swept over the quarter and made people forget the case and the criminal who had escaped. A man of noble birth was pushed off his mule and fell to the ground. A stone struck the head of Sami Shukri the private secretary, while surrounded by his guard, and split it open. Priceless jewels disappeared from the governor's house. A fire broke out in the lumber warehouse. Harassment of women in the marketplaces increased. Terror pursued the high and the low, while all the time Fadil Sanaan rushed headlong on his rugged path, intoxicated by despair and madness.

The governor Abbas al-Khaligi met up with Sheikh Abdullah al-Balkhi and with the doctor Abdul Qadir al-Maheeni and the mufti. He said to them, "You are the elite of our quarter and I want to seek guidance from your opinions in what is occurring. What is your diagnosis and what treatment do you suggest?"

"It is no more than a gang of evil persons operating with cunning and resourcefulness," said the doctor, "and we are in need of increased vigilance where security is concerned."

He thought for a while and then continued, "We are also in need of revising the distribution of the alms tax and charity."

"I believe," said the governor, "that the problem is more serious than you suppose. What is the opinion of Sheikh Abdullah?"

The man answered tersely, "We lack true faith."

"But the people are believers."

"Not at all," he said sadly. "True faith is rarer than the unicorn."

At this the mufti said in a harsh voice, "There is someone who is practicing black magic against us. I accuse no one but the Shiites and the Kharijites."

XIII

Everyone who was under any sort of suspicion was taken off to the prisons. Many homes were shaken by doubts. For the first time Fadil Sanaan awoke from his state of despair. He was astonished at himself and wondered whether he still had in his heart any room for contemplation and regret. Old memories revived in him, like breezes blowing on a blazing fire, and he began thinking about directing his frivolous action in some new direction. However, the owner of the cap appeared to him with a warning look and inquired, "Are you not yet cured of your old disease?"

Though overcome by rage, he controlled himself humbly and said, "To effect the escape of these men would be the height of frivolity."

"Remember our agreement."

"What good is there behind rescuing the enemies of religion?" he inquired sharply.

"They are in your opinion the leaders, and you are merely one of them, so don't try to play games with me."

"Let me do what I want," he said with determination and hope. "Then after that I'll do what you like."

The cap was then torn from his head and he assumed corporeal form amid the crush of passersby in Shooting Square. He was scared at the sudden change that had occurred, but before he could recover from his terror the other had replaced the cap on his head, saying, "Stick to our pledge so that I may continue to treat you in the same manner."

XIV

He did not have the good fortune to escape. A feeling of bitterness took hold of him. He wondered how he could save his brothers and comrades. He was choked by the steel grip which enwrapped him. He was both the slave of the cap and its owner, as well as the prisoner of darkness and nothingness. No, he did not have the good fortune to escape and was ashamed to do so. Even despair seemed beyond him: however many stupidities he committed they were unable to pluck out its old tunes from his heart. He yearned to resurrect the old Fadil at any price. Yes, the old Fadil was over and done with, but along the way there was still room for action. From the depths of the darkness there was a gleam of light. For the first time in ages his spirit was refreshed as he charged his willpower with fresh life. His courage burst forth in the shape of mounting aspirations. A wave of challenging scorn raised it above considerations of life and death and he found himself gazing from on top of a peak to horizons of promise; horizons that promised a noble death. Thus would Fadil Sanaan be restored, be it even as a lifeless corpse.

Without hesitation he set off with new resolve toward the governor's house. The madman passed by him, repeating the words "There is no god but God. He brings to life and makes to die, and He is capable of everything."

He had reached an extreme of intoxication and recklessness and was not frightened when the owner of the cap appeared to him.

"Keep away from me," he said, and he seized the cap from his head and threw it into the other's face with the words "Do what you like."

"They'll tear you to pieces."

"I know my destiny better than you do."

"You will regret when regret will be of no use."

"I am stronger than you," he shouted.

Fadil expected fearfully that he would strike him, but he vanished as though vanquished.

XV

The trial of Fadil Sanaan provoked more speculation than any previous one. His confessions burst upon the city like a storm. As the elite still considered him one of their sons, and because the common folk saw him as one of theirs, minds and hearts were utterly confused.

Punishment Square received a steady flow of men and women of all classes. Whispers of pity mingled with gloating shouts, while the moaning of the rebab mixed with the boisterous revelry of the drunk.

When the young man was seen from afar all eyes strained toward him. He approached in the midst of his guards with firm step, a calm face, and humble resignation. In front of the leather execution mat memories surged over him in a single wave of blazing light. The faces of Akraman, al-Balkhi, Gamasa al-Bulti, Abdullah the porter, and the madman came and went before him. Love and adventure, propaganda leaflets and the thousands of meetings held in darkness in underground cellars and out-of-the-way places—all were welded together in his mind. The cap and its owner were dispersed like some stumbling step he had taken. Finally, his tragic triumph was revealed, drawing with it Shabeeb Rama the executioner. He met it in a matter of seconds with extraordinary power and startling speed; he refused with disdain to show distress and faced his destiny with cool self-possession, seeing beyond death a dazzling brilliance. But he also saw one of the signposts of the other world in the form of Master Sahloul the bric-a-brac merchant. As he recovered from his astonishment at seeing him, he asked, "And what brought you, master?"

"I was brought by that which brought you," he replied.

"You are the Angel of Death!" Fadil exclaimed in even greater surprise.

But Sahloul did not reply.

"I want justice," Fadil said brusquely.

"God does what He wishes," said Sahloul quietly.

Ma'rouf the Cobbler

I

Nothing surpassed his outward merriment except his inner apprehensions. His earnings were meager and his wife Firdaus al-Urra was greedy, covetous, and ill-tempered, a woman of strength and violence. His life was hell, divided between the daily toil and marriage. Not a day went by without his being subjected to blows and curses as he trembled before her, frightened and humiliated. He hoped for the strength with which to divorce her and would dream of her dying; he would have liked to flee, but how and where to? He told himself that he was a prisoner, just as Fadil Sanaan had been the prisoner of the Devil. Perhaps, as with him, he had no escape except through death.

One night he swallowed an excess of narcotics and went off to the Café of the Emirs with the world not big enough to contain his feeling of well-being. He looked into the faces of his companions and said in a voice that was heard by all the customers, "I'll tell you a secret that shouldn't be hidden from you."

Ugr the barber was about to make fun of him but he remembered his own sadness and abstained.

"I'll tell you the truth," went on Ma'rouf. "I've found Solomon's ring."

"Show some sense in front of your superiors, you ass," Shamloul the hunchback called out to him.

"It seems you've made good use of it," Ibrahim the water-carrier said to him. "Where are the palaces and servants? Where's the pomp and splendor?"

"Were it not for my fear of God," he said, "I would have done what would never occur to human minds!"

"Give us one example so that we may believe you," Ragab the porter said.

"That's easy!"

"Fine—rise up toward the sky, then come down safely."

"O ring of Solomon, raise me up to the sky," said Ma'rouf in a whisper.

At this Suleiman al-Zeini shouted, "Stop muttering rubbish."

But suddenly he fell silent. Ma'rouf himself was swept by a strange sense of terror. He felt a power dragging him from where he was sitting; slowly and steadily he found himself rising up into the air. Then all the customers were standing up in awe. Moving toward the door of the café, he went through it, shrieking, "Help me," then continued upward till he disappeared into the darkness of the winter night. The customers all gathered in the street in front of the café with people shouting out about the extraordinary happening. The news of it spread like the sun's rays on a summer day. Then, ever so slowly, he came down until his form appeared in the darkness and he returned to where he had been sitting, though in an indescribable state of fright and exhaustion. Everyone, high and low, stared at him and he was bombarded with questions:

"Where did you find the ring?"

"When did you find it?"

"What are you going to do with it?"

"Describe the genie to us."

"When will you make your hopes come true?"

"Don't forget your friends," Ugr said.

"And your poor comrades," Ibrahim the water-carrier called out.

"Make things as they should be," said Ragab the porter.

"Forget not God, for He is the Sovereign Power."

He understood nothing of what was said and did not know how what had happened had come about. What secret had he taken possession of? What miracle had been achieved at his hands? Should he confess the truth to them? An instinctive wariness made him keep quiet. He wanted to be on his own, to get back his breath, to think things over. He rose from where he was sitting without saying a word, with several voices protesting, "Don't leave us in bewilderment. Say something to satisfy our curiosity."

Without a glance at anyone, he left the café.

II

He went toward his house in a procession of men and women who filled the street. They vied with each other to get near him; some of them fell and others were trodden underfoot.

"Get away," he shouted at them, "or I'll send you to the next world."

In less than a minute they had all dispersed in frightened disarray until their voices were lost and he found no one before him but Firdaus al-Urra, his wife, waiting for him in front of the door, a lamp in her hand.

"He gives dominion to whom He wants," she was saying.

For the first time in ages she was smiling at him. He glared at her and gave her a slap that rang out in the silence of the night.

"You are divorced!" he shouted at her. "Go to hell."

"You enslave me with your poverty and throw me out as soon as good fortune comes."

"If you don't go immediately, the genie will carry you off to the valley of the jinn."

The woman screamed out in alarm and rushed away. He also smiled serenely for the first time in ages as he entered his home, which consisted of no more than a room and a corridor.

III

What is the meaning of this, Ma'rouf? Is it a dream or reality? Has something mysterious truly happened to you? He looked around him in the almost bare room and muttered cautiously, "O ring of Solomon, raise me up one arm's length above the ground."

He waited anxiously, but nothing happened. He was downcast at his failure. Did I not soar into the air? Did not the people of the quarter witness it? Had not al-Urra been defeated for the very first time?

"O ring of Solomon," he said from a wounded heart, "bring me a dish of green wheat and pigeon."

All he saw was a beetle making its way at the edge of the worn rug. He looked long at it, then burst into sobs.

IV

His bitter frustration was interred deeply within him. He made of it a hidden secret, erecting a barrier between it and his tongue. He told himself that he should allow things to proceed as God willed. Should he not, though, continue to go to his shop to repair shoes, slippers, and sandals? Would people be able to stomach such behavior from someone who owned Solomon's ring? And if he did not do so, would he be giving himself over to death by starvation? However, he happened to meet Khalil Faris the chief of police at the gate to his alley, who seemed to have been waiting for him. Faris greeted him with an unusually friendly smile and his intelligence told him that people were looking at him in the light of being the owner of Solomon's ring. His heart beat with a new hope and he was determined to play his role with due skill until God should cast the die for him.

"May God make your morning a happy one, Ma'rouf," Faris said amiably.

"And may He grant you such a morning, O chief of police," he said with an aloofness that astonished him. He spoke with the confidence of someone possessing power that no human being could aspire to.

"The governor of the quarter would like to meet you," said the man.

"With great pleasure," Ma'rouf said indifferently. "Where?"

"Wherever you like."

You groveling cowards! "In his house," he said, "as is only right and proper."

"You will receive due attention and protection," Faris assured him.

"I have nothing to fear from any power on earth!" he said with a contemptuous laugh.

Concealing displeasure—and perhaps fear—Khalil Faris said, "We shall be waiting for you at noon."

V

He saw from the great attention people paid him that there might soon be a fresh gathering around him, so he returned to his humble dwelling. He saw Ugr the barber, who informed him that he had become the talk not merely of the quarter but of the city and that the miracle he had performed had shaken the sultan himself. Knowing of the imminent meeting between him and the governor, Ugr said, "Don't worry about anyone, for you are the most powerful man in the world. People are now divided—there are those who fear your power because they wish to retain their own might, and those who hope that it will prove to be a protection for their weakness."

Hiding his sorrow with a smile, Ma'rouf said, "Remember, Ugr, that I am one of God's obedient servants."

His friend wished him victory and success.

VI

Waiting for him in the reception hall were Abbas al-Khaligi the governor, Sami Shukri the private secretary, and Khalil Faris the chief of police, as well as the mufti and a group of leading citizens. Though they regarded his ragged clothes with astonishment, the governor invited him to sit down by his side and greeted him warmly. He sat down confidently, a target for glances burning with curiosity.

"I have learned that you possess Solomon's ring," said the governor.

"I am prepared," he said confidentially and in a slightly threatening tone, "to convince anyone who has any doubt in his heart."

To which the governor said, "In fact I wanted to know—within the scope of my official responsibility—how it was that you came into possession of it."

"I am not permitted to reveal that secret."

"As you think best. The fact that you have honored my house by coming here gives proof of your confidence in me, for which praise be to God."

"The truth is that it has nothing to do with my confidence in you, for neither you nor anyone else can harm me," he said craftily.

The governor bowed his head to show agreement and to hide his feelings at the same time. "I and my colleagues," he said, "have thought that it is our duty to exchange views with you. God raises whom He will and humbles whom He will, but it is demanded of us that we worship Him in all circumstances."

"It is more appropriate for you to direct your words to yourself and your colleagues," said Ma'rouf boldly.

The governor's face flushed. "It is true that we took over power following bitter events, but we have been committed to the law since then."

"The proof is in the ending."

"No one will experience from us other than what is pleasing. Let His Majesty Sultan Shahriyar be an exemplar for us."

"It is not to be denied that he opened a new page, even if he has not as yet attained the hoped-for perfection."

"Perfection is with God alone."

The governor looked toward the mufti, who said, "I have a word for you, Ma'rouf, that I hope you will accept from a man who fears none but God. God puts His servants to the test in good times and bad, and

He is always and ever the most powerful. He brings the strong to trial through his strength, just as He brings the weak to trial through his weakness. Others have come into possession of Solomon's ring before you, and it was a curse on them. May your possession of it be an example to the believers and a warning to the polytheists."

Ma'rouf smiled, puffed up with the power of someone in command of the situation.

"Listen, you men of eminence," he said, "it is indeed fortunate that Solomon's ring should fall to the lot of a believing man who has the name of God on his lips morning and evening. It is a power which yours cannot prevail against, but I keep it for times of necessity. It is within my ability to order the ring to construct palaces, to fit out armies, and to gain control of the sultanate, but I have resolved to follow another path."

The assembled group breathed a sigh of relief for the first time and words of praise were showered upon Ma'rouf from every side. At which, with throbbing heart, he said, "But I should not neglect to benefit from a blessing that God has accorded me."

They all gazed at him expectantly. "I require immediately," he said, "a thousand dinars with which to improve my state of affairs."

"I shall check the account of money that is at my disposal," said the governor with relief. "If it is not sufficient I shall seek assistance from His Majesty the Sultan."

VII

Ma'rouf obtained the money he wanted and the leading citizens loaded him with gifts. He bought a palace, charging the furnishing of it to Master Sahloul, who made of it a veritable museum. He married Husniya Sanaan, the sister of Fadil. He made Ugr the barber, Ibrahim the water-carrier, and Ragab the porter his close companions and showered the poor with his generosity. He induced the governor to provide for their livelihood and to show them care and respect so that smiling faces replaced those once lined by hardship. They came to love life as they loved Paradise.

VIII

One day Ma'rouf was asked to meet the sultan Shahriyar. He went to him muttering, "There is no god but God" and "There is no strength or power except through God," hoping he would come to no harm. The sultan met him in his winter palace, in what was known as the Coral Reception Hall. He assessed him quietly, then said, "Welcome to you, Ma'rouf. I have heard with my own ears during my night excursions the praise of God's servants for you, and this has filled me with a desire to see you."

Overcoming the beating of his heart, Ma'rouf said, "For me the blessing of this meeting is more precious than Solomon's ring itself, Your Majesty."

"A noble sentiment from a noble man."

Ma'rouf lowered his head, while all the time wondering what he would do were the sultan to demand a miracle. Would you in that event, Ma'rouf, depart from the palace to the leather mat of execution?

"How did you come across the ring, Ma'rouf?" inquired the sultan.

"I have pledged myself to keep that a secret, Your Majesty," he answered with quaking heart.

"You have good reason not to tell me, Ma'rouf, but can I not see it from afar without touching it?"

"Not that either, Your Majesty. How miserable I am not to be able to fulfill your wish!"

"It doesn't matter."

"Thank you for your kindness, Your Majesty."

"I wonder at you," said the sultan after some thought. "Were you to want to sit upon my throne, no power on earth could stop you."

Ma'rouf exclaimed in disavowal, "God forbid, Your Majesty. I am nothing but a believing servant of God, who is not tempted by any power to oppose God's wish."

"You are a believer, truly—and it is a blessing that the ring is in the hand of a believer."

"Thanks be to God, Lord of the Worlds."

"Have you gained happiness, Ma'rouf?" asked the sultan with concern.

"Limitless happiness, Your Majesty."

"Does not the past sometimes spoil your happiness for you?"

"What has passed was a series of unhappy occurrences that I experienced at the hands of others, but I myself did not do anything to regret."

"Do you enjoy love, Ma'rouf?"

"Thanks be to God I do—I have a wife who gives me happiness with every breath she draws."

"And all of this is by virtue of the ring?"

"By virtue of God, Your Majesty."

The sultan was silent for a while, then asked him, "Are you able to grant happiness to others?"

"There is no limit to the power of the ring, but it cannot invade people's hearts."

In the depths of Shahriyar's eyes there showed a listlessness that revealed his disappointment. However, he smiled and said, "Allow me to see you rise up into space until your turban touches the decorations in the dome of the hall."

The request hit him like a mountain toppled by an earthquake. His hopes were scattered like dust and he knew for sure that he was doomed.

"It is not appropriate," he said vehemently, "to act other than with decorum in the sultan's presence."

"You will be flying only at my request."

"Your Majesty, I am your slave, Ma'rouf the cobbler."

"Do you owe me allegiance, Ma'rouf?"

"God is my witness to that," he croaked.

"Then I am giving you an order, Ma'rouf."

He got up from where he was sitting and sat cross-legged in the middle of the hall. He communed with his Lord secretly. "My Lord, let it be Your wish—don't let everything vanish like a dream." From a wounded and despairing heart he murmured, "Rise up, body of mine, until my turban touches the ceiling."

He closed his eyes and gave himself up to his black destiny. When nothing happened he called out from a tortured heart, "Mercy, Your Majesty!" But before he could utter another word an inspired energy had stolen into his heart, he had grown light, and his fear had disappeared. Then an unknown force quietly and gently took him up as he sat cross-legged on nothing, until his turban touched the coral dome, while the sultan followed him with his eyes in helpless astonishment, his composure cast aside. Then, slowly, Ma'rouf began to sink down until he was again settled in his seat.

"How trivial is being a sultan! How trivial all vanity!" exclaimed the sultan.

Ma'rouf was unable to say a single word, for his own astonishment was even greater than the sultan's.

IX

He was utterly incapable of taking in what was happening to him. He had tried to exploit his hidden power at home but it had not responded to him. However, he thanked God for his escape. Let his power be as it might. Let it disappear as it wanted so long as it hastened to his rescue in critical situations. He drove off his misgivings and put his trust in God.

He was sitting out in the sun in the garden of his house when a stranger came and asked to see him. Thinking he might be in need of something, Ma'rouf asked for him to be shown in. The stranger entered, swaggering in a fine Persian robe; he had a tall turban, a well-trimmed beard, and a haughty air; there was no doubt that he was a man of high rank. Ma'rouf greeted him and invited him to sit down.

"Who might our honorable guest be?" he asked.

"I am the owner of this palace," the man answered brusquely, in a tone like the falling of a hammer on metal.

Ma'rouf, taken aback, said furiously, "What rubbish!"

"I am the owner of this palace," the man repeated with even greater force.

"I am its sole owner."

"You are nothing but a deceiving charlatan," said the other, challenging him with an insolent look.

"You're a crazy, impudent madman," shouted Ma'rouf angrily.

"You have fooled everyone, including the stupid sultan, but I know you better than you know yourself."

"It is in my power to reduce you to chaff to be scattered to the winds."

"You're good at nothing but patching and mending shoes. I challenge you to do me harm."

His heart sank, robbing him of confidence. Then in a voice whose tone betrayed him despite its firmness, he asked, "Perhaps you did not hear of the miracle at the Café of the Emirs?"

"I did not hear of it because it was I who staged it, so don't try to deceive me. It was I too who saved you from failure in the sultan's presence."

He pleaded inwardly to Solomon's ring to exterminate the man utterly. When nothing happened his body collapsed under the weight of his despair. "Who are you?" he asked fearfully.

"I am your master, your benefactor."

He groaned and shrank into silence.

"It is in your hands to retain the blessing if you wish," said the other.

"What do you want?" he asked in a voice that could scarcely be heard.

"Kill Abdullah al-Balkhi and the madman," said the stranger quietly.

Overcome by terror, Ma'rouf said dejectedly, "I am incapable of killing an ant."

"I'll arrange things for you."

"Why do you seek my help when it is you who are the powerful one?"

"That's none of your business."

He recalled the trap that Fadil had fallen into; he brought to mind, too, the tragedies of Sanaan al-Gamali and Gamasa al-Bulti.

"I entreat you by God to free me from your demands."

"Nothing," said the other derisively, "would be easier than for me to persuade the governor of your deception. People do not feel safe from you and would welcome your ruin in order that they may be freed from your subtle subjugation. You will soon be called upon to perform a miracle in front of them and if you fail—as you must—they will pounce on you like tigers."

A sad and blindly despairing look came to his eyes, but the stranger had no mercy on him and said, "I am waiting for your decision."

"Get away from me," he cried sharply. "I cannot think properly in your presence."

"I shall leave you for a while," he said, rising to his feet. "If you do not call me, the chief of police will come in my stead."

Having said which, he made off.

X

He left Ma'rouf in a state of blazing hell. Was he to kill Abdullah al-Balkhi and the madman? Yes, he was keen to retain his good fortune, yet he was a good and weak man, also a true believer. Imagination pulled him this way and that, but always he held firm to the ground at the edge of the abyss. In the darkness of agony there shone a happy thought: why did he not escape with Husniya and the money?

He rushed home and ordered his wife to put on her cloak for going out, and he made his money into a package. His wife asked what it was all about and he told her that she would know once they arrived safely at their destination. They mounted two mules and went off, his intention being to go to the river quay. But, approaching the end of the street, he saw Khalil Faris the chief of police coming toward him at the head of a force of troops.

XI

The scandal broke and the drumming of it resounded into the corners of the city. The gossips spread the news of Ma'rouf the cobbler's confessions. Some hearts were reassured, while others sank into the abyss. It was known that the execution mat would soon be receiving Ma'rouf and that he would be joining Fadil Sanaan and Aladdin. The poor and the miserable left their huts for the city squares. They rushed off, following their anxious and deeply-rooted emotions. In vast gatherings they found themselves as one giant boundless body, roaring their protests and their fears for the future. With the demise of Ma'rouf their daily bread would disappear. Once again faces grew gloomy and groans of complaint were exchanged in hoarse whispers. Such force was engendered, such unrelieved anger, that they felt themselves to be an irresistible flood that could burst forth.

"Ma'rouf is innocent."

"Ma'rouf is compassionate."

"Ma'rouf must not die."

"Woe to those that do him harm."

No sooner had a voice called out that they should go to the governor's house than the crowds surged forth like a torrent unleashed from the highest mountain, letting loose a great roar. At the first street their way was blocked by heavily-armed troops. Quickly a battle ensued with arrows and stones, a battle waged fiercely under a cloud that threatened rain. Before sundown a rumble of drums was heard and a town crier shouted, "Stop the fighting—His Majesty the Sultan himself is on the way."

The two sides pulled back and silence fell. The sultan's procession came with a large force of cavalry. Shahriyar entered the governor's residence surrounded by his men of state. The official inquiry went on the whole night. Before dawn the town crier emerged as drizzle was falling, softly washing the faces drawn with anxiety. Many were the expectations of the people, but what actually happened had never occurred to them in their wildest dreams.

"It is the wish of the sultan," called out the town crier, "that the governor be transferred to take charge of another quarter and that Ma'rouf the cobbler should take command here."

Cheers rang out as the people became intoxicated with their resounding victory.

Sindbad

I

Ma'rouf the governor of the quarter suggested with all modesty
to the sultan that he transfer Sami Shukri the private secretary and Khalil
Faris the chief of police to another quarter, and that he should be
gracious enough to appoint Nur al-Din as personal secretary and the
madman as chief of police under a new name—Abdullah al-Aqil, which
is to say, "Abdullah the Sane." It was extraordinary that the sultan
should grant his request, although he did ask him, "Are you really happy
about the madman being your chief of police?"

"Absolutely so," answered Ma'rouf confidently.

He wished him all success, then asked, "What about your policy,
Ma'rouf?"

"I have spent my life, Your Majesty," the man said humbly,
"mending shoes until mending has become lodged in my blood."

The vizier Dandan was disturbed by this and said to the sultan after
Ma'rouf's departure, "Do you not think, Your Majesty, that the quarter
has fallen into the hands of a group of people with no experience?"

"Let us venture," said the sultan gently, "upon a new experience."

II

The habitués of the Café of the Emirs were whiling away the evening in merry conversation in keeping with the change that had happened in their quarter, when a stranger appeared at the entrance to the café. Of slender build, rather tall, with a black and elegant beard, he was dressed in a Baghdad cloak, a Damascene turban, and Moroccan sandals, while in his hand he held a Persian string of prayer beads made of precious pearls. The people were tongue-tied and all eyes gravitated toward him. In spite of the fact that he was a stranger, he let his smiling eyes roam familiarly among the people there. Then suddenly Ragab the porter leapt to his feet, shouting, "Praise the Lord, it is none other than Sindbad!"

The newcomer guffawed loudly and took his old comrade in his arms. The two embraced warmly, and soon hands were being grasped in friendly handshakes. Then he went to an empty place beside Master Sahloul, drawing Ragab with him, who protested in whispered embarrassment, "That's the place for the gentlemen!"

"As of now, you're my business agent," said Sindbad.

"How many years have you been away, Sindbad?" Shamloul the hunchback asked him.

"In truth, I've forgotten time!" he said in confusion.

"It seems like ten centuries," said Ugr the barber.

"You have seen many worlds," said the doctor Abdul Qadir al-Maheeni. "What did you see, Sindbad?"

He savored the great interest being taken in him, then said, "I have delightful and edifying tales, but everything in its due time. Have patience until I settle down."

"We will tell you our own tales," said Ugr.

"What has God done with you?"

"Many have died and have had their fill of death," answered Hasan al-Attar, "and many have been born and have not had their fill of life. People have fallen down from the heights, and other people have risen up from the depths; some have grown rich after being hungry, while others are begging after having been of high rank. Some of the finest and the worst of jinn have arrived in our city, and the latest news is that Ma'rouf the cobbler has been appointed to govern our quarter."

"I had reckoned that wonders would be restricted to my travels. Now I am truly amazed!"

"It is clear," said Ibrahim the water-carrier, "that you have become rich, Sindbad."

"God bestows fortune upon whom He will without limit."

"Tell us," said Galil the draper, "about the most extraordinary things you encountered."

"There is a time for everything," he said, swinging his string of Persian prayer beads. "I must buy a palace and I must open an agency for putting up for sale the rare and precious objects I have brought from the mountains and from the depths of the seas and unknown islands, and I shall shortly invite you to a dinner at which I shall present to you strange foods and drinks, after which I shall recount my extraordinary journeys."

III

Immediately his choice fell on a palace in Cavalry Square. He entrusted to Sahloul the task of furnishing and decorating it, while he opened a new agency in the market, over which Ragab the porter was put in charge from the first day. Meanwhile he visited the governor. They were no sooner alone than they embraced like old friends. Ma'rouf told him his story, while Sindbad related what had happened to him during his seven voyages.

"You are deserving of your position," Sindbad told him.

"I am the servant of the poor under God's care," answered Ma'rouf with conviction.

He visited Sheikh Abdullah al-Balkhi, his teacher when he was a young boy. Kissing his hands, he said to him, "I was under your tutelage only so long as was necessary for my primary schooling, but I gained from it some words that lit up the darkness for me when I was faced by misfortune."

"It is useless to have good seed unless it is in good earth," said the sheikh amiably.

"Perhaps, master, you would like to hear my adventures?"

"Knowledge is not gained by numerous narratives but through following knowledge and using it."

"Master, you will find in them things to please you."

"Blessed is he who has but one thing to worry about," answered the sheikh with little enthusiasm, "and whose heart is not preoccupied by what his eyes have seen and his ears heard. He who has known God is abstemious about everything that distracts from Him."

Having made his arrangements to settle down, Sindbad invited his friends to a feast. There he recounted what had happened to him on his seven voyages. From them the stories spread to the quarter and then to the city, and hearts were stirred and imaginations kindled.

IV

One day Ma'rouf the governor of the quarter asked him to pay a visit.

"Rejoice, Sindbad, for His Majesty the Sultan Shahriyar wishes to see you."

Sindbad was delighted and went off immediately to the palace in the company of the chief of police, Abdullah al-Aqil. As he presented himself before the sultan only at the beginning of the night, they took him to the garden. There he was shown to a seat in profound darkness, while the breaths of spring brought to the depths of his being a blending of the perfumes of flowers under a ceiling that sparkled with stars. The sultan talked gently, so he was put at ease and his sense of awe was replaced by feelings of love and intimacy. Shahriyar asked him about his original occupation, about sciences he had acquired, and about what it was that had caused him to resolve to travel. Sindbad answered with appropriate brevity, frankly and truthfully.

"People have told me of your travels," said Shahriyar, "and I would like to hear from you what you learned from them, whether you have gained from them any useful knowledge—but don't repeat anything unless it is necessary."

Sindbad thought for a time, then said, "It is of God that one seeks help, Your Majesty."

"I am listening to you, Sindbad."

He filled his lungs with the delightful fragrance, then began:

"The first thing I have learned, Your Majesty, is that man may be deceived by illusion so that he thinks it is the truth, and that there is no safety for us unless we dwell on solid land. Thus when our ship sank on our first journey, I swam, clinging to a piece of wood until I reached a black island. I and those with me thanked God and we set off wandering about all over it searching for fruit. When we found none, we gathered together on the shore, with our hopes set upon a ship that might be passing by. All of a sudden someone shouted, 'The earth is moving.'

"We looked and found that we were being shaken by the ground. We were overcome with terror. Then another man called out, 'The earth is sinking!'

"It was indeed submerging into the water. So I threw myself into the sea. It then became apparent to us that what we had thought was land was in fact nothing but the back of a large whale which had been disturbed by our moving about on top of it and was taking itself off to its own world in stately fashion.

"I swam off, giving myself up to fate until my hands struck against some rocks and from these I crawled to a real island on which there was water and much fruit. I lived there for a time until a ship passed by and rescued me."

"And how do you make a distinction between illusion and truth?" inquired the sultan.

"We must use such senses and intelligence as God has given us," he answered after some hesitation.

"Continue, Sindbad."

"I also learned, Your Majesty, that sleep is not permissible if wakefulness is necessary, and that while there is life, there is no reason to despair. The ship crashed against some projecting rocks and was wrecked, and those on it moved onto an island, a bare island that had no water and no trees, but we carried with us food and waterskins. I saw a large rock not so faraway and I told myself that I could sleep in its shade for a while. I slept and when I awoke I could find no trace of my companions. I called out but heard no answer. I ran toward the shore and saw a ship slipping beyond the horizon; I also saw waves surging and giving out an anthem of despair and death. I realized that the ship had picked up my comrades, who, in the ecstasy of being saved, had forgotten about their friend sleeping behind the rock. Not a sound issued from a living soul, not a thing was to be seen on the surface of the desolate land except for the rock. But what a rock! I looked, my eyes sharpened by terror, and I realized that it was not a rock, as it had seemed to my exhausted sight, but an egg—an egg the size of a large house. The egg of what possible bird? Terror seized hold of me at that unknown enemy, as I plunged into the void of a slow death. Then the light of the sun was extinguished and a dusk-like gloom descended. Raising my eyes, I saw a creature like an eagle, though hundreds of times bigger. I saw it coming slowly down until it settled over the egg. I realized that it was taking it up to fly off with it. A crazy idea occurred to me and I tied myself to the end of one of its legs, which was as big as a mast. The bird soared off with me, flying along above the ground. To my eyes everything looked so small and insignificant, as though neither hope nor pain pulsated there, until the bird came down on a mountain peak. I untied myself and crawled behind a towering tree, the like of which I had never seen before. The bird rested for a while then continued its journey toward the unknown, while I was vanquished by sleep. When I awoke the noon sun was shining. I chewed some grasses to assuage my hunger, while I quenched my thirst from a hollow that was full of clear water. Then I noticed that the earth was giving out beams that dazzled my eyes. When I investigated, the surface of the ground revealed uncut diamonds. Despite my wretchedness, my avidity was aroused and I tore out as many as I could and tied them up in my trousers. Then I went down from the mountain till I ended up on the shore, from where I was rescued by a passing ship."

"It was the roc, which we have heard of but not seen," said Shahriyar quietly. "You are the first human to exploit it to his own ends, Sindbad—you should know that too."

"It is the will of Almighty God," said Sindbad modestly. Then he went on with what he had to say.

"I also learned, Your Majesty, that food is nourishment when taken in moderation but is a danger when taken gluttonously—and this is also true of the carnal appetites. Like the one before, the ship was wrecked and we found ourselves on an island which was governed by a giant king. He was nevertheless a generous and hospitable man and gave us a welcome that surpassed all our hopes, and under his roof we did nothing but relax and spend our evenings in conversation. He produced for us every kind of food and we set about it like madmen. However, some words that I had learned of old in my childhood from my master Sheikh Abdullah al-Balkhi prevented me from eating to excess. Much time was afforded me for worship, while my companions spent their time in gobbling up food and in heavy sleep after filling themselves so that their weight increased enormously and they became barrel-shaped, full of flabby flesh and fat. One day the king came and looked us over man by man. He then invited my companions to his palace, while to me he turned in scorn.

" 'You're like rocky ground that doesn't give fruit,' he said.

"I was displeased by this and it occurred to me that I might slip out at night and see what my companions were doing. So it was that I saw the king's men slaughtering the captain and serving him up to their ruler. He gobbled him down with savage relish and the secret of his generosity was immediately borne upon me. I made my escape to the shore, where I was rescued by a ship."

"May He maintain you in your piety, Sindbad," murmured the sultan. Then, as though talking to himself, he said, "But the ruler too is in need of piety."

Sindbad retained the echo of the sultan's comment for a minute, then continued with what he had to say:

"I learned too, Your Majesty, that to continue with worn-out traditions is foolishly dangerous. The ship sank on its way to China. I and a group of those traveling with me took refuge on an island that was rich in vegetation and had a moderate climate. Peace prevailed there and it was ruled over by a good king, who said to us, 'I shall regard you as my subjects—you shall have the same rights and the same obligations.'

"We were happy about this and gave up prayers for him. As a further show of hospitality to us he presented us with some of his beautiful slave-girls as wives. Life thus became easy and enjoyable. It then happened that one of the wives died and the king had her prepared for burial and said to our comrade who was the woman's widower, 'I am sorry to part from you but our traditions demand that the husband be buried alive with his dead wife; this also goes for the wife if the husband happens to die before her.'

"Our friend was terror-struck and said to the king, 'But our religion does not require this of us.'

" 'We are not concerned with your religion,' the king said, 'and our traditions are sacrosanct.'

"The man was buried alive with the corpse of his wife. Our peace of mind was disturbed by this and we looked to the future with horror. I began to observe my wife apprehensively. Whenever she complained of some minor indisposition my whole being was shaken. When she became pregnant and was in labor pains, her state of health deteriorated and I quickly fled into the forest, where I stayed. Then, one day, a ship passed by close to the shore, so I threw myself into the water and swam toward it, calling out for help. When I was almost on the point of drowning they picked me out of the water."

As though addressing himself, the sultan muttered, "Traditions are the past and of the past there are things that must become outdated."

It seemed to Sindbad that the sultan had something more to say, so he kept silent. However, Shahriyar said, "Continue, Sindbad."

"I also learned, Your Majesty, that freedom is the life of the spirit and that Paradise itself is of no avail to man if he has lost his freedom. Our ship met with a storm which destroyed it, not one of its men escaping apart from myself. The waves hurled me onto a fragrant island, rich with fruits and streams and with a moderate climate. I quenched my hunger and thirst and washed, then went off into the interior to seek out what I could find. I came across an old man lying under a tree utterly at the end of his resources.

" 'I am decrepit, as you see, so will you carry me to my hut?' he said, pointing with his chin. I did not hesitate about picking him up. I raised him onto my shoulders and took him to where he had pointed. Finding no trace of his hut, I said, 'Where's your dwelling, uncle?'

"In a strong voice, unlike that with which he had first addressed me, he said, 'This island is my dwelling, my island, but I need someone to carry me.'

"I wanted to lower him from my shoulders, but I couldn't tear his legs away from my neck and ribs; they were like a building held in place by iron.

" 'Let me go,' I pleaded, 'and you will find that I am at your service when you need me.'

"He laughed mockingly at me, ignoring my pleas. He thus condemned me to live as his slave so that neither waking nor sleeping was enjoyable, and I took pleasure in neither food nor drink, until an idea occurred to me. I began to squeeze some grapes into a hollow and left the juice to ferment. Then I gave it to him to drink until he became intoxicated and his steel-like muscles relaxed and I threw him from my shoulders. I took up a stone and smashed in his head, thus saving the world from his evil. I then spent a happy period of time—I don't know how long—until I was rescued by a ship."

Shahriyar sighed and said, "What many things we are in thrall to in this world! What else did you learn?"

"I learned too, Your Majesty," said Sindbad, "that man may be afforded a miracle, but it is not sufficient that he should use it and appropriate it; he must also approach it with guidance from the light of God that shines in his heart. As before, my ship sank and I took refuge on an island that deserves the name 'island of dreams': an island rich with beautiful women of every kind. My heart was taken by one of them and I married her and was happy with her. When the people felt they trusted me they fastened feathers under my arms and told me that I could fly any time I wanted. I was overjoyed and rushed to embark upon an experience that no other man had tried before me. But my wife said to me secretly, 'Be careful to mention God's name when you are in the air or else you will be burnt up.'

"I immediately realized that the Devil was in their blood and, shunning them, I flew off, determined to escape. I floated in the air for a long time with no other objective but to reach my city. I went on until I reached it, having despaired of doing so, so praise be to God, Lord of the Worlds."

The ruler was silent for a while, then said, "You have seen such wonders of the world as no human eye has seen, and you have learned many lessons, so rejoice in what God has bestowed upon you in the way of wealth and wisdom."

V

Shahriyar rose to his feet, his heart surging with overpowering emotions. He plunged into the garden above the royal walkway as a faint specter amid the forms of giant trees under countless stars. Voices of the past pressed in on his ears, erasing the melodies of the garden; the cheers of victory, the roars of anger, the groans of virgins, the raging of believers, the singing of hypocrites, and the calling of God's name from atop the minarets. The falseness of specious glory was made clear to him, like a mask of tattered paper that does not conceal the snakes of cruelty, tyranny, pillage, and blood that lie behind it. He cursed his father and his mother, the givers of pernicious legal judgments and the poets, the cavaliers of deception, the robbers of the treasury, the whores from noble families, and the gold that was plundered and squandered on glasses of wine, elaborate turbans, fancy walls and furniture, empty hearts and the suicidal soul, and the derisive laughter of the universe.

He returned from his wanderings at midnight. He summoned Shahrzad, sat her down beside him, and said, "How similar are the stories of Sindbad to your own, Shahrzad!"

"All originate from a single source, Your Majesty," said Shahrzad.

He fell silent as though to listen to the whispering of the branches and the chirping of the sparrows.

"Does Your Majesty intend to go out on one of his nightly excursions?"

"No," he said listlessly. Then in a lowered voice, "I am on the point of being bored with everything."

"A wise man does not become bored, Your Majesty," she said with concern.

"I?" he asked with annoyance. "Wisdom is a difficult requirement —it is not inherited as a throne is."

"The city today enjoys your upright wisdom."

"And the past, Shahrzad?"

"True repentance wipes away the past."

"Even if the ruler concerned himself with killing innocent young girls and the cream of the men of judgment?"

"True repentance . . ." she said in a trembling voice.

"Don't try to deceive me, Shahrzad," he interrupted her.

"But, Majesty, I am telling the truth."

"The truth," he said with resolute roughness, "is that your body approaches while your heart turns away."

She was alarmed—it was as if she had been stripped naked in the darkness.

"Your Majesty!" she called out in protest.

"I am not wise but also I am not stupid. How often have I been aware of your contempt and aversion!"

"God knows . . ." she said, her voice torn with emotion, but he interrupted her. "Don't lie, and don't be afraid. You have lived with a man who was steeped in the blood of martyrs."

"We all extol your merits."

Without heeding her words, he said, "Do you know why I kept you close by me? Because I found in your aversion a continued torment that I deserved. What saddens me is that I believe that I deserve punishment."

She could not stop herself from crying, and he said gently, "Weep, Shahrzad, for weeping is better than lying."

"I cannot," she exclaimed, "lead a life of ease and comfort after tonight."

"The palace is yours," he said in protest, "and that of your son who will be ruling the city tomorrow. It is I who must go, bearing my bloody past."

"Majesty!"

"For the space of ten years I have lived torn between temptation and duty: I remember and I pretend to have forgotten; I show myself as refined and I lead a dissolute life; I proceed and I regret; I advance and I retreat; and in all circumstances I am tormented. The time has come for me to listen to the call of salvation, the call of wisdom."

"You are spurning me as my heart opens to you," she said in a tone of avowal.

"I no longer look to the hearts of humankind," he said sternly.

"It is an opposing destiny that is mocking us."

"We must be satisfied with what has been fated for us."

"My natural place is as your shadow," she said bitterly.

"The sultan," he said with a calm unaffected by emotions, "must depart once he has lost competence; as for the ordinary man, he must find his salvation."

"You are exposing the city to horrors."

"Rather am I opening to it the door of purity, while I wander about aimlessly seeking my salvation."

She stretched out her hand toward his in the darkness, but he withdrew his own with the words "Get up and proceed to your task. You have disciplined the father and you must prepare the son for a better outcome."

VI

Sindbad thought he would be able to enjoy the pleasures of work and evening conversation until the end of his life, but there came to him a dream. When he awoke he could not forget it and its effect did not disappear. What was this yearning? Was he fated to spend his life being tossed about by sea waves? Who was it who was calling to him from beyond the horizon? Did he want from the world more than it had already given him? He closed his warehouse in the evening and set off for the house of Abdullah al-Balkhi, telling himself that the sheikh would have the solution. On the way to the sheikh's room he caught a glimpse of Zubeida his daughter, and the ground shook under him. His visit took on a new perspective, one that had not previously occurred to him. He found that the sheikh had with him the doctor Abdul Qadir al-

Maheeni. He sat down, hesitant and confused, then said, "Master, I have come to ask for the hand of your daughter."

The sheikh pierced him with a smile and said, "Not at all—you came for another reason."

Sindbad was taken aback and said nothing.

"My daughter, since her husband Aladdin was killed, has devoted herself to the Path."

"Marriage does not divert one from the Path."

"She has said her final word on this."

Sindbad gave a sad sigh and the sheikh asked him, "Why did you really come to me, Sindbad?"

There was a long silence, which seemed to divide pretension and truth. Then he whispered, "Anxiety, master."

"Has your business been hit by a slump?" asked Abdul Qadir al-Maheeni.

"He who finds no tangible reason for anxiety is nonetheless anxious," said Sindbad.

"Speak out, Sindbad," said the sheikh.

"It is as though I have received a call from beyond the seas."

"Travel," said Abdul Qadir al-Maheeni simply. "For in journeys there are numberless benefits."

"I saw in a dream the roc fluttering its wings," said Sindbad.

"Perhaps it is an invitation to the skies," said the sheikh.

"I am a man of seas and islands," said Sindbad submissively.

"Know," said the sheikh, "that you will not attain the rank of the devout until you pass through six obstacles. The first of these is that you should close the door of comfort and open that of hardship. The second is that you should close the door of renown and open that of insignificance. The third is that you should close the door of rest and open that of exertion. The fourth is that you should close the door of sleep and open that of wakefulness. The fifth is that you should close the door of riches and open that of poverty. The sixth is that you should close the door of hope and open the door of readiness for death."

"I am not of that elite," Sindbad said courteously. "The door of devoutness is wide open for others."

"What you have uttered is the truth," said the doctor Abdul Qadir al-Maheeni.

"If you want to be at ease," the sheikh said to Sindbad, "then eat what falls to your lot, dress in what you find at hand, and be satisfied with what God has decreed for you."

"It suffices me that I worship God, master," said Sindbad.

"God has looked into the hearts of his saints and some of them are not suited to bearing a single letter of gnosis, so He has kept them busy with worship," said the sheikh.

"He has seen and he has heard," said the doctor, addressing the sheikh. "I am happy for him."

"Blessed is he who has but one worry and whose heart is not occupied with what his eyes have seen and his ears heard," said the sheikh.

"Calls have poured down from a thousand and one wondrous places."

The sheikh recited:

> "I in exile weep.
> May not the eye of a stranger weep!
> The day I left my country
> I was not of right mind,
> How odd for me and my leaving
> a homeland in which is my beloved!"

Al-Maheeni looked at the sheikh for some time, then said, "He is traveling, master, so bid him farewell with a kind word."

The sheikh smiled gently and said to Sindbad, "If your soul is safe from you, then you have discharged its right; and if people are safe from you, then you have discharged their rights."

Sindbad bent over his hand and kissed it, then looked at the doctor in gratitude. He was about to get to his feet when the doctor placed his hand on his shoulder and said, "Go in peace, then return laden with diamonds and wisdom, but do not repeat the mistake."

A confused look appeared in Sindbad's eyes and al-Maheeni said to him, "The roc had not previously flown with a man, and what did you do? You left it at the first opportunity, drawn by the sparkle of diamonds."

"I hardly believed I would make my escape."

"The roc flies from an unknown world to an unknown world, and it leaps from the peak of Waq to the peak of Qaf, so be not content with anything for it is the wish of the Sublime."

And it was as if Sindbad had drunk ten drafts of wine.

The Grievers

I

He abandoned throne and glory, woman and child. He deposed himself, defeated before his heart's revolt at a time when his people had forgotten his past misdeeds. His education had required a considerable time. He did not venture on the decisive step until the fear within him had gone out of control and his desire for salvation prevailed. He left his palace at night, wearing a cloak and carrying a stick and giving himself over to fate. Before him were three possibilities: to travel as Sindbad had done; to go to the house of al-Balkhi; or to take time to think things over.

His feet led him to an empty space close by the green tongue of land where a strange sound came to his ears. He listened under a crescent moon in a clear sky and was sure that it was the sound of a group of people mourning. Could it be someone was lamenting in this open space? He moved cautiously toward the sound until he came to a stop behind a date palm. He saw a rock like a dome, with men sitting squat-legged in front of it in a straight line. They continued their lamentation. His curiosity aroused, various thoughts came to his mind by turns. Then one of the men rose, went to the rock, and rained down blows upon it with his fist. Then, after returning to where he was sitting, he continued his lamentation with the others. Shahriyar looked keenly at the men and recognized several who had previously been his subjects: Suleiman al-Zeini, al-Fadl ibn Khaqan, Sami Shukri, Khalil Faris, Hasan al-Attar, and Galil al-Bazzaz. He thought of intruding upon their session to find out what they were about but caution restrained him. Before dawn one of them rose and said, "The time has come for us to return to the abode of torment."

They stopped wailing and rose to their feet as they promised one another to meet up the next day. Then, like specters, they made off toward the city.

II

What was the meaning of this?

Drawing near to the rock, he circled right round it. It was nothing but a rock in the form of an uneven dome, a place anybody would pass by without noticing. Going up to it and feeling its surface, he found it to be rough. Several times he brought his fist down upon it, then was about to turn away when there came a strong sound that seemed to come from several directions. Underneath the rock an arched entrance revealed itself. He drew back, trembling with fear, but then he saw a gentle light and breathed in a fragrant and intoxicating smell. Fear left him. It was this door that the men were yearning to open and for which they had shed tears. He approached and put his head inside; he looked around and was captivated by the atmosphere. Hardly had he entered than the door closed behind him. He found himself in a passage, the charm of which took hold of him completely: illuminated though without any apparent light, sweet-smelling though without any window; redolent with a beautiful fragrance though there was no garden. Its floor was shining white, carved out of some unknown metal, its walls emerald, its roof embellished with coral of complementary colors; at the end of the passage was a gateway, shining as though inlaid with diamonds. Forgetting what was behind him, he proceeded unhesitatingly. He thought he would reach the gateway in a matter of a minute or two, but he found himself walking for a long time while the passage remained as it was, becoming no shorter and with temptation pouring out from its sides. He was apprehensive that it might be a road without an end, but he did not think of returning, nor of stopping; he enjoyed the fruitless never-ending walk. When he was about to forget that his walk had a purpose, he found himself drawing close to a limpid pond, behind which stood a burnished mirror. He heard a voice saying, "Do what seems good to you."

Quickly he obeyed his sudden desires, stripped off his clothes, and plunged into the water. The throbbing water massaged him with angelic fingers, penetrating right inside him. Emerging from the water, he stood in front of the mirror and saw himself as new in the skin of a beardless young man, with a strong and perfectly proportioned body and a handsome face that breathed youthful manliness, with parted black hair and with a mustache just sprouting. "Praise be to the Almighty who is capable of everything!" he whispered.

He looked to his clothes and found trousers of Damascene silk, a Baghdadi cloak, a Khurasani turban, and Egyptian slippers. Putting them on, he became a wonder to behold.

He continued walking and found himself in front of the gateway. Before him was an angelic young girl he had not seen before.

"Who are you?" she asked with a smile.

"Shahriyar," he answered in confusion.

"What is your trade?"

"A fugitive from his past."

"When did you leave the place you live?"

"An hour ago at the most."

"How weak you are at arithmetic," she said, unable to stop herself from laughing.

They exchanged a long look, then the young girl said, "We have waited for you a long time—the whole city is expecting you."

"Me?" he asked in astonishment.

"It is expecting the bridegroom promised to its exalted queen."

She made a gesture with her hand and the gateway opened, giving out a sound like the plaintive moaning of the rebab.

III

Shahriyar found himself in a city not of human making: in beauty, splendor, elegance, cleanliness, fragrance, and climate. In all directions were buildings and gardens, streets and squares, decorated with all sorts of flowers, the saffron ground spread over with pools and streams. The city's inhabitants were all women, not a man among them, and they were all young with the beauty of angels. Noticing the newcomer, they hurried to the royal highway leading to the palace.

IV

As though he were a vagabond among his own people, he was dazzled by the palace. He believed now that his old palace was nothing but a filthy hut. The young girl led him to the throne room, where the queen sat resplendent on her throne between two flanks of pearl-like young maidens.

The young girl prostrated herself before the queen and said, "Your promised bridegroom, Your Majesty."

The queen gave a smile that made him lose his heart. He, in turn, prostrated himself with the words "I am nothing but Your Majesty's slave."

"No, you are my partner in love and the throne," said the queen in a voice like the sweetest of tunes.

"Duty demands I reveal to you that in the past I lived a long life until I approached old age."

"I don't know what you're talking about," said the queen sweetly.

"I am talking about the grip of time, Your Majesty."

"We are acquainted with time only as a faithful friend who neither oppresses nor betrays."

"Praise be to the Almighty, Who is capable of everything," whispered Shahriyar.

For forty days the city celebrated the marriage.

V

The time was passed in love and contemplation—and worship too has its time, and it can be expressed in drinking, singing, and dancing.

It appeared to Shahriyar that he was in need of a thousand years to uncover the hidden secrets of the garden, and a thousand years or more to know the reception hall of the palace and its wings. Then, one day, in the company of the queen, he passed by a small door of pure gold, in whose lock was a key of gold decorated with diamonds; on it was a card on which was written in black handwriting "Do not approach this door."

"Why this warning, my beloved?" he asked the queen.

"We live here in complete freedom," she answered with her usual sweetness, "so that we regard mere advice as an unforgivable insult."

"Or does it issue from you as a royal command?"

"The form of the imperative," she said quietly, "is used with us only in matters of love, which has existed as you see it for millions of years."

VI

Once when embracing her, he had asked his wife, "When will we have a child?"

"Do you think of this when we have been married only a hundred years?"

"Only a hundred years?"

"No more than that, my love."

"I had reckoned it as a matter of days."

"The past has not yet been erased from your head."

"Anyway," he said, as though apologizing, "I am happier than a human being has ever been."

"You will know true happiness," she said to him as she kissed him, "when you forget the past completely."

VII

Whenever he passed by the forbidden door he looked at it with interest, and whenever he had been away from the wing where it was, he returned to it. It pressed upon his mind and his emotions and he began to say to himself, "Everything is clear except for this door."

VIII

One day his resistance weakened and he submitted to a secret call. Seizing an opportunity when the servants were not attentive, he turned the key. The door opened easily, giving out a magical sound and releasing a delightful fragrance. He entered, his heart agitated but full of hope. The door closed and there appeared before him a giant more terrible than anything he had seen. Pouncing upon him, the giant lifted him up like some little bird between his hands. In remorse Shahriyar called out, "Let me go, by your Lord!"

Complying with his plea, he returned him to the ground.

IX

Shahriyar looked about him wildly.

"Where am I?" he asked.

The desert, the night, the crescent moon, the rock, the men, and the continued wailing. Shahriyar and his stick and the polluted air of the city.

"Mercy! Mercy!" he screamed from a wounded heart, and brought his fist down on the rock several times until the blood flowed from it.

But the truth took hold of him and he was overcome by despair. His back became bowed and he became old. There was no choice. He went toward the men with faltering steps and threw himself down at the end of the row. He soon broke into tears like them under the crescent moon.

X

Before dawn the men went away as usual. He did not go nor did he cease to weep. Then someone, walking in the night alone, approached him and asked, "What makes you weep, man?"

"That is no business of yours," answered Shahriyar crossly.

"I am the chief of police," said the other, searching his face, "and I have not overstepped the bounds of my authority."

"My tears," said Shahriyar, "will not disturb the peace."

"Leave that for me to judge and answer me," said Abdullah al-Aqil, as he went on scrutinizing his face.

"All creatures weep from the pain of parting," said Shahriyar after a silence. It was as though he were heedless of the whole situation.

"Have you no place of abode?" asked Abdullah al-Aqil with a mysterious smile.

"None."

"Would you like to dwell under the date palm close to the green tongue of land?"

"Perhaps," he said with indifference.

Said the man gently:

"I give you the words of a man of experience, who said: 'It is an indication of truth's jealousy that it has not made for anyone a path to it, and that it has not deprived anyone of the hope of attaining it, and it has left people running in the deserts of perplexity and drowning in the seas of doubt; and he who thinks that he has attained it, it dissociates itself from, and he who thinks that he has dissociated himself from it has lost his way. Thus there is no attaining it and no avoiding it—it is inescapable.' "

Then Abdullah al-Aqil went off in the direction of the city.

ABOUT THE AUTHOR

Naguib Mahfouz is the most prominent author of Arabic fiction published in English today. He was born in Cairo in 1911 and began writing when he was seventeen. A student of philosophy and an avid reader, he has been influenced by many Western writers, including Flaubert, Balzac, Zola, Camus, Tolstoy, Dostoevsky, and, above all, Proust. He has more than thirty novels to his credit, ranging from his earliest historical romances to his most recent experimental novels. In 1988, Mr. Mahfouz was awarded the Nobel Prize for Literature. He lives in the Cairo suburb of Agouza with his wife and two daughters.

ABOUT THE TRANSLATOR

Born in Vancouver, Denys Johnson-Davies began studying Arabic at the School of Oriental Studies, London University, and later took a degree at Cambridge. He has been described by Edward Said as "the leading Arabic-English translator of our time," and has published nearly twenty volumes of short stories, novels, and poetry translated from modern Arabic literature. He lives much of the time in Cairo.